A Twist of FATE

Bindarra Creek A Town Reborn

ERIN MOIRA O'HARA

This book is dedicated to Eric,
a true gentleman with a big heart,
who I'm extremely lucky to call my dad.

Chapter One

Burning with its usual intensity, the midday sun bore down on Chelsea's dusty white ute. No glamorous sports car for this country girl. An aging mare named Muscat, a motorbike missing third gear and a twenty-year-old ute were her standard means of transport around the farm and Bindarra Creek.

Last day of December. Last day of another far from dull year in Bindarra Creek. Last day for Reid Sullivan to get it through his thick skull that she, Chelsea Morgan, was his perfect mate. Yet the dolt couldn't see what was right in front of his beautiful green eyes.

They'd been raised on neighbouring farms, in a community where everyone pitched in to help those less fortunate—as had happened numerous times over the years. Drought, floods, bush fires, car accidents, arson attacks and hailstorms. Any number of natural disasters had brought out the best in the people of Bindarra Creek. He knew her to be reliable, hardworking, stable. Not flighty or cruel like his mother.

She checked the dashboard clock. Reid still had eleven hours and fifty-three minutes to make the dream she'd clung to for twelve years come true. Otherwise, she'd have to honour her promise to her mother, aunt, gran and two best friends.

She would move on, forget Reid, bury her dream and get drunk. Well maybe not drunk, but it *was* New Year's Eve. If she did drink a little too much, no one would suspect that Chelsea Morgan—kindergarten teacher, swim coach and Jillaroo of the Year—was drowning her sorrows, and about to shock the community by going on a real date. Lots of dates. Mountains of dates. With every unattached man within fifty miles.

A giggle escaped. "It will certainly shock the shirt off Reid Sullivan's broad shoulders."

Whompwhompwhompwhomp.

"Damn." She eased the ute to the side of the road, released her belt and swung the door wide.

Heat bounced off the newly sealed road, smacking her in the face and snatching her breath. The weather bureau had forecast temperatures in the mid-thirties, but she'd wager her father's stamp collection it had reached forty. Grabbing her Akubra, she placed it on her freshly braided hair then paced around the car, not surprised to see the rear tyre as flat as a tack.

"Damnation, Reid." If she hadn't been determined to make one last bid for his attention, she wouldn't have driven to Armidale to have her hair styled and purchase an alluring red sheath of a dress. One the sales assistant guaranteed would make any man drool. "If only."

The tyre wasn't going to change itself. With a huff of disgust, she glanced down at her new white dress and sandals—an impulse buy, along with new underwear. Any other day, she would have been dressed to deal with a flat tyre, or at least have her riding boots, pants and a shirt in the ute. A cloud of billowing red dust rose in the distance, residue from a vehicle on Wallaby Flats Road, which meant it could only belong to a Morgan or Sullivan. Her heart lifted. It might be Reid.

The vehicle made a left-hand turn onto Reservoir Road, coming her way. "Yes."

Her excitement faded somewhat when she recognised Hunter Sullivan's white Landcruiser. Reid's younger brother by twenty months. At thirty-one, Hunter ran the only real estate agency in town. He'd be dressed for the office, so wouldn't be thrilled about changing a tyre in this heat. Maybe he'd send for Reid.

Hunter slowed then pulled onto the wrong side of the road and parked nose to nose with her ute. His grandmother, Kathleen Sullivan sat in the passenger seat. She gave Chelsea a wave.

With a wide grin, Hunter unfolded his tall frame from the Landcruiser, leaving the engine running. "Chelsea, don't tell me, you're a damsel in distress."

"Of course not. I was about to change the tyre myself, but as you're here you may as well help. Or..." She eyed his pressed pants, shiny leather shoes and spotless short-sleeved shirt. "You could radio Reid and ask him to give me a hand."

His lips twitched. "Reid's drenching his rams. I wouldn't dream of interrupting him."

Damnation. The rams were becoming an obsession with Reid.

"It's all he thinks about. Diversifying. Cattle, sheep, crops." Hunter opened the rear door of his car, leaned in and retrieved his Akubra and a picnic rug. Closing the door, he placed his Akubra on his head then strolled towards her, leaving Kathleen watching keenly from inside the airconditioned vehicle.

"What's the rug for?"

He raised an eyebrow. "If I'm going to change your tyre, I'll need to protect my pants from the melting tar." He passed her the rug.

"With your notorious reputation, I was half afraid you meant to seduce me in front of your grandmother."

"Don't believe everything you hear, Chelsea. If I were to seduce you, it wouldn't be on the side of a road or in front of Gran."

"Where would it be?" How easily they fell into their usual light-hearted banter. If he wasn't a womanising harlot, he'd almost give Reid a run for her affection.

Without answering, Hunter retrieved her spare tyre, spanner and jack. She lay the rug out for him then held the spanner while he fitted the jack under her ute. Their eyes met as he reached for the spanner. "*If* I seduce you, it would only be because you wanted me with a desperation that made you reckless and wanton."

She blinked, surprise snatching her breath. She licked her lips. "Wanton?"

He grinned. "Yes, Chelsea, wanton. It's a term my grandmother uses, but very apt."

"I'm a kindergarten teacher. I have a reputation to uphold, and I wouldn't know the first thing about being...wanton."

"Pity. Pass me the spanner." He loosened the nuts then jacked the ute up. "I hear there's a big New Year's Eve party in town tonight. You going?"

"No. My parents and I are coming out to Tulachmhor. Antonia and your dad are hosting their own New Year's Eve party. Aren't you going to be there?"

"I wasn't, but I guess if it means I get a chance to thrash your brothers in a game of pool, I might drop in."

"Riley's on duty tonight, and Jake has taken Ali and Jasmine to Coffs Harbour. They're spending a couple of weeks by the beach. Riley, Samantha and Elise are joining them tomorrow. I would have thought you would know that, seeing Ali and Sam are your sisters."

"I knew they were going on holidays. I didn't realise it was so soon. I've been out of town on business. Aren't your parents and grandmother going on a cruise with Antonia, Dad and my grandmother tomorrow?"

"Yes, why?"

"Who has your dad got looking after the farm?"

She stiffened. "Me. It's school holidays. I don't go back to work until the end of January." She narrowed her eyes. "Don't you think I'm capable, Sullivan?"

"Oh, you're capable, Chelsea. I just find it hard to believe they're going away without you. Couldn't your dad hire a few locals to oversee things?"

"I didn't want to go." Not when she had one last chance for Reid to realise marriage to her would be the polar opposite to what his father went through with his first wife. For Reid to realise their future children would be safe with her. "I have to prepare for my swimming classes starting in a fortnight. The children are all around six. You can help, if you want?"

"I'm extremely fond of my two nieces, but I draw the line at getting in a pool with six-year-old monsters."

"One day Elise and Jasmine will be six too. Do you know how many country kids get into difficulty because they can't swim?"

"A lot, I imagine." He removed the flattened tyre and replaced it with her spare. "What would I have to do?"

Chelsea couldn't help the smile spreading across her face. "I will teach you everything you need to know."

He tightened the nuts, the muscles in his arms flexing and rippling as he strained. She frowned. A pity she couldn't talk Reid into helping. Young boys responded better to male role models.

"All done." Hunter stowed her jack, spanner and flat tyre then wiped his hands on the rag she handed him. "I'll think about it."

"Thanks, Hunter." She stretched up and kissed his cheek. "You're a star."

Chapter Two

Hunter watched Chelsea Morgan drive away. She was a conundrum he couldn't fathom. Even with her family's disapproval, she'd worn her heart on her sleeve for years. He could understand Reid's stance against marriage, yet Chelsea would make an ideal wife. She adored children and didn't have a cruel bone in her body. She loved animals and farm life. She'd stubbornly maintained a friendship with their sister, Aleisha, even though the Sullivans and Morgans were—at best—only polite to each other. It had been that way since their ancestors had first settled in Bindarra Creek. Unfortunately, Reid had no desire to marry, thanks to their mother's cruelty and sordid affairs.

He returned to his car and reached for his seatbelt.

"Hmm." His grandmother raised a white eyebrow. "Careful, darling. If one believed in legends, our families are fated to fall out over a woman every generation. We're overdue."

He laughed, accelerating along the shimmering tarred road. "It almost happened when Samantha arrived in town looking for her birth mother. I still can't believe she fell for a bloody Morgan."

Kathleen, matriarch of the Sullivan clan, gave him a pointed glare. "Senior Sergeant Riley Morgan is a good man, and you know it."

Hunter turned onto Kings Road. "We almost had another falling out with the Morgans when Aleisha surprised us all by giving birth to Jake Morgan's baby."

"Yes, but to be fair, he didn't know your sister was pregnant and it turned out to be a big misunderstanding, that you were responsible for."

"Hmm." The guilt he felt over that still niggled. "I admit married life seems to suit them and he's a good vet."

Kathleen smiled. "How do you feel about your father's marriage to Antonia?"

"I'm happy for them. Things would have been vastly different if my mother hadn't split them up in the first place. Antonia has been more of a mother to us over the years than that witch ever was."

"So very true." She sighed. "So... Chelsea Morgan?"

"She's flogging a dead horse. Reid will never trust a woman to be faithful or to care properly for his children. He'll never marry her." Hunter rolled his shoulders.

"What of you, darling? I know your mother had an adverse effect on you too."

"I'm more like her than you think."

"What?" The shocked surprise in his grandmother's voice made him smile.

"I'd never hurt a child, but I'd make a lousy husband."

"Not to the right woman, darling. You're more like your father than you realise."

They crossed the Kingfisher bridge then passed the Riverside pub. He gave a wave to Dan Molyneaux, who stood leaning against a verandah post, a broom in one hand, laughing at something his wife, Alice, was saying. She'd helped Dan turn the Riverside Pub into a really nice place to have a meal or a drink.

"Gran, I'll drop you at Samantha's house, then I have to get back to the office."

"Of course, darling. Thank you for coming to get me. I wouldn't dare interrupt your father and Reid while they're drenching the rams."

Hunter looked out his side window and scowled. Running the real estate, stock and station office was as important as drenching a mob of bloody over-sexed rams. He drove around the Anzac Cenotaph then turned onto Mt Ingalls Road. "Here we are."

"Thank you, darling. I'll catch a ride home with you when you're finished at the office."

There goes any chance of a beer at the pub before the crowd descended for New Year's Eve. "Sure."

"You've a good heart, darling, don't let it go to waste." She opened her door. "It's not too late to go after what you truly want."

"And what's that, Gran?"

She gave him a sad smile. "Chelsea Morgan."

Bloody hell. "Gran... I've got as much interest in marriage as Reid, and Chelsea Morgan is not the kind of girl to play around with."

"No, she certainly isn't, but a man with your skills must have some idea how to gain her attention. Or is your reputation all smoke and no fire?"

"Have a nice afternoon with Samantha, Gran."

"I will, darling. Think about what I said. Bye." She closed the door and made for Sam and Riley's front gate. He noted the trim lawn and freshly painted window trims. The historical house was ideal for raising a family. The same thought had prompted him to buy and renovate Samantha's old rental in Willow Tree drive. A ridiculous purchase for a bachelor. He should at least rent it out.

He parked out the front of his office and strode in to find Lewis, his offsider, behind a newspaper with his feet up on the desk. "Don't you have anything better to do?"

Lewis squawked, his feet crashing to the floor. "I thought you'd be gone for hours."

"I don't pay you to sit on your arse. Get around to the Bindarra Bugle and give them our listings for next week. You can check the post office box for mail too."

"Sure thing, boss." Lewis snatched up the listings and bolted out the door.

Sinking into his own leather chair, Hunter picked up his to-do list and stared at it, but the print didn't compute as his gran's words flitted around his brain. Chelsea deserved better than Reid, or at least a chance to meet a guy who'd give her the family she craved.

Hell, there were other single guys in Bindarra Creek. From what Ali let slip, Chelsea was considering dating other men, but if Reid asked her to dance with him tonight, it would raise false hope and prolong her pain, which meant—as a friend—Hunter had to do something.

Chapter Three

As far as makeovers went, the Sullivan's barn had been turned into a twinkling wonderland where a girl could easily believe her dreams might come true. Chelsea gazed up into the rafters where fairy lights dotted its entirety, resembling millions of stars in a desert sky. The Sullivans and Samantha had indeed been busy over the last few days. It was a pity Riley, Jake and Ali wouldn't be here to enjoy New Year's Eve.

Every wall had been sheathed in mountains of midnight blue calico, dyed by Ali and Samantha. The effect added to the magic, especially as sparkling lights glittered high across every wall, giving the impression the sky extended far into the horizon.

Hay bales had been set up on the right side of the barn where Tom Sullivan played barman. Tables and chairs surrounded the timber dance floor that her father and Tom had created. A Sullivan and Morgan working on a project together. Would wonders never cease? Music blasted out of two huge amplifiers, compliments of Shane Picton, shearer by day and DJ on Saturday nights. His dreadlocks and bushy red beard gave him a bush ranger appearance.

Laughter and conversation filled the barn. There were many more neighbours and friends than she'd expected, especially with the big New Year's Eve party in town.

Strolling through the crowd, Chelsea couldn't miss the prolonged and thorough examination from guys she knew to be single or in several cases, married. It seemed her daring red dress was having the promised effect. Hopefully it worked on Reid. She waved to her cousin, Emma, who'd recently resigned from her position at a Sydney hospital to accept a permanent appointment in Bindarra Creek's new maternity ward. As a gynaecologist and neonatal doctor, Emma had been welcomed with open arms.

Chelsea searched for Samantha. Having a friend to dance and talk with would flit away the hours until eleven-fifty-nine. If her dress hadn't worked on Reid before the magical hour, she had one minute to corner him and take matters into her own hands. If she dared. Hunter had suggested wanton. She'd show him wanton.

"Chelsea..."

Heart pounding, she swung to face the deep drawling voice. "Hunter?" Damn, did two brothers have to sound so alike? "You came."

"I did." He gave her an amused smile, before sweeping his gaze over her dress then down her legs to land on the red high heels and painted toenails. She almost squirmed under the intensity of his gaze, relieved when he finally raised his eyes to her face again. "Chelsea...you look..."

"What?" Why his opinion mattered so much, she didn't know, but it did.

"Spectacular. Come dance with me?"

"Um, I...okay." What else was she supposed to do? He'd changed her tyre.

Hunter took her hand, surprising a squeak from her at the trail of heat shooting up her arm. That couldn't be right.

He chuckled. "At the horror I see in your parents' eyes, they're not happy I'm claiming a dance."

"Do you blame them, Hunter? You only dance with ladies you intend to seduce."

"I've danced with you at three weddings in the last few years, and I haven't seduced you...yet."

Surely, he couldn't mean anything by that pause. "That's different and you know it. We were part of the wedding party. Plus, Reid cut in on each of our dances. That must say something?"

"Yes. He should mind his own damn business." Hunter drew her closer, his warm breath feathering her ear. "I might even steal a kiss at midnight."

"Good luck with that. My father is already glaring daggers at you."

"He's not the only one."

Chelsea sneaked a peep past his broad shoulder. Even in high heels, she had to stretch up. Sure enough, her grandmother and mother were frowning heavily, as were several of their neighbours. Her gaze found Reid, as tall and broad and handsome as ever, with his back to the dance floor, talking to Emma. *Turn around, Reid.*

As if he heard her plea, he looked over his shoulder, his gaze drifting over her and Hunter then shooting back.

Yes, he's seen us. Now he'll cut in and we will dance the night away.

Emma touched Reid's arm and his attention returned to the twenty-nine-year old, willowy doctor who then handed him a beer. Chelsea stiffened. It came as little consolation that her cousin, thanks to a two-timing ex, wasn't the least bit interested in establishing another relationship. But one could hardly be annoyed with her for being polite, or Reid for continuing their conversation.

Emma had a fragile, ethereal beauty and she was extremely intelligent, whereas her younger sister, Lindsay, was more of a free spirit. Thankfully Emma had no interest in farming, sheep or Reid Sullivan.

"I challenge you to a game of pool?"

"Pardon?" Chelsea looked up at Hunter, belatedly realising the song had ended and they were the only two left on the dance floor. "Sure, that is, if you can handle being thrashed by a Morgan."

"If you think you're that good, we should make a wager."

"A wager?"

"Hmm."

The sturdy pool table stood on the far left of the barn with a large dart board and antique Space Invaders machine. All relics from a pub that had closed down years ago. Tom Sullivan had created a male-only space, where he, Reid and Hunter could escape Julia, the witch they once called wife and mother.

Chelsea shook off the reminder of that nasty piece of work and grinned at Hunter. "Ali and I used to sneak in here and play pool and darts whenever we got the chance."

"That would explain why the feathers on our darts were often mangled beyond recognition. We blamed it on rats or one of the dogs having a chomp."

She giggled. "We got better with time."

"You must have. Now, what are you prepared to give me when I win?"

Unable to help it, she chortled. "What are *you* prepared to give *me*?"

"My body."

"Wha—" Heat infused her face. Damn the man, she couldn't let him tease her into a beetroot-faced, stuttering twit or he'd win for sure. Reaching for a cue, she took a moment to ponder a witty reply, something to shock the cocky grin off his far too handsome face. "Hmm. Not good enough, Sullivan. I don't want something you give away without the slightest thought. I'll decide what you shall give me when I win." To add emphasis, she raised an eyebrow and calmly leaned her hip against the table. "And, it will be something you've never given any other woman." She thought she'd stumped him, until he bellowed with laughter. "I'm serious. Best of three games."

"You're on, sunshine. And, when I win, I'm claiming a kiss."

"Shush, Hunter, someone will hear you."

Unlikely with the loud music, but best not to wave a red cape in front of her father. Good thing her brothers weren't here. They'd have warned Hunter off by now.

The only reason her father hadn't intervened yet was he loathed gossips. Confrontations between Sullivans and Morgans were legendary. If rumours were to be believed Dan Molyneaux ran a wagering book at his pub for such events.

Hunter strolled around the table. "Do we have a deal?" Amusement flitted over his lips, as his deep green eyes taunted her to accept his wicked challenge.

Curse him. She'd wager her grandmother's pearls he was enjoying baiting her. This wasn't the time to show any weakness. She needed to appear unflappable, even if her heart was galloping under her rib cage. Her sister-in-law's younger brother often bragged about thrashing Hunter—and anyone else silly enough to challenge the seventeen-year-old—but then Harry was a killer pool player.

Chelsea attempted a sultry smile. Harry's coaching skills rarely lost her a game. If she could beat her twin brothers, she could certainly beat Hunter. And, if not, it was only a kiss. "Deal." She held out her hand.

He raised an eyebrow, took her hand and kissed it. "Deal."

Tingles leapt along her fingers, shooting up her arm, quickly followed by a tremor that racked her whole body. "What are you doing?"

"Sealing the deal." He picked up his cue. "Oh, and I've never kissed a lady's hand before, so that's uniquely yours. Want to break, or shall I?"

Chapter Four

Damn you, Hunter, what the hell are you up to? Against his better judgement, Reid had agreed to attend this New Year's Eve party. One...because it was being held in his family barn. Two...because he needed to speak to Shane Picton regarding the next shearing. Three...because he didn't trust his brother not to make a move on Chelsea Morgan. And four... because he hadn't wanted to disappoint Antonia. This was her first New Year's Eve party as Mrs. Tom Sullivan, the mother he'd always wanted.

As a child, he'd run to her cottage for refuge and her home-cooked shortbread biscuits. When she moved away, he'd often hidden in the caves on Eagle Rock to avoid his mother's temper. Then Antonia moved back to Bindarra Creek as a widow and opened her heart and home again to three children who would forever adore her.

Now, although he'd been keeping a distant eye on Chelsea Morgan, he would have to go and interact with her, which would only put stars in her eyes. Completely out of character, she'd turned up in a blazing red dress that clung to every tantalising curve. He knew why, but the V-shaped neckline drew every bloody male eye to her enticing cleavage. As if that wasn't bad enough, it clung to her perfect arse, and when his brother had twirled her on the dance floor earlier, a slit in the damn dress opened, revealing thighs to make a man go weak at the knees.

He frowned. The crowded dance floor kept obstructing his view of her and Hunter. A game of pool shouldn't bother him, but if she kept bending over the table, drawing eyes to her cleavage or backside, she'd invite the wrong kind of attention. Hunter being the worst example. Hell, Hunter knew better than to toy with Chelsea, so this had to be a ploy to get him to march over there and extract her. Was his whole family working against him?

"Excuse me, Reid?" He glanced back to Chelsea's cousin, Emma Fahey. A slender blonde with huge brown eyes and a gracefulness few women could claim.

She narrowed her eyes. "If you would rather dance with Chelsea or play a game of pool with her, then please, don't let me keep you."

"Believe me, I do not want to go anywhere near Chelsea unless I have to."

"Oh?"

"Sorry, that came out badly. I've known Chelsea all her life. She's my sister's best friend, and as you know, her brothers are married to my sisters, but that's as far as it goes."

"You do realise she's had a crush on you since she was fifteen?"

"I do, but I have no intention of marrying her, or anyone else."

"I see." Emma glanced across the dance floor. "And your brother?"

Reid sighed. "Hunter is a notorious flirt, but I doubt he'll cross the line with Chelsea. She's attempting to annoy me into marching over there to rescue her."

"Are you sure? They look like they're enjoying each other's company."

Reid shot another look across the dance floor to see Chelsea doing some sort of victory dance then she raised her arm and palm-slapped Harry's hand. "It appears she has beaten my brother at pool."

"Reid, it's obvious you'd rather be over there than talking to me."

"No, I wouldn't." The pretty doctor intrigued him.

"If this is how you honestly feel, then you have to tell Chelsea."

He ran a hand through his hair. "It's not that easy. From the moment she was born, Chelsea has lived in a bubble of happiness, protected and sheltered by a family who adore her. No one has ever hurt a single hair on her head, let alone shredded her heart. I don't want to be that person."

"Oh." Emma exhaled, the empathy in her intelligent eyes easing the tension strumming through his body. She stepped closer. "Then I suggest you stay clear of her tonight. My grandmother told me New Year's Eve is your last chance to stake a claim on Chelsea. Apparently, if you don't, she's made a pledge to move on."

"Move on to what?"

"She will date someone else."

An icy finger ran down his spine. "Has she someone in mind?" He watched Hunter rack up another game. "Please tell me it's not my brother?"

"Of course it's not Hunter, but she's promised her mother she will look around, and unlike some of us, Chelsea wants to get married."

The pretty doctor's words surprised him. "You don't?"

She smiled. "I take it you don't listen to gossip?"

"Not if I can help it."

"I left a four-year relationship because my partner, another doctor, had a problem with faithfulness. As is usually the case, I was the last person to hear about his affairs. Hence, I took a secondment to Bindarra Creek, so I didn't have to see his face every day."

"You prefer the city?"

"After growing up in Armidale, I loved the fast pace of city life. It's only since I came to Bindarra Creek, that I realised how much I miss country hospitality and the slower pace of life. Here I have quality time with my patients and my ideas are listened to and acted on."

"So, you plan to stay?"

"Yes, I do."

A shout went up from across the barn. Reid glanced over to see Hunter punching the air. They were drawing a crowd. "I should go over there and see what he's up to."

"That would be a mistake, if you're not interested in Chelsea."

The pretty doctor was right. "Very well. Would you care to dance?"

"I...sure, why not?"

Chapter Five

One game each. She would have won the second game if Hunter hadn't broken her concentration. Chelsea chalked her cue. She couldn't fault his strategy. Placing his hands on her waist to move her slightly might have passed for an innocent interaction, except he'd lingered, squeezing slightly before whispering where he intended kissing her. Why he was fixated on her collarbone, she couldn't fathom, but the thought had lost her the game.

Harry hovered close, whispering advice. She would have had Sam's support too, except five minutes ago, Kathleen Sullivan stole her away because Elise had woken. Still, Chelsea had the king of pool in her corner and Harry knew all Hunter's weaknesses.

They'd drawn a crowd and, knowing Hunter's competitive streak and love of outlandish wagers, the spectators were curious to discover what he wanted. At least she didn't have to run down main street in the middle of the night naked. Jake might have been nineteen at the time, but Hunter wore that win like a badge of honour.

"Rack them up, Miss Morgan." He grinned. "Let's raise the stakes and make it the best of five games. *If* you win, you can claim two extra bonuses."

She would win, but curiosity got the better of her. "And, if I lose?"

"I win…a date with you."

Everyone gasped, including Chelsea. Why would Hunter want a date with her?

He cast an annoyed frown at the crowd. "I said *date*. Chelsea has already assured me she doesn't want my body."

Raucous laughter broke out.

"That must have dented your ego," called Paddy Cullen. "She's a wise woman."

"What's the wager *when* she wins?" asked Harry.

Chelsea glanced across the barn. Reid and Emma were dancing and yelling at each other over the music. The dress wasn't working. Chelsea needed help from an expert. "Okay, Hunter, best of five games, but I get five hours of your time."

"Please let it be something wanton?" A wicked smile flitted across his lips.

"In your dreams, Sullivan. It could entail coming with me to the sale yards to buy a new stock horse, or painting the verandah, or replanting the vegetable garden."

After the laughter died down, Hunter strolled around the table. "I accept your terms, but if I lose you agree to a rematch Saturday night?"

"Do I get another five hours of your time?"

"Yes, but if I win, you're mine for two full days, doing anything I choose."

Silence met his challenge as their spectators' eyes shot to her. Chelsea tapped the edge of the table. "It has to be something you've never done with any other woman."

All eyes shot to Hunter.

"You have my word." Not one hint of mischief glinted in his eyes as he took her fingers in a firm handshake. "Your turn to break, Miss Morgan."

Chelsea narrowed her eyes. She'd wager both her brothers' horses he was stringing her along. All hell would break loose if she spent two days with Hunter. Their families would never allow it. Except they'd be away for the next three weeks. Still, within an hour the grapevine would work its runners into every corner of town. Hell would freeze over before he got his two days. In the meantime, she'd soak up his expertise.

"I'm taking you down, Sullivan. And there will be no third rematch."

She took her shot, sending the cue ball slamming into the racked balls, just like Harry had taught her, sinking the green solid.

Loud applause broke out.

"Looks like you get the stripes, Hunter." She glanced at Harry to see him grinning widely. He mouthed 'orange five'. Finding the number five, she rounded the table, making sure to stay clear of Hunter. "Number five in the middle pocket." She set up the shot, calmed her breathing, blocked out all noise then took the shot, sinking the orange. She glanced at Harry. He mouthed 'red three'.

And, so it went. She sank the black without Hunter

taking a single shot. Cheers drowned out the music. Their crowd had grown, but still Reid hadn't approached. He stood by the bar talking to Shane Picton. Most likely about shearing the bloody rams. She checked her watch. Still plenty of time. Reid's sheep were important to him. Once he'd talked business, he'd wander over to see what all the cheering was about.

Hunter racked up the balls. "My turn."

And damn it if he didn't win the game. Two games each. She needed to concentrate.

It was close, but she won the fifth game to the crowd's delight. If Reid hadn't made his move by eleven-fifty-nine, and her act of desperation didn't work, she would conscript Hunter's services. He'd certainly be shocked, but he would have to give her five hours of his expertise in flirting and attracting the opposite sex.

If that failed to bring Reid to heel, then she'd date every unattached guy in Bindarra Creek. A laugh escaped her. It would certainly set the grapevine ablaze.

Tom Sullivan clanged a saucepan lid. "Attention everyone. My beautiful wife tells me supper is served. Help yourselves to a plate and whatever takes your fancy. Then you can get back to the dancing."

All their spectators moved off to the smorgasbord of finger food that had been set up outside the barn doors. Chelsea looked for Reid, but he'd disappeared.

"What's my punishment, sunshine?" Hunter's cheeky grin drew a laugh from her.

"I will tell you tomorrow. Meet me at the foot of Eagle Rock at seven o'clock."

"What? In the morning?"

"Yes, in the morning, Hunter. I ride early every day, and I have to be back home by eight-thirty to have breakfast with my parents and grandmother before they leave. They're taking the train from Armidale to Sydney. For the cruise, remember?"

"I'm not likely to forget. I've been roped into driving them all to Armidale. Three weeks without our parents and grandmothers. What mischief can we get up to?"

Chapter Six

It came as no hardship spending time with Hunter. His witty comments on the goings-on in Bindarra Creek made her laugh, and as Harry and Samantha had joined them, no one else paid them much attention. Not even Reid, which did surprise her.

After they'd eaten, she had a dance with Harry then another with Hunter, before excusing herself to go up to the house. As Reid was avoiding her, she might as well spend some time with Elise. One of life's true pleasures was cuddling Elise and Jasmine. Both nieces had been born on the same night, almost two years ago. Their mothers Sam and Ali, were Chelsea's closest confidants. Even they insisted she move on and forget Reid.

Elise had the grumps and Sam looked exhausted.

"Go lie down, Sam, I'll look after this little cherub."

"I will, thanks, Chelsea."

"My pleasure." She rocked Elise in her arms.

It was a pity Riley had to work tonight, but as

Senior Sergeant, he usually did the New Year's Eve shift and wouldn't finish until well after midnight. By then Chelsea would be floating in a romantic haze of rose-scented clouds. Or be set on a course of action that could damage her reputation. But that could gain an adverse reaction from Reid, turn brother against brother, and restart the feud between the Sullivans and Morgans. Hopefully it wouldn't come to that. She crossed her fingers and cooed at Elise.

"Hello, sweetie. If all goes to plan tonight, your aunt is going to be one very happy lady, and if it doesn't then…then it's not meant to be."

It took an hour for Elise to succumb to sleep. Settling the toddler in her portable crib, Chelsea tiptoed from the bedroom and returned to the barn. Upbeat, lively music belted out from the speakers. Most of the oldies had adjourned to Tulachmhor homestead's verandah for coffee, tea or port, leaving the young-at-heart dancing, and the drinkers boozing. She squeezed past a few blurry-eyed, unsteady guys, waving off their slurred attempts at conversation. She couldn't stand drunks hitting on her, their breaths reeking of spirits, their inappropriate behaviour or comments so out of character to their sober personas.

Where is he? She bumped into her father, who gave her a wink then continued his conversation with Tom Sullivan. Fate had conspired by having Tom's two daughters marry James' two sons, and they now shared two granddaughters, but they were also becoming friends, something unheard of a few years ago. Hunter stood behind the bar serving drinks. She couldn't see Reid anywhere. "Blast, he's avoiding me."

She found Emma talking to Antonia, which at least meant Reid hadn't gone off with her. Giving them a wave, she wound her way through the crowd. Time was running out, where was he?

"This sucks." She spied the open door at the rear of the barn. Reid wasn't big on parties, so of course he'd be outside, probably talking to another farmer about shearing sheep, or drenching sheep, or breeding bloody sheep.

He wasn't outside.

She marched to the water tank and looked up at the full moon high above Eagle Rock. Strange things were supposed to happen on a full moon. What would be stranger than Reid declaring his love or kissing her?

"Wanna talk?" The deep voice brought her back to earth with a snap.

"Hunter?"

"At least you know it's me this time." He leaned his broad shoulders against the tank. "I followed you."

"Why?"

"What is it you want in life, Chelsea? And don't say Reid. Think about it for a minute. Dig deep. What do you *really want*?"

She looked up at the golden moon, taking his advice to delve deep. No one had ever asked her what she wanted. "To be loved by a man who treats me as an equal, appreciates my opinion and cherishes me. I want children and romance." She gulped. "I deserve that."

"Yes, you do, so stop wasting your time. There are plenty of nice guys in town."

Poor Reid, even his brother thought him a hopeless case. "Thanks for the pep talk, Hunter, but I don't want to miss the count down." She swung away, set on proving them all wrong. Her hem caught, jerking her back. A maliciously long tearing sound resonated through the still air.

"That did not sound good." Hunter met her gaze then they both looked down.

Her delicately scalloped slit had gone from mid-thigh to waist, the jagged slash, showcasing her red lacy panties.

They both stared dumbly at the ruined dress then Chelsea groaned. "That was a complete waste of money. At this rate, I'll be lucky to get a marriage proposal from Paddy Cullen."

Hunter bellowed with laughter. "Chelsea, you're one in a million. Any other woman would be crying in despair. You make a joke. If I wasn't tarnished by my parents' marriage, I might propose to you myself."

"I'd kick you into the next galaxy if you did." She couldn't help chuckling. "Or, I might accept and become your worst nightmare. No dating other women. No kissing other women. No sleeping with other women."

His lips twitched. "I don't tend to sleep when I'm—" His breath caught at the impact of her fist against his abs. "Hell, Chelsea, I've known you twenty-seven years and you've never punched me before."

"You bring out the best in me." She stilled. How was it possible to banter with Hunter, with her dream slowly slipping away? Her now ruined dress hadn't worked on Reid. She frowned. "You may be a rogue, Hunter, but don't let your parents' marriage rule your life. If you open your heart, like your sisters and father have, and stop with the Casanova act, the right woman will fall in love with you."

"Will she?"

"Yes. But it won't happen while you're playing the field, so stop it."

"Whatever you say, Miss Morgan."

"Argh." She threw up her hands. "You're not taking this seriously. We are friends, yes?"

"I guess so." He watched her warily.

"Good. As friends, we're going to help each other, but it means you can't flirt, kiss or hook up with any other woman for three weeks."

"What?"

"You won't have time."

"What the hell does that mean?" He loomed over her.

"I'll tell you in the morning, but I've got to go pin my dress. It's almost midnight. See you tomorrow at seven." She clutched the torn material and ran to the homestead's back verandah as fast as her heels would allow. She'd use some safety pins to hold the dress together. There was not a minute to lose.

Chapter Seven

The tea, coffee and port drinkers had deserted the house, so the countdown would begin any second. Chelsea threw her red heels under the verandah lounge and leapt down the back steps two at a time, overtaking Samantha and Elise to sprint across the lawn.

"Why the mad dash?" called Sam. "You've got two minutes to see the new year in."

"Exactly." Two minutes to find the love of her life. Two minutes before she shocked him and everyone else to the soles of their feet.

The normally latched garden gate hung open, surely a positive sign. Light spilled from the barn, creating a golden pathway for her to follow, bringing to mind a yellow brick road. She might have tossed away her red shoes and be older than Dorothy, but she knew the way home and she had both a brain and a heart. What she needed was courage to kiss Reid Sullivan. Hopefully at the stroke of midnight she'd have a wizard in her corner.

"Hold up," called Sam.

"Can't."

She forged her way through the mass of singing, swaying revellers. Of course, they'd choose this moment to link arms and sing *Auld Lang Syne*. She searched for Reid's dark wavy hair and broad shoulders. Going up on her toes, she swivelled left then right, catching a glimpse of his blue shirt disappearing out the rear of the barn.

"Oh, no you don't."

She ducked and weaved, dodging a few merry guys with opportunity glinting in their eyes. There was only one man she intended kissing at the stroke of midnight.

After the bright lights of the barn, the blanket of darkness had her squinting and silently cursing. A crude oath alerted her to his direction. He'd gone into the woodshed, which was where Tom had stashed the ice tubs and excess beer.

Her father's tipsy voice bellowed over the sound system. "Okay, folks, get ready. Here we go. Ten, nine, eight..."

Chelsea ran. Why Reid chose the countdown to collect more beer was beyond her.

"Seven, six, five..." The crowd had joined in the countdown.

The woodshed had no light, but thanks to the moonlight, she could make out his frame as he bent to pat his dog, Gypsy.

"Four, three, two..."

Dragging up every ounce of courage she possessed, Chelsea darted into the shed, seized Reid's muscly bicep and swung him round. With her heart hammering in her ears, she only just heard his gasp on the count of one.

"Happy New Year." She launched her body against his hard chest, wrapping her arms around his neck.

Amazingly he didn't detangle her limbs. Instead, he groaned then locked his arms around her, lifting her feet clear off the ground, then lowered his head, capturing her lips in a startlingly predatory kiss. Spine tingling tremors followed his hand gliding down her back. She gasped as he cupped her backside and lifted her higher, joining them intimately from lips to thighs.

She jerked, gasped for breath, gloried in the heated exchange as he deepened the kiss, his tongue ravaging her mouth, drawing her into a duel of exploration. She hadn't known what to expect, but it certainly wasn't this. She had no resistance to his seductive caress. She'd waited too long to be kissed and touched like this. Alarm bells clanged in her head. Something wasn't right. Why now? Yet she couldn't, wouldn't end this wondrous moment.

"I'll get more beer." The slurred call tore them apart.

Chelsea landed on her feet, stumbling backwards. He caught her arms, steadied her then propelled her out the doorway. "Go!"

She didn't think to argue. God knew, Reid loathed being fodder for gossips and she'd wager Bindarra's water supply his primary thought would be to protect her reputation. Chelsea darted behind the water tank as Paddy Cullen appeared in the moonlight, making an unsteady path towards the woodshed.

With her heart singing and her lips tingling, Chelsea ducked out of her hiding place and darted for the barn. This was the best New Year's Eve ever. Powerless to keep the ridiculous grin off her face, she stepped into the barn, letting the booming beat of the music and out of key singing wash over her.

Most of the crowd had taken to the dance floor. She waved to her parents, still in love after thirty-three years. She glanced over the other dancers and froze.

Reid was slow dancing with Emma. How could he be in two places at once?

He couldn't.

"Who the hell did I kiss?" Who looked enough like Reid for her to make such a monumental mistake? "No." Dreading the answer, Chelsea slowly turned and locked eyes with Bindarra Creek's notorious womaniser. "Oh my God."

An all too knowing, wicked smile formed on Hunter Sullivan's lips then he winked. "Happy New Year, sunshine."

She shook her head. "This isn't happening. You...you..." She touched her lips, softly swollen from his ravishing kisses. "You should have stopped me."

"I should have, but—" His heated gaze dropped to her lips. "You gave me permission."

"I did not."

He raised an eyebrow. "You said, I'm not to flirt, kiss or hook up with any *other* woman for three weeks."

Chelsea opened her mouth to agree, then gaped at him in horror. "I meant..." She swallowed. "That's not what I meant."

"Does this mean you're releasing me from my five hours of hard labour?"

Damn. With her monumental mistake, she now needed Hunter more than ever. "You're not getting out of it that easily. Meet me in the morning and we'll negotiate."

He roared with laughter, drawing unwanted attention. "Sweet dreams, Chelsea." He sauntered off as if he hadn't monopolised most of her evening and sabotaged her magic moment.

Heat infused her face. Her magic moment far exceeded anything she'd imagined. Chelsea groaned. "Damn you, Hunter. If this gets out, I'll never live it down."

"If what gets out?"

"Argh, Reid. Don't sneak up on me."

"What happened to your dress, Chelsea?"

She dropped her gaze, terrified the bodice had shifted and her breasts were on public display. Everything looked fine. "My dress?"

"It's torn and held together by safety pins."

"Oh, I caught it on the water tank."

His eyes narrowed. "What did my brother do that you will never live down?"

Blinking furiously, she willed the hard-packed earth to open up and swallow him. It didn't of course. Reid wasn't going anywhere. "We made a wager."

"I heard, but that doesn't answer my question."

Think girl. Something close to the truth or he won't give up. Chelsea shrugged. "Hunter owes me five hours to do whatever task I ask."

"Which is?"

"I'm still deciding."

His gaze drilled her. "What aren't you telling me?

Chelsea rolled her eyes. *Now* he deemed to speak

to her, and in a censorious tone, as if she were a naughty little girl. "Not that it has anything to do with you, Reid Sullivan, but as Hunter's friend, I have decided to help him reform."

He let out a bark of laughter. "Hunter does not have female friends and will never reform. If you value your reputation, stay away from him."

Her mouth dropped open, disbelief wrangling with rage as he turned his back on her, heading straight back to Emma at the bar. Her until now dormant temper rose like a monster serpent, surging through the waves to exact justice. "Stop right there, Sullivan. How dare you tell me to stay away from Hunter. What gives you any right to interfere in my life? Hunter is my friend, and he's not afraid to…to…"

Reid swung back to face her, his lips a thin slash across his stony face. "To what?"

That's when she realised the music and singing had ceased. Not even a whisper of breeze came to her rescue. All eyes were glued on her and Reid. Some like Edwina Lette and Kathleen Sullivan in fascination. Some like her mother, Pamela Brown and Florrie Miller, in absolute horror. There was no coming back from this.

"Talk to her." Hunter pushed through the crowd. "I'm not afraid to spend half an hour talking to Chelsea." He winked at her. "Thanks for sticking up for me, Chelsea, but it's wasted effort. I am what I am."

Her newly-found temper rose again. "You might deceive ninety-nine-point-nine percent of people, Hunter, but not me. You owe me five hours. I will see you tomorrow." Holding her head high, Chelsea stalked out of the barn.

"You're deluded, Miss Morgan." His deep amused voice followed her.

Without slowing, she glanced over her left shoulder. "Don't be late."

Chapter Eight

Having his own cottage on Tulachmhor had its upside and downside. The up being Reid had complete ownership of the remote control, he could leave dishes in the sink, and bring a woman home whenever the urge hit, as he had last night. The downside being he missed his grandmother's and Antonia's cooking, his evening discussions with his father, and having family around him.

Gypsy whined at his feet. The dog had been another of Chelsea's rescue missions. She'd first dumped the pup on her brother, Jake. When it became obvious he didn't have the time or patience to train the pup, she'd confiscated the boisterous scamp and brought it to Tulachmhor. It had taken Reid months, but finally Gypsy understood and obeyed his every command, just as Chelsea had predicted.

Guilt niggled at his conscience as he mounted his quad bike. He should have left well enough alone last night. Calling Chelsea out like that had been callous.

Yet, he couldn't forget the way that red dress clung to her curves, or her ruffled braid and bemused dark eyes as she stood in the barn doorway, looking sexy as hell. Any sober person with half a brain could see she'd been kissed.

Gypsy jumped on the back and Reid pressed the starter button then put the quad into gear. He traversed the bumpy track toward Tulachmhor homestead, the home that would one day be his, but never filled with his children.

Reid's thoughts returned to Chelsea and the absolute shock in her eyes when she'd focused on him, as if he was the last person she'd expected to see. Something had happened, obvious by her altercation with Hunter in the doorway. What wouldn't she live down if it got out? "Bloody hell, Hunter, what did you do?"

As if thinking about his brother could summon him, Hunter stepped out of the tack shed, carrying his western saddle. Reid's gaze shifted to the bay gelding tethered to a hitching post. Monty belonged to Hunter, and as such was only ridden when they had cattle work to do and all hands were needed on deck. For Hunter to be saddling Monty on New Year's Day was unheard of, and this early in the morning, it could only mean one thing.

Reid parked beside the lunging yard then climbed off the quad. Gypsy followed at his heels. "Morning, little brother. Unusual to see you out and about this early. What's up?"

Hunter adjusted the saddle before looking over his shoulder. "Can't a bloke go for a morning ride without a royal inquisition?"

"Your morning rides usually involve a woman and, as it's New Year's Day, I'd have thought you'd be out cold for another few hours. Don't tell me you couldn't find some gullible lady to share your bed?"

"Shove off, Reid. I slept here last night. Alone."

"Are you saying you didn't stop by the big party at the Riverside Pub?"

"Is that so hard to believe?" He cinched the girth then patted Monty's rump. "A ride is exactly what I need this morning."

"Like hell it is." Reid vaulted the fence. "Chelsea Morgan rides every morning about this time. Are you meeting her?"

Hunter looked over his shoulder. "How do you know she rides every morning?"

Heat warmed Reid's face. "I often see her in the distance."

"But you're too damn stubborn to acknowledge her or join her." Hunter shook his head. "Our mother has a lot to answer for, but you're cutting off your nose to spite your face. Chelsea is about to give up on you. Is that what you want, after all the years she's worshipped you?"

"You know better than anyone how I feel. I'm not about to change my mind."

Hunter fitted his left boot into the stirrup then hauled himself onto the saddle. "If that's your last word, don't be surprised when she starts dating other guys."

"I don't give a fig who she dates, as long as it's not you."

"Spoken like a mule with his head buried in the sand. She won't date me, but I did warn you, Reid.

You're going to lose her, and you've got no one to blame but yourself." He kicked his heels against Monty and the gelding surged forward, cantering out of the yard.

Reid watched his brother cross the house paddock before Monty broke into a gallop, horse and rider moving in perfect accord towards Eagle Rock. What were the chances Chelsea wouldn't be riding today? Her final words from last night rang in Reid's mind.

See you tomorrow. Don't be late.

She could have fixed to meet Hunter early because of the wager. Reid laughed. If Hunter's first job was riding the Morgan's boundary fences, checking for holes or damage, there was no way he'd admit it, even to his older brother. Hunter loathed fixing fences.

Shaking his head, Reid whistled to Gypsy then climbed on his quad again. If his guest hadn't woken yet, he might tempt her to indulge in a morning ride of a different sort. First, he'd check his precious flock. Since investing in six merino stud rams and two hundred ewes, he'd taken the first steps in bringing Tulachmhor back to its original purpose. A Merino stud.

With the lambs born in October and November, they now had four hundred and twenty-six merinos, which they'd set aside one thousand hectares for. The restored shearing shed had stood up well to its first shearing four weeks ago, and with the new dams, and bores, Tulachmhor could handle the drought years better than most farmers in the surrounding district.

He traversed the steep climb up to Henry's Plateau then pulled up under a red gum. From here, he had a one-eighty-degree view of the south-west and south-east paddocks, Eagle Rock, the Akuna River and Bindarra Creek in the far distance.

A calmness settled over him. White dots covered the paddocks. Tulachmhor still ran four-hundred head of Hereford cattle on one thousand hectares to the north-east, while three-hundred hectares to the north-west had been set aside for maize, barley and oats.

Forced to buy feed during the last few years of drought had bankrupted many farmers and would have put the Sullivans back years, if it hadn't been for Antonia. Her infusion of funds and her faith in Reid's dream was coming to fruition. If all went well over the next couple of years, Tulachmhor would once again be a rich source of income. The key was diversifying.

Unable to help himself, Reid's gaze fell on the neighbouring property from which he usually observed Chelsea riding about this time. The Morgans' also fronted the Akuna River and although they only ran cattle, Hickory Ridge contained two thousand hectares of premium land. Riley and Jake Morgan showed little interest in taking on their father's legacy. Jake loved being a Vet, and Riley took his role of Senior Sergeant seriously, which meant Chelsea stood a good chance of inheriting Hickory Ridge. The irony wasn't lost on Reid, but he wouldn't marry her for her land. That low act belonged to vipers like his mother.

A rider and chestnut horse emerged from a forest of pines then smoothly cantered along the riverbank. Reid's breath caught as horse and rider flew effortlessly over his locked gate. They did it most days unless Chelsea crossed the bridge to ride on McGregor land.

Reid narrowed his eyes, searching for his brother and Monty. Both horses would meet at the intersecting trails, out of sight. "Damn it, Chelsea. What are you up to?"

Chapter Nine

A buzz of anticipation welled in Hunter's chest. She might have got him out of bed at the crack of dawn but strike him down if it wasn't a pleasure to watch her ride towards him, her engaging smile like a beaming ray of sunshine.

"Hello, Hunter. Happy New Year." She patted Muscat's neck then released the reins so the mare could munch on the dew-covered grass. "Isn't it a beautiful morning?"

"Happy New Year, Chelsea." He glanced at the native trees and scrub around them, and drew in a breath of crisp, clean air. He knew and loved every inch of Tulachmhor, but rarely took the time to appreciate it. "It is a beautiful morning, although I could have done with another hour in bed. Now I'm here, what's my punishment?"

Her husky laugh stirred a familiar response, one he quashed immediately.

"It's not punishment, Hunter. I told you, we're

going to help each other. Let's walk the horses to the river and I'll tell you all."

Urging Monty forward, Hunter considered Chelsea's mare. "Muscat must be getting on in years. How old is she?"

"Twenty-two, going on eight. She still loves cattle work and our morning ride, but I don't jump her over anything above four feet these days." Chelsea grimaced. "I've been thinking about buying a younger horse for working the cattle, but I don't want to offend Muscat."

He couldn't help but laugh. "Honey, horses don't get offended."

She whipped around so fast her blonde plait coiled about her neck. "What did you say?" Her velvety-russet eyes looked astonished.

"Horses don't get offended."

"Muscat would, but that's not what I meant. You called me 'honey'."

"Did I?" Hunter adjusted his Akubra, using the movement to hide his surprise.

"Yes, you did." She slapped his thigh, jibbing Monty. "Don't you dare use your lovey-dovey, fake endearments on me, Sullivan."

He almost choked. "Lovey-dovey? I'll have you know, Chelsea, I have never called another woman 'honey'. It slipped out. I meant to call you 'Miss Morgan'."

She huffed then returned her attention to the trail. "I've made a new year's resolution. I'm going to date every unattached man who meets my criteria, within a twenty-mile radius of Bindarra Creek."

"What?" Hunter couldn't hide the horror in his voice.

She shrugged as if it were no big deal. "I've made a chart, but I need your help with fine-tuning it. What should I use to rank my dates, and where should we go for the initial date, etcetera?"

"Why would you want to date every *single* guy in town?"

"I would have thought that obvious. Reid doesn't want me, so I plan to meet a man who does want me, marriage and children."

"Chelsea—"

"You owe me five hours of help in whatever I choose, and in return I will assist you to become a better man. Remember, three weeks with no other woman's company but mine. We shall help each other."

He stared at Chelsea in stunned disbelief. "You're serious."

She looked ahead again as they negotiated a slight decline. "Where do *you* take a lady on your first date?"

To bed. He cleared his throat. "Coffee, in a public place." Feeling rather pleased with himself, Hunter suppressed his grin and adopted his best impression of sincerity. "If you're bored or uncomfortable, you say thanks for the coffee and forget him."

"Do I let him hold my hand?"

"Absolutely not." He was warming to this project.

"What do *you* do if you enjoy a lady's company?"

Take her to bed. "I... This is not about me. If you enjoy his company, your next date should be...the movies. If he asks your preference, that's a good sign. If he doesn't, then he'll probably never consider your preferences. And don't let him make out with you in the dark. It's too soon for that."

Her gaze dropped to the pommel of her western saddle and she frowned. "I should be taking notes. Where should we go after the movies?"

It was killing him not to laugh. "Dinner at a restaurant in town. Not your place, and definitely not his. See what his table manners are like, and if his conversation holds your attention. Is he funny or a whinger? If you've nothing in common, it's not saying much for married life."

"That's so true. I knew you were the right person to help me."

"Yes, you're probably right. Another thing to consider is his generosity. You don't want a tight arse. If he offers to pay for dinner that's a good sign. You don't have to agree, but it shows the type of man he is."

"Right. If dinner goes well, I'll let him kiss me."

"No, at least not on the mouth." The thought of any man kissing Chelsea put a sour taste in his mouth. "You want to play hard to get. He can kiss your cheek."

"That's not what you would do." Her arched eyebrow had him chuckling.

"I don't date respectable ladies, sunshine." Although one tempted him.

"Okay, I like him enough to let him kiss my cheek. What next?"

"You attend a local event as a couple. A football match, the Saturday markets, the Riverside Pub if there's a band playing or it's karaoke night. If the guy is proud to be seen with you, he's less likely to be in a relationship already."

"That makes sense. When do I let him kiss me on the lips?"

Never. Again, with the sour taste, yet he couldn't avoid her question. "You need a minimum of six dates before you allow a guy into your bed."

"Hunter, I said a kiss, not sex."

He eased Monty to a stop then stared at her. "Exactly how far have you gone with Reid?"

Her lovely eyes flared as a slow blush covered her face and neck. "I kissed Reid once in the cave on Eagle Rock after he was tied up by those men who robbed the petrol station. I did it to sneak him a knife without the men noticing."

If an earthquake hit at this very second, it wouldn't rock him as much as her matter-of-fact statement. Delight, relief and bewilderment zapped through his brain. "That's it? You've kissed Reid once?"

"Yes. I know my infatuation was ridiculous. You're not telling me anything anyone else hasn't over the last ten years."

Hunter wondered if Chelsea realised she'd used the past tense. There was hope for her yet. Then the rest of her words penetrated his foggy brain. "Good God, Chelsea, are you saying you're a...a..."

She dropped her reins to clamp both hands on her hips. "It's not a dirty word, Hunter. I was saving myself for the man I loved. Now I damn well have some catching up to do."

She was right, 'virgin' wasn't a dirty word, but could karma get any more sardonic? How the devil did a man like him steer a passionate, vibrant, tempting woman like Chelsea through a dating schedule without taking liberties? He didn't bother to hide his groan.

She bristled. "Don't you dare renege on our deal. I need you to show me how to flirt, and how to recognise a decent guy from a philanderer out to gain scalps. I want you to teach me everything you know."

He was going to hell. "Take your feet out of the stirrups."

"Pardon?"

"If you want my help, take your feet out of the stirrups now."

Chapter Ten

Puzzled but intrigued, Chelsea did as he requested then frowned as he dismounted and reached for her. "What—"

She gasped, clutching his upper arms, momentarily distracted by the hard muscles under her palms as he lifted her down. She gasped again when he pushed her Akubra off her head, allowing her to see his intense green eyes.

"Hunter?"

"Lesson number one—never place yourself in a vulnerable position or a philandering scalp-gatherer will take advantage."

Before she had a chance to figure out his intention, Hunter cupped her chin and kissed her. Not like last night, but in a gentle exploration. With a soft moan, she opened her mouth to his probing tongue, unable to deny this newfound considerate side of him. He would teach her and keep her safe at the same time.

Gradually he deepened the kiss, caressing the

hollow of her back, hips and bottom in slow, delightfully sensual strokes. As if tasting a drop of water after days in the desert, Chelsea pressed closer, winding her arms around his neck, desperate for more of this life-giving source.

He made a growling sound deep in his throat, pulled her hard against his chest and locked his arms about her. If he thought she'd try to escape, he'd be very wrong. Every nerve in her body bloomed with anticipation and wonder.

Suddenly she was against Muscat's shoulder with Hunter's hands clasped around her waist, his breathing ragged as he glared at her.

"Let that be a lesson in what can happen, if you're not careful."

She blinked. "Good God, Hunter, if you're trying to warn me away from such a pleasurable activity, this is definitely not the way to do it."

His lips twitched. "Are you saying you enjoy kissing me, Chelsea?"

"Your ego is outrageous, Sullivan." She pushed his hands away then swiped up her Akubra. "I'm saying kissing is nice." Strangely her legs felt unsteady. "I think we should allow kissing on the second date."

"No. If you want help, we do things my way. Trust me, I have far more experience in how men think and behave than you could ever imagine."

"But—"

"My way, Chelsea, or not at all."

"Fine, no kissing until date four. At this rate I'd wager my mother's Royal Dalton tea set that I'll still be a virgin at thirty." She rammed her Akubra on her head.

He laughed. "Then your mother is going to be very annoyed. I guarantee with my assistance, you won't be a virgin much longer, honey." The wicked glint in his eyes should have rung alarm bells, but for the life of her, she couldn't disguise the tremor of excitement, and it had nothing to do with her prospective dates.

Several sharp squawks had her raising her gaze to the cloudless blue sky. A wedge-tailed eagle swooped low over the tops of the gum trees. Its timely appearance taking her mind off Hunter's addictive kisses.

"He's magnificent, isn't he?" The awe in Hunter's voice mirrored her own thoughts.

"Yes. I see him or his mate most mornings." She sighed. "Did you know it's estimated a pair of wedge-tailed eagles can bring two hundred rabbits to their nest over the nesting period?"

"No. I guess that's why we don't have a rabbit or feral cat problem on Tulachmhor or in the National Park. Now that the lambs are older, Reid's moved them from Shady Glen to Martha's Meadow. We've never lost a lamb to the eagles."

Chelsea watched the impressive raptor soar across the river. "They mate for life, unless one dies. He's the largest eagle I've seen."

"I call him Victor." Hunter pointed up the mountain beside them. "Victor and Victoria have had a nest on top of Eagle Rock for fifteen years or more. Some of their offspring have nests in the National Park." He swung up onto his saddle.

"We've had a pair of Whistling Kite eagles on Hickory Ridge for years." Collecting Muscat's rein, Chelsea swung up onto her saddle. "I have to get back.

Once you drop our folks and grandmothers in Armidale, we should meet to work out a strategy. Today's Wednesday, so I want my first coffee date tomorrow."

"Tomorrow?" He urged Monty into a trot beside her.

"Yes, Hunter, tomorrow. I will invite Craig Sanders first. He's the year six teacher at my school and has been asking me out on and off for almost a year."

"I don't know the guy, tell me about him?"

"Um...he's about twenty-eight, dark hair, easy-going and great with kids."

"Where does he come from and what colour are his eyes?"

That stumped her. She'd worked with Craig for a year and had no idea of his eye colour. Slowing to walk, she frowned. "I don't know about his eyes, but Craig is from the Blue Mountains. He went home for Christmas, but I saw him in town yesterday."

"All right. Who else is on your list?"

"Shane Picton and Jerry Eckford. I've known them both for years." Although easy-going and nice enough, neither had sparked her interest like Reid. In fact she knew very little about both men.

"Both decent guys who could do with a wife to whip them into shape. Who else?"

"Reece Nolan and maybe Steve Eckford. He's asked me out a few times over the years, but I wasn't interested. I know he's a bit full of himself, and his mother spoils him rotten, but he's Jerry's brother, so he can't be that bad."

"Reece is even-tempered and a good farrier. He's been shoeing our horses for years, but he tends to date several women at once. As for Steve Eckford, he drinks like a fish and had a nasty streak at school."

"See, I knew working together would get results."

"That remains to be seen. You could consider Leroy Murdoch and Nigel Clemons."

Chelsea searched her memory for either man. For some reason his casual suggestion bothered her, especially after that kiss. "I don't know them."

"Leroy is a bank teller and Nigel's a clerk at the Council Chambers. They're both quiet, but I haven't heard anything disreputable about them."

"Okay, I need a few more."

"Don't worry, sunshine, once word gets out, your phone will run hot with contenders eager to charm their way into your heart."

"I don't want this to become a circus. We have to keep it low-key, or my brothers will cut their holiday short. Meet me at the Cyprus Café at twelve and I'll show you my graph."

He groaned. "Not the café. After last night, that will only fuel the rumour mill."

"You're right. Come to the farm. You can help me paint the back verandah."

"Wow, sunshine, you said our wager didn't include hard labour."

"It doesn't, I'll have all the prep work done. You just have to wield a paint brush for an hour or two. And, if anyone asks what I've got you doing, you can tell them the truth."

"That's a form of black—" His eyes narrowed. "What's that bloody gate doing open?"

Chelsea followed the direction of his finger pointed to the boundary gate between Tulachmhor and the National Park, which should be shut. "Could the fire brigade have accidentally left it open?"

"Not a chance. Kel Jones and every member of his crew know better than to leave a gate open." Hunter kicked Monty into a canter, riding towards the gate.

Chelsea followed, scanning the surrounding trees and scrub. Stock were never kept in this area as they were impossible to muster off Eagle Rock, but it was a safety net in case of a broken fence. If stock got into the National Park, they'd never be located.

Reaching Monty, she slid off Muscat and joined Hunter at the gate post. His face was set like stone. "The chain's been cut with bolt cutters."

"You're kidding." Her eyes widened at the cleanly cut thick links. "Hunter, check out the tyre prints. A vehicle has come in and out. Maybe they were after firewood."

He dropped to his haunches and studied the deep prints. "Look how wide and deep these tracks are. It's a small truck, heading straight towards Martha's Meadow. I reckon some bastard helped himself to a few of Reid's sheep."

"Who would do that?"

"These are desperate times, honey. A drought can bring out the worst in people."

"You need to tell Reid and get a thicker chain on that gate."

"Hmm, but first I want to check the sheep. There could be lambs without mothers."

"I'll go, you secure this gate." Chelsea swung up onto Muscat then cantered beside the deep tracks to the next gate, which also had a broken chain. She swore at the wide groove gouging the earth. Hunter was right, a ramp had been lowered.

"Damn." Rising in the stirrups, she searched

Martha's Meadow, so named after a Sullivan ancestor received it as part of his bride's dowry. One small lamb, bleating its little heart out, caught her attention. She waited for its mother to respond. She didn't, which meant at least one ewe had been stolen. Reid would have removed the rams until the next breeding cycle in April or May. Even so, it was unlikely thieves would take a ram, as they were huge, heavy, and dangerous if cornered. Rustlers would need dogs and a fenced run to get one of those brutes on a truck.

Dismounting, she opened the gate, shut it again then set out on foot for the bleating lamb. It was much smaller than the other lambs and still had a tail, which meant a late arrival. The little mite was extremely lucky the eagles hadn't noticed it.

With Tom, Antonia and Kathleen away, Reid wouldn't have time to bottle feed a lamb, which meant this little orphan needed a foster home.

The lamb didn't run as she approached, just gave a broken-hearted bleat and waited.

"Hello, sweetling." She picked up the lamb and checked its sex. "Male. Damn, if Reid gets his hands on you, he'll band your bits then it's off to the sale yards, little piggy. I'll have to raise you myself, then when you're a big handsome ram, Reid can rent you."

"Still conversing with animals, Dr. Dolittle?"

"Doesn't everyone?" She grinned at Hunter as he approached. "This little fella is on his own."

"Okay, I'll let Reid know. He'll want to check the mob himself."

They walked back to the gate then Chelsea slipped through and waited for Hunter to close it. "Here, hold Stanthorpe while I mount Muscat."

"Stanthorpe?" Amusement shone in his eyes as he took the tiny lamb.

"Prize winning rams need regal names." She settled in the saddle, collected the rein then held out one arm. "I'll take him home with me."

"Reid might have something to say about that." He passed the lamb to her.

"He'll thank me one day." She huffed. "Well, he would if he could say two civil words to me. See you later, Hunter, and don't forget your old clothes." With a nod, she clasped the lamb across her thighs then nudged Muscat into a gentle canter. She wanted to have breakfast with her parents and Gran before they left for the cruise.

"Dad is going to kill me."

Explaining the lamb would raise eyebrows unless she snuck it into an empty stable. As if hearing her thoughts, Stanthorpe began bleating again.

Chapter Eleven

Hunter's chest tightened as Chelsea cantered away. Kissing her had been a low act and totally uncalled for, yet after last night's frantic kiss, it had been vital. In all his years of pursuing the fairer sex, he'd never experienced such an explosion of desire. And, God help him, he wanted more of her kisses, more of her.

She'd made it plain what she thought of his womanising ways, but damn it if she didn't intrigue him. She had since the age of fourteen, when she'd berated Reid, her brothers, and him for risking their necks and horses in a race through Akuna National Park.

The following weekend, at the Moree Show, Chelsea had chased down a spooked mare, leaning dangerously far out of her saddle to grab its bridle, rescuing a boy, without any thought to her own safety.

"Bloody tenacious woman."

He strode to Monty, mounted, then sprang him straight into a gallop. Assisting Chelsea would be all kinds of hell, so why torture himself and every other man rash enough to put his hand up? God only knew what would ensue if prospective suitors turned her plan into an all-out, winner takes all, duel to the altar.

"Hell."

The Morgan men would use him for target practice, the women from both families would draw and quarter him. Worse still, Chelsea could get hurt. He had to talk her out of this mad scheme.

A revving engine drew his attention up the rise to Henry's Plateau where his brother sat atop his quad. "Damn, that's all I need."

If Reid had witnessed the kiss, he'd knock Hunter's head off, and there was no telling what he'd do to keep Chelsea's reputation intact. The vice around his chest intensified. If Chelsea didn't get the love and children she craved, it would slowly dim her spirit and break her heart. He really had no choice but to help her find a decent husband who could give her everything she deserved.

"Hold up, boy." With the softest of jerks, Hunter brought Monty to a trot then walk and stopped beside the quad. "I need to talk to you."

Reid's gaze flicked from the valley below to Hunter. "What was that about?"

Looking over his shoulder, Hunter searched the river trail and found Chelsea, still seated on Muscat, but closing the gate between their properties.

"At least she didn't jump it this time." He scanned the trail leading to the base of Eagle Rock, searching for the spot where he'd kissed Chelsea. His tension eased a fraction. Without binoculars, it would be difficult to see that far and—thanks to the trees—

pretty much impossible. Holding in his relief, Hunter turned back to Reid. "Some bastard cut the outer gate chain then stole at least one ewe."

"You're kidding?" Reid snatched up a pair of binoculars from the toolbox on the back tray. The vice around Hunter's chest constricted again. He prayed the trees had concealed him and Chelsea from sight.

"I found the outer gate open. The chain on the gate to Martha's Meadow has been cut too. Chelsea spotted a lamb on its own. Its tail hasn't been banded, so it must be new. She's taken it home to bottle feed. With Gran and Antonia away, she thought you'd appreciate it."

"I do. I'll drop over one day next week and dock its tail. Was it male or female?"

"Male, but I can do it when I call in to pick them up. What are we going to do about the thief?"

"We?" Reid raised an eyebrow. "You didn't want any part of my Merino venture?"

"It hasn't stopped you hijacking me to help with the docking, drenching and shearing." Hunter looked across Tully Flats to the homestead and beyond to the grazing Herefords. "Tulachmhor has been a cattle stud for fifty years. My argument has always been, if you want to run sheep and grow crops, we need to buy more land and take on extra labour. Now that Aleisha's a mother and part time vet, she's out of the picture. And, it's too much for two. Dad's getting older, and I have a business to run, not that anyone seems to take that seriously."

Reid rubbed his jaw. "Selling houses and stock might make you rich, Hunter, but your heart will never be in it. You love Tulachmhor, and working the land is in your blood." His gaze shifted from Hunter to the distant grasslands of Hickory Ridge. "If we bought the Morgan and Eckford properties, we could graze cattle on Hickory Ridge, sheep here and grow crops on the Eckford's land."

"Are you stark raving mad?" Hunter swiped his Akubra off and ran a hand through his hair. "That's at least ten million dollars, not that James Morgan would ever sell to us."

"Maybe, maybe not. Our sisters married his sons, so Hickory Ridge could be split three ways or put up for sale."

"You're forgetting Chelsea. She could inherit the lot."

"I can't see it unless...she marries a man her father trusts to help her run a cattle property that size. Someone they know, born and bred in this region."

Hunter's heart began pounding. "It wouldn't be a man after her land."

Reid's eyes narrowed. "Nor a skirt-chaser who'd break her heart."

"No."

They both glared at each other until Reid's lips twitched. "That rules us out then."

"We were never in contention." Hunter grinned. "The Morgans would do away with us long before we popped the question."

Reid chuckled. "Jake would shoot us using tranquilisers loaded with lethal toxins."

"James would string us up for target practice then let the crows peck our bones clean." Hunter chuckled as he visualised the Morgans chasing them across paddocks firing randomly, dirt flying as bullets sprayed about their feet. "Senior Sergeant Riley Morgan would take great satisfaction in digging a hole and burying us."

They belly-laughed so hard Gypsy began barking and Monty shied.

"Woah, boy." Hunter swiped at the tears running down his face. "Our family might wonder what happened to us."

"Don't bet on it. Now the Morgans are related by marriage, our parents and sisters only have eyes for the babies. It would take years for them to notice us missing." Reid held his side, gasping for air. "Chelsea would end up taking over Tulachmhor *and* Hickory Ridge with the blessing of the whole bloody town."

Hunter sobered. He hadn't laughed like this with Reid in years. It felt good. If a guy couldn't trust his brother, who could he trust? "I met Chelsea this morning, at her request, to discuss the wager."

Reid's grin widened. "I can't wait to hear this. What's your five hours of punishment?"

"I'm painting their back verandah, but that's only a cover. She's retained me in an advisory capacity to recommend and assess potential suitors. She's even created a bloody graph to gauge their suitability. And, I'm not permitted to flirt, kiss or bed any women for three weeks, because she plans to reform me as payment for my advice."

Reid's mouth opened, shut then opened again. His eyes boggled. "You agreed?"

"What choice did I have? I lost the wager."

Reid bellowed so hard with laughter he lost his balance then rolled sideways, falling off the quad.

"I should have kept my mouth shut." Hunter sat back in the saddle, crossed his hands over the pommel and waited.

Several minutes passed before Reid's mirth calmed enough for him to roll onto his knees, snatch up his Akubra then stand. "Damn it, if this isn't going to be the most entertainment Bindarra Creek has had in years."

"Put a sock in it, Reid. What are we going to do about protecting your bloody sheep?"

"Secure the gates and put out an alert. I did have more pleasurable plans, but let's get back to the house and talk to Dad." He began chuckling again. "It pains me to say this, Hunter, but Karma has finally caught up with you. Now you must play the roles of fairy godmother *and* chaperone."

"What the hell are you talking about?"

"Under no circumstances can you let Chelsea be hurt or humiliated, because if she is, your head will roll."

"This wasn't my idea."

"Maybe not, but you didn't have to agree to it."

"I lost the wager." He looked towards Hickory Ridge and the distant rider. She'd always been out of reach, until now. And after two kisses, she enthralled him more than ever.

Chapter Twelve

"Coffee, movie, dinner and a public outing." Chelsea tapped her black marker on the dining table as she considered the headings across her graph. "Conversation, company, humour, interests, generosity, attraction and chemistry." She'd leave a couple of columns in case Hunter suggested something more. "Name, age and occupation can go under...contenders."

She filled in the square then racked her brain for guys within her age bracket who fit her criteria. She didn't know any well, except for Craig Sanders.

"Chelsea, love, Hunter's on his way up the road." Her mother stuck her head around the door. "What are you doing?"

"Designing a...a schedule." Chelsea covered the graph with another piece of cardboard. "Lots to do before school starts."

Her mother frowned. "Love, you've still got four weeks holiday. Why don't you join your brothers and the girls on the coast? They'd love your company. We can ask Jerry or Angus to keep an eye on things here."

"I can't. I brought an orphan lamb home this morning. Rustlers cut the chain on the Sullivan's back gate and came in through the National Park. They stole the lamb's mother."

Her mother's eyes widened. "Rustlers? Does your father know?"

"Tom will tell Dad the minute he arrives, however, it's unlikely rustlers will prey on our cattle if I'm about."

"A young woman on her own is not going to deter rustlers. I'm sure our neighbours won't mind dropping by occasionally. They'll need to keep an eye on their stock too. Maybe I should ask Jake or Riley to come home for a few days each week to stay with you."

"No, don't. They need this holiday."

"That's true. What about Harry? I know he planned a camping trip with your cousins, but I'm sure they wouldn't mind camping here."

The thought was enough to make Chelsea quake. Harry would be fine, but her seventeen-year-old cousins were pranksters. "No, don't spoil Harry's fun. He's been looking forward to the camping trip."

"Very well, but promise me you'll lock the doors, otherwise I'll worry myself sick?"

Chelsea frowned, unable to remember ever locking the doors. "Where's the key?"

Her mother's gaze flitted around the room. "We must have one somewhere."

"Don't worry, I'll find it." She hugged her mother. "If it eases your mind, I'll keep Lola and Reggie inside at night. Only an idiot would attempt to break into a house containing two snarling Blue Heelers and a woman with a shotgun."

"Did I miss something?" asked Chelsea's grandmother. Therese Morgan stood in the doorway looking between her daughter-in-law and Chelsea. "Who wants to break in?"

"No one, Grandy." Chelsea herded both women back to the kitchen. "The Sullivans have had a sheep stolen. Mum is worried the rustlers might target Hickory Ridge next."

"Oh dear."

"Don't worry, Grandy. Word will be out within hours. The rustler wouldn't be stupid enough to hang around, and Lola and Reggie *will* turn vicious if anyone threatens me."

As if hearing their names, Lola and Reggie padded into the kitchen. Unfortunately, Stanthorpe trotted in behind them. By the lopsided grin on Lola's face, she was delighted to show off their find. The lamb bleated, butting its tiny head against Reggie.

Chelsea groaned. "I forgot Lola can open stable gates."

Heavy footsteps along the verandah proclaimed her father's imminent arrival. James Morgan stopped in the doorway, staring at the dogs and their new best friend. "Where the devil did *that* come from?"

"Tulachmhor."

Her father glanced over his shoulder as Hunter's Landcruiser pulled up at the garden gate. "Do the Sullivans know you have one of their lambs?"

"Hunter does."

"Hunter?" Her father's eyebrows rose, creating

deep furrow across his forehead. He stepped into the kitchen. "Are you saying, you rode onto Sullivan land this morning, stole a lamb, and Hunter, who just happened to be out and about on New Year's Day, witnessed your actions but didn't stop you?"

"No, that is not what happened, Dad. What a fanciful imagination you have."

"Thank God for that." Her father's shoulders relaxed.

Chelsea swallowed. "I rode along the river and *then* onto Tulachmhor to meet Hunter in regard to the wager I won last night. That's when we noticed the chain on the gate to Akuna National Park had been cut. Further investigation revealed a second gate had been compromised and the lamb's mother missing."

Her father's mouth opened, but he didn't get a chance to reply. Tom Sullivan stepped into the kitchen and clamped a hand on his shoulder. "It's all under control, James. I've notified our neighbours and put heavy duty chains on my external gates. Reid's installing cameras, microwave dishes and solar panels. If the bastards come near our stock, we'll see them."

"Isn't that a bit over the top for one ewe?" Her father's gaze shifted to Hunter, who had squeezed past his father and stood frowning at Chelsea.

Tom shook his head. "The cameras are part of Reid's modernisation strategy. We can check dam levels and stock without running all over the place. We just hadn't got around to putting them up. Reid did a tally. We're missing fifty heifers, ten ewes and nine lambs."

That got her father's attention. "I haven't noticed any of our stock missing."

"Reid will check your cattle later, and we've advised Angus and Jerry to check theirs. It's possible we're all missing stock and wouldn't have noticed for weeks."

Chelsea picked up Stanthorpe. "You would have noticed a lamb on its own though."

"I doubt it." Tom grimaced. "A new lamb wouldn't last long without its mother, not with eagles and foxes about. We'd better get going. Don't worry about your cattle, James. The boys will keep an eye on them and Chelsea."

Chelsea bit her lip as her father scowled at Hunter. "As long as that's all they do. I heard about the wager you lost last night, among other things."

"You should be pleased, James." Antonia pushed her way into the kitchen, smiling broadly. "Hunter is going to paint your verandah and any other chores Chelsea can squeeze into five hours."

Hunter groaned. "I'm the laughing-stock of Bindarra Creek."

Chelsea almost collapsed in relief when her father spluttered with mirth. "Haven't you Sullivans learned anything in the last two hundred years? Never challenge a Morgan."

"Yeah, yeah." Tom followed Chelsea's father onto the back verandah. "Seems to me, the Morgans continue to underestimate the Sullivans. We win through in the end."

As everyone followed, the two men's banter continued to Hunter's Landcruiser, where he stowed the luggage.

Chelsea chuckled. "It's hard to believe you're all going on a cruise together."

"Miracles happen every day, love." Her mother hugged her. "I want you to make the most of your holidays. Go out and enjoy yourself. Don't work too hard on your graph."

"Graph?" Behind them, Hunter appeared to be having a coughing fit.

Chelsea glared at him. "As astounding as you seem to find it, Sullivan, I often prepare work during the holidays."

"Sorry, sunshine." He gave her what she assumed was his interpretation of a contrite grimace then held the passenger door open for Grandy. "I'll work off my wager later."

"Do it another day. You've got plenty to do on Tulachmhor." Tom yelled as he claimed the seat in the rear cabin. Chelsea's mother and Antonia slid along the middle seat.

Her father wrapped an arm around Chelsea's shoulders then kissed her forehead. "Take care, sweetheart. Ring your brothers if you have any concerns."

"I will. Enjoy the cruise."

"Hmm." He hesitated. "How long has Hunter been calling you 'sunshine'?"

"Years, why?"

"I'm probably barking up the wrong tree, but you haven't transferred your affection from one brother to the other, have you?"

"What? Are you out of your mind?" His question hit a raw nerve, especially after the confusing dreams she'd had last night.

"Sorry." He held his hands up. "I won't say another word." He slid into his seat and closed the door.

Hunter gave a toot, and the others waved at Chelsea as he drove off, leaving Lola and Reggie staring adoringly at Stanthorpe. He lay sound asleep in Chelsea's arms.

"What nonsense. Exchanging one Sullivan for the other. As if I would do anything so ridiculous." She swallowed. Hunter gave away kisses at a dime a dozen. They meant absolutely nothing. She would do well to remember that.

Chapter Thirteen

An attack of the guilts hit Hunter as he parked beside the rear garden gate of the Morgan homestead. Five-thirty was too late to start painting their verandah but securing the sheep had been a priority. Chelsea would understand.

She stood at the top of the steps, hands on hips, lips pursed, glaring. "Hunter."

Maybe not. "Sorry, I'm late. We were installing cameras, microwave dishes and solar panels. It takes a while."

"You could have let me know."

"Sorry. Angus found a panel of fencing peeled back. He thinks he's lost a dozen steers."

"Has he let the police know?"

"Yeah, Abby's organised for an officer from Armidale to come out and take a mould of the tyre prints."

"Good. At least the grapevine is good for something. By tomorrow everyone in Bindarra will be on the lookout for anything suspicious."

He nodded. "I've brought an expander and two bands for the lamb."

"Stanthorpe is not having his testicles banded. How would you like it, if I grabbed yours and stuck a tight band around them?"

Hunter couldn't help himself. He roared with laughter. Chelsea's indignation was priceless. He battled for composure, but it was near impossible. "Keep the bands, but any time you want to handle my balls, just say the word."

"You...you..." She threw her hands up and stormed along the verandah. "You may as well leave the expander and go home. Since you failed to show up on time, I started without you. I've only got a couple of hours left before dark."

"I'm here now, and I'm in my work clothes, so I may as well help." Hunter surveyed the upper boards of freshly painted olive-green, against the lower, faded, off-white boards. "If you're making such a dramatic change, won't you need to paint the whole house?"

"Your powers of observation are astounding, Sullivan. Yes, I will now have to paint the whole house." She dipped her brush in the paint can then attacked the panel in front of her with a vengeance. "Grandy ordered the paint, but the colour card Mum showed me, definitely wasn't grey."

"Soft olive-green."

"What?"

"It's soft olive-green. I like it."

"You have no idea what a relief that is, Sullivan." She bent to dip her brush again.

"Sarcasm doesn't suit you, Chelsea. Shelve your

dating agenda, and I'll work my five hours helping you paint the whole house."

"No thanks. You need to help me find my ideal man. I have three weeks to paint the house before my parents return. I shall do perfectly well on my own."

Hunter's gaze rose to the upper story and he shuddered. She'd have to stand on the wrap-around verandah roof to paint, but still wouldn't reach the higher boards. He sighed. "All right. I'll help on both counts." He picked up a roller.

"You will?" She faced him, chewing her bottom lip. "It will take more than five hours."

He shrugged. "If I lose our next wager, you can subtract the hours."

"Next wager?" A wide smile spread across her face, transforming her anxious dark eyes to pools of velvet devilment. "The rematch. Yes, ten hours should do nicely."

He wouldn't be surprised if she did a victory dance. Immense satisfaction washed off her in waves. Hunter dragged his gaze from her lips. Kissing her was out of the question. "Yes, but if I win, you're mine for two full days."

"Doesn't matter, I'll still win." She attacked the wall with renewed vigour. "The house gets painted, and I get my man. What can you do with me over two days that you haven't done with any other woman?"

"Race our horses across Tully Flats then up through Red Gum Gully to a dam where a family of ducks live. Ride through Akuna National Park then take the horses swimming in one of the deep watering holes. Lie side-by-side under the stars on a clear summer night and search out all the constellations." *Make out under those same stars then fall asleep in each other's arms.* That fist tightened around his chest again. Meaningless hook-ups had lost their attraction since a case of mistaken identity almost destroyed his sister's life.

At the time he'd thought it amusing to be mistaken for the local vet. He'd accepted the flirty pharmaceutical rep's advances, until he'd discovered she was married. When the peeved woman stalked out of the surgery, rearranging her clothes, he'd had no idea she'd spoken to Aleisha, or that his sister and Jake Morgan were involved.

Fortunately fate intervened, yet twenty months later, he was still perceived as a man without scruples. The thought didn't sit well of handing Chelsea over to some clot who didn't have a clue how to satisfy a vibrant woman, or a rat after her land.

The absolute silence impinged on his brain. He glanced up from his work boots, to see Chelsea holding her paintbrush in the air, staring at him. Droplets of olive-green paint dotted the boards in front of her bare feet.

He frowned. "What?"

"Are you saying, you've never made out with a woman under the stars, or woken up with her in your arms?"

"Shit. I didn't mean to say that aloud."

"Well you did, so which is it?"

"I've never done either." Hunter ran the roller through the paint tray and went to work. "If you want to get this wall finished tonight, stop gawking and paint."

She huffed. "Seems to me you're one big phoney, Sullivan. If you want to win our wager, you'd better ask Harry for some pointers."

He chuckled; thankful she'd lightened the mood. "The Morgans continue to underestimate the Sullivans."

She laughed. "Let's put it to the test. If we finish this wall by seven, I'll make dinner. If not, these two-hours don't count, and you still help me with the graph tonight."

Hiding his grin, Hunter coated his roller again. "Do I still get dinner, or do you plan to starve me? I missed lunch."

"You still get dinner, but you have to dock Stanthorpe's tail then feed him."

"What about the testicles?"

"If you want me to dock *your* testicles, Hunter, it will have to be after we work on the graph, because I won't be able to concentrate with your high-pitched screaming."

"*Touché*, honey." Hunter chuckled. They settled into an easy rhythm, painting and bantering in a light-hearted fashion, sometimes debating more serious topics, giving him a whole new insight to Chelsea's clever mind. Deep and meaningful conversation was something he'd never encouraged with women who were not related to him. The thought humbled him. He truly was his mother's son. If Chelsea could reform him, it would be a miracle, but she was welcome to try. He had nothing to lose.

"Sorry, Hunter, we aren't going to finish by seven."

Her overly cheerful voice brought him out of his despondency to find they only had five minutes. It amused him to see Chelsea valiantly trying to keep a straight face as her brush strokes slowed to a snail pace. He could easily finish the last two boards in time, but he was having too much fun to cut the evening short.

"I can finish these, why don't you start on my dinner?"

"What?" She checked his progress. "You're almost finished."

"You'd be amazed what I can do with a little incentive."

Her velvety eyes widened. "Oh wait, you misunderstood me. I meant we have to clean up by seven. You're out of time, Sullivan. I win again." With a smug grin, she ran her brush along the board, humming merrily.

No, honey, I win. Hunter turned away to hide his own satisfied grin.

Chapter Fourteen

Anticipation buzzed through Chelsea's veins as she waited for Hunter. He had to be the messiest painter she'd ever come across. Once they'd finished the back verandah, he'd been speckled with olive-green paint from head to foot. At his insistence, she left him cleaning the brushes to come inside and make a simple pasta, only to discover his method of washing brushes left his shirt and trousers drenched.

They'd eaten on the back steps then she'd sent him off to shower and change. She'd yet to tell him she'd secured two coffee dates for the morning. Another in the afternoon would be most helpful.

"Okay, how can I be of assistance?" His deep voice and warm breath beside her ear sent a pleasant tingle through her.

"You...you can tell me what I've forgotten." She pointed at her headings. "And, who else I should consider."

He slid onto the chair beside her, picked up a black

marker pen and studied her graph. "So, you've decided Craig Sanders and Shane Picton are your first contenders?"

"Yes, I rang them today. Craig is meeting me at the Cyprus Café at nine and Shane at eleven. Is two hours long enough for a coffee date?"

"Struth, you don't waste time. Half an hour would be plenty." He sounded rather gruff, but she relaxed as he began writing in her neatly ruled squares. "You need to consider irritating habits, possessiveness and temperament. If the guy's jealous, possessive or has a nasty temper, you want to steer clear."

"I agree. That gives me...ten means to rate them. What else?"

He picked up her ruler and began drawing back-slashes under all the headings in every square. "For every attribute you give a score out of ten, which gives each contender a total score out of one hundred per date, for example..."

Chelsea leaned closer as Hunter used a pencil to give Craig Sanders differing scores under her headings. She giggled when the final score for their coffee date totalled twenty-five. "You're a tough marker. I'm sure Craig would reach at least seventy."

He huffed. "As I don't know the guy, I can't comment. Was he surprised you called?"

"At first, but he thinks I want to talk about school stuff."

"What about Shane Picton?" Did Hunter sound annoyed or was it her imagination?

"Yes, he was definitely surprised, but seemed eager to have coffee with me."

"Of course he is," Hunter muttered as he erased

the pencilled scores. "After each date is recorded in pen, rub out your scores for the next date."

"That's brilliant. Who else should I consider?" She tried to sound excited, when really an attack of nerves assailed her. Or it could be Hunter's proximity. Maybe this wasn't such a good idea.

"Nigel Clemons and Leroy Murdoch." He wrote in their names and occupations. "I can't be sure about their ages, but they're under thirty. You'll have to ask them."

"No problem. Hey, why did you rub out Jerry Eckford."

"He's got to be forty."

"He's thirty-seven. I asked my mother.

"Nice fella, but too old for you, and he's under his mother's thumb."

She snatched the pen. "I'm writing him in. What about the guy who works for you?"

Hunter's eyes narrowed. "He's not suitable."

"Does he have a drinking problem, or a nasty temper? Is he a womaniser?"

"No, but I see him every day. I don't want to hear about your escapades."

It was not her imagination. Hunter definitely had the grumps. She laughed. "Okay, I'll speak to Edwina Lette." She clutched Hunter's arm. "Edwina has a sixth sense. I don't think any of her predictions have ever been wrong."

He groaned, dropping his head into his hands. "I don't want you talking to Edwina."

She rubbed his shoulder consolingly. "It will be fine, Hunter. Edwina may give me a heads up on my ideal man."

"Bloody hell."

A low growling drew their attention. Chelsea frowned. "That's Lola. A fox or dingo could be about." She pushed back the chair and ran into the kitchen then out onto the dark verandah. "Lola, come here girl."

The low growling continued from behind the barn, except now Reggie had joined Lola.

"Something is definitely out there." Hunter brushed past her. "Pity you dismantled the verandah lights. They would have illuminated the yard. I've got a torch in my car."

She grabbed his arm. "Put your boots on, I don't want you standing on a snake."

He chuckled. "It's nice to hear someone besides my grandmother and Antonia think my hide is worth saving."

As he pulled on his thick socks and boots, Chelsea found herself pondering his words. "Hunter, do *you* think your hide is worth saving?"

"No, I don't." He jumped down the steps then strode to his car.

"Well you are." Chelsea called after him. "Everyone deserves a second chance." Finding her own socks and boots, she dragged them on and ran after him.

Hunter kept the torch on low beam as they rounded the side of the barn.

Lola and Reggie stood alert and growling as they stared into the darkness. Two beams of light drifted over a far paddock down near the river then disappeared. Chelsea clutched Hunter's arm. "Did you see that?"

"Could it be Angus?"

"Angus wouldn't be driving through our bottom paddock, especially at this time of night, but someone is. I'll get my ute. We need to investigate."

"No." He caught her hand. "Your lights will alert them, and it's too dangerous to drive in the dark. We'll go on foot. If it's rustlers, we'll phone the police."

"Let's take the horses and Lola. She'll lead us straight to them."

"Okay. Lock Reggie in the barn."

Chelsea called both dogs, then put Reggie in a stall with Stanthorpe. While she saddled Muscat, Hunter saddled Buck. With Lola leading the way, and light from the moon, they cantered along the dirt trail beside the home paddock. The closer they got to the river the more Chelsea's apprehension grew. She hadn't seen light beams for a while, but the paddock they were headed to contained ten breeding bulls, all worth their massive weight in gold. Hunter drew Buck to a stop then motioned for her to dismount.

Once they'd tied the horses to the gate, he pressed his mouth to her ear. "Stay here, I'm going to cross the paddock on foot."

"I'm coming with you."

"If it is rustlers, I may need you to go for help."

"Hunter, you're scaring me." Chelsea frantically searched the dark for any sign of movement. "They must be below the dip. This paddock has all our bulls in it."

"Give me ten minutes. I'll send three flashes if it's safe to follow. If you don't see any, go for help."

"Hunter, be careful. Your hide *is* worth saving."

"Thanks, honey." He bounded over the gate and ran off into the dark.

"Lola." She glanced behind, surprised Lola hadn't whined or licked her fingers. "Lola?"

No response. Her gaze shot to the black outline of trees along the river. The more she stared, the easier it became to make out a group of large black shapes in the far corner. The low growls verifying the agitated state of the bulls. She counted nine then found Hunter and Lola stealthily making their way across the middle. It would take more than one person to coerce a fully-grown Hereford Bull onto a cattle truck. Or a dog and electric prod.

"Please be careful, Hunter."

An engine spluttered to life then headlights lit up the distant trees. Relief surged. The rustlers had either seen Hunter and were fleeing, or they'd succeeded in loading a bull. It didn't matter, they'd be caught. All that mattered was Hunter and Lola were safe.

The terror that had seized her gradually ebbed away, leaving an astounding realisation. She cared about Hunter. Her infatuation with Reid had never caused this level of angst. "Ridiculous. It doesn't mean anything. I would be just as terrified if it were Reid, or one of my brothers."

With her dilemma resolved, Chelsea considered the rustler's escape route. They could cross the bridge then go through the McGregor place, but unless they were familiar with the river bends and trees at night, finding the bridge would be near impossible. And, to exit Craigellachie, they'd have to pass close to the homestead, which would alert Angus.

"They won't go that way."

Their second option would be through Tulachmhor,

but with the gates heavily chained, they'd probably take an easier route.

"Big time waster."

That left the most likely option. They'd drive north along the eastern boundary fence of Hickory Ridge, opening unlocked gates to cross three large paddocks. They'd then use the main drive to exit onto Wallaby Flats Lane. If she took Muscat and stuck to the ridge trail, she could watch the rustlers progress and damn near beat them to the front gate. All she needed was a number plate. Decision made, she untied Muscat then swung up into the saddle.

Chapter Fifteen

Agitated bulls were not on Hunter's list of favourite things to tussle with on a star-studded night, but then neither were vicious dogs or rustlers. He rubbed his chin as the truck's taillights vanished. The rustler's dog had alerted them to his and Lola's approach, and they'd made a run for it, which meant he'd had to skirt an aggressive bull to shut the gate. At least the bastards were going home empty-handed. Lola whined at his side.

"I know how you feel. Come on, I need you to divert the bull, so I can close the gate."

Taking her cue, Lola made a wide circuit of the hostile bull. He shifted with her, his head lowered as he pawed the ground, growling low in his throat. The electric prod and a snapping dog at his hind legs had taken their toll. The brute was in a foul temper.

Moving slowly, Hunter backed towards the gate while Lola darted left and right, keeping the bull's attention riveted on her. Once he had the gate secured,

Hunter whistled, and she came hurtling across the field and under the fence. "Good, girl. Find Chelsea.

As he sprinted behind Lola, Hunter ran his gaze along the connecting fence line until it reached the dark silhouette of a single horse. Frantically, he searched further afield, until movement caught his attention. Chelsea and Muscat cantered along a higher ridge, their silhouette so clear, anyone looking up would see them.

"Shit." He pulled out his phone and rang his brother. He began to think Reid wasn't home until he finally answered.

"This had better be important, Hunter, I have company." Reid sounded as grumpy as an old man with gout, but then he'd been fencing under the blazing sun all day.

"It is." Hunter kept his gaze glued to Chelsea. "Rustlers just tried to steal a bull from Hickory Ridge. The bastards are making their way along the Morgan's eastern boundary in a small cattle truck." He dragged in a deep breath. "Chelsea's hell-bent on intercepting them. God knows what they'll do, if she recognises them."

"Why didn't you stop her? If anything happens to her, I'll—"

"Damn it, Reid, quit the lecture. I thought she was safe, out of harm's way. I need your help. I won't catch her in time."

"On my way. I'll ring the cops then try to cut off the rustlers' escape."

"Thanks."

The phone went dead and a little of Hunter's anxiety eased. Reid's cottage was close to Tulachmhor's front gate. He'd make it in time. He had to. Climbing over the corner post, Hunter sprinted to Buck, mounted, then took off after Chelsea and Lola.

Buck was stronger and younger than Muscat, so Hunter pushed him as far as he dared. The ridge trail was well-maintained and easily negotiated under moonlight, but Jake would never forgive him if Buck broke a leg.

The horse shied then reared, almost unseating Hunter. "Easy boy, easy." He brought Buck round, but the gelding flattened his ears and refused to take another step forward.

"What's up?" Movement on the side of the trail caught his eye then a six-foot King Brown slithered across their path and into the bush. "Woah, easy boy." He patted Buck's quivering shoulder. "It's gone now. Let's go." Digging in his heels, Hunter sprang the gelding into a gallop. The thundering hooves would scare off other snakes.

From the top of the ridge, Hunter could see the dimmed lights of the truck nearing another gate. In the far distance, on Tulachmhor, a set of headlights moved north. It would be close.

Reid's headlights turned onto Wallaby Flats Lane. Hickory Ridge and Tulachmhor were side by side, yet their driveways were ten kilometres apart. With kangaroos tending to feed alongside the road, it was never wise to drive above sixty kilometres, especially at night, but Reid's ute tore along the dirt road.

Hunter couldn't see Chelsea, although he caught up to Lola, panting, her tongue hanging out. Overtaking her, Hunter followed the winding dirt road down from the ridge. When Chelsea had talked her father into putting a road system through Hickory Ridge, most folks argued it a waste of valuable grazing land. Chelsea had stood her ground, maintaining moving vehicles without having to open then close gates or disturb stock made sense.

Galloping along one of the internal roads, Hunter silently applauded her foresight. He was too far behind Chelsea. The ridge hid the rustler's lights, but they couldn't be far away.

Coming to a crossroad, he turned left onto the main driveway leading past the homestead. The truck hadn't passed while they were painting, which meant it must have cut through the front paddocks and along the far side of the ridge between the two properties.

He reached the front gate and eased Buck to a stop. The gelding snorted and pranced, his neck and shoulders caked in sweat. Hunter searched the road ahead and the dark paddock to his right. This was where Reid and Chelsea should have been.

A wailing siren sounded in the far distance. The cops were on their way, which meant they would meet the rustlers—if the bastards hadn't changed direction.

"Damn it." He'd always admired the high ridge dotted in hickory trees, especially when the sun set behind it, but right now it was a bloody nuisance and the rustlers were using it to their advantage. Where was Chelsea?

A large mob of heifers and calves occupied the paddocks fronting Wallaby Flats Lane. Most scattered as he rode through. Others, well used to stockmen, watched with mild curiosity. Hunter cantered over the dry grass, alert for lights or noise other than the siren. A sharp yap, drew his attention to a group of trees, where Lola stood panting beside Muscat. Chelsea and the dog must have taken the same shortcut down from the ridge.

"Thank God." His relief was short-lived. There was no sign of Chelsea. "I'm going to strangle her. Where the hell is Reid?"

Lights dipped on the far side of the next group of trees, heading north. The rustlers were making for the front boundary fence. He could only pray Chelsea didn't get too close. If anything happened to her, it would shred him to the bone.

Chapter Sixteen

Slowing for a bend, Reid noticed a panel of the Morgan's fence down. He swerved in behind a clump of trees on the other side of the road. Movement on the ridge above caught his attention. The dark silhouette of a horse and rider came cantering down the fire trail then jumped a gate and made for a clump of trees.

"Christ almighty."

Chelsea Morgan had been the bane of his life for far too long. She'd never had anyone raise their hand or voice to her in anger, never been sent to bed without dinner, or locked in the woodshed for defiance. Never been reined in from doing whatever she bloody well wanted.

Chelsea had led a fairy-tale existence, idolised by every member of her family. As an adult, she spent five days a week with six-year-old children who showered her in adoration. She naively believed everything could be fixed with a hug or kiss.

Reining in his temper, Reid leapt out of his ute and ran across the road. Using the cattle as a shield, he jogged across the field. Reaching the clump of trees, he found Muscat tethered to a low hanging branch and no sign of Chelsea. "Shit."

With only moonlight to aid his sight, Reid searched the distance then ran towards another group of trees.

By the time he reached the trees, she was running out in the open. The siren wail grew louder, but the cops would go up the main drive. A spluttering engine caught his attention. He searched the darkness finding a pair of dimmed headlights coming from the south. Breaking into a full sprint, he chased after the bane of his life as she rounded a huge mass of blackberries. Behind him came the sharp bark of a dog and hoof beats.

Rounding the tangle of blackberries, Reid's heart gave a start. The bloody woman was out in the middle of the paddock. If she expected them to stop for a friendly chat, she'd lost her marbles.

Reid's legs pumped under him as he chased her, his heart thundering within his chest and ears, perspiration swamping his forehead, and black fear rose like a tidal wave. Bindarra Creek without Chelsea Morgan would be a bleak place.

A Blue Heeler pelted past as thundering hooves came surging up behind. Buck's huge frame overtook him, gaining fast on Chelsea. He could only pray Hunter made it in time. Gasping, Reid bent over, clutching his knees as he dragged in air and watched in horror as the truck's speed increased.

"Chelsea, *no*." Hunter bellowed a stream of

profanities as he bent low over Buck's neck, galloping at a nerve-racking speed. They were all on a collision course.

Having long ago given up on miracles, Reid tensed for the impact, a deadening dread preventing him from taking another step. All he could do was watch in horror as Chelsea realised the rustlers' intention and turned to flee.

Hunter bellowed again, but Reid couldn't make out his words, only the blind terror in his brother's ragged voice.

Chelsea burst into action, sprinting towards Buck as Hunter galloped towards her. Seconds passed, but it felt like a lifetime as Reid urged her to run faster, praying Buck didn't trample her, vowing to tear the rustler's limbs from their bodies, if any harm came to Chelsea.

Almost on top of Chelsea, Hunter pulled a stunt they'd witnessed Jake and Riley perform years ago. He hauled down on the right rein, bringing Buck to a skidding halt, then reached out as Chelsea jumped. Against all odds she caught his arm and swung up behind him, just as Buck's massive hind legs bunched. Without missing a beat, the gelding leapt forward, veering away from the truck to gallop in a wide arc, then slowing to a canter towards Reid.

Lola went into a frenzied barking, chasing the truck.

The truck's gears crunched as the driver dropped to third then flattened the accelerator, making for the break in the fence. The headlights went out with the unmistakable approach of a siren, seconds before the flashing red and blue lights appeared along Wallaby Creek Lane.

As Reid expected the paddy wagon swung into the main drive and sped towards Hickory Ridge homestead, while the truck, now with its lights on, rocketed towards Reservoir Road.

"Shit." With no outlet for his fury, Reid clenched his fists and jaw, his body vibrating with frustration as Hunter drew Buck to a stop.

"Chelsea Morgan, I'm going to wring your bloody neck then put you on the first train to the coast. Once I inform your damn brothers of what you've been up to, they won't let you out of their sight for the next year. With any luck it will be five years. What the hell were you trying to prove?"

"Stow it, Reid, she's winded. I hope I didn't crack her ribs with the impact." Hunter lifted his right leg over the saddle and slid to the ground then reached for Chelsea.

A new fear clutched Reid. "We'd better get her to the hospital."

"I'm just winded." Chelsea took several short breaths then turned her face into Hunter's chest. "Thank you for saving me. I wasn't trying to prove anything. I thought if I recognised them, we could get Reid's sheep back."

Reid silently cursed. "A few sheep are not worth your bloody life, Chelsea." Witnessing her seeking comfort from Hunter raised a grain of concern. They looked a little too comfortable for his liking, which didn't improve his temper.

Chelsea shuddered. "The first part of the number plate is WOS, and I caught a glimpse of the driver. He wore a beanie and leaned over the steering wheel with scary intent. He...he would have mowed me down."

Reid ran a hand through his hair. "After we speak to the police, you're leaving town until the rustlers are caught or your brothers return."

"You can let me go now, Hunter." She wriggled until he obliged then she faced Reid with both hands fisted on her slim hips. "I've wasted years waiting for you to show me the slightest bit of interest. I might as well have been a scrawny sparrow, waiting for a crumb of your affection or concern. *You* do not tell me what to do. I decide what's best for me. Come on, Hunter, we have an agenda to finalise."

Leaving him gobsmacked, she stalked off with Lola trotting behind.

Hunter shook his head. "At least *I'm* still in her good books."

Reid clamped his fingers about Hunter's bicep, forestalling him from following the indignant little fireball. "Hurt her in any way, and I'll beat you to a pulp."

"You're a fool, Reid." Hunter jerked his arm away. "She'd give you the world if you let her. And, no matter what you believe, neither of us are capable of our mother's vicious abuse. We don't hurt women or children."

"How can you, of all people, say that?" Reid couldn't hide his distaste for Hunter's lifestyle. After all, it had ended their sister's relationship with Jake Morgan, until the truth had emerged the night their baby was born.

"Damn you, Reid. Most of my reputation is hearsay, and I've never dallied with married women or virgins. Chelsea is in no danger from me."

"She can't *still* be a virgin." He glanced after Chelsea,

watching as she stalked towards Muscat. "She must have dated guys at Uni."

"She might have dated one or two, but she only ever wanted you."

"Bloody hell." Was there no end to his mounting guilt?

"Don't fret." Hunter clapped his shoulder. "By this time next year, I'll have her married to a decent guy and with luck, pregnant. She'll get everything she's ever wanted."

Reid rolled his shoulders. "It'll take a bloody miracle, or a man with the patience of a saint."

"Probably, but I'm committed now, so don't go throwing a spanner in the works. Let's fix that fence before the cattle wander onto the road."

"I can do it. You talk to the cops. Tell them to stop on their way out and I'll give my statement. We'll have to go into town tomorrow and do it formally. I'll ring Riley and Jake when I get home."

"Tell them I'll keep an eye on her."

Reid huffed. "Is that supposed to mollify them?"

"Okay, tell them she's staying in town. I'll make sure she does." He'd shadow her if necessary. No rustlers or prospective coffee dates would get within a foot of her if he had his way.

Chapter Seventeen

Rattled by her close encounter with death and Reid's fury, Chelsea flung herself into the saddle. She couldn't stop shaking, or still the images and sounds flooding her mind. The driver's intent stare, the churning gears, Buck bearing down on her, his hooves thundering. Hunter's ragged roar or the torment in his eyes as he risked his own life and Buck's to save her. She nudged Muscat into a canter, reaching the gate with Lola only to find Hunter still talking to Reid.

"What are those two planning now?"

It wasn't hard to hazard a guess. She'd bet her grandmother's vinyl record collection they intended to ring her brothers, which meant Jake and Riley would turn up sometime tomorrow, and that would definitely hamper her dating agenda. Unless she got in first. It didn't matter what she promised them as long as they stayed away.

Still pulsating from her close encounter with

death, and Hunter's heroic rescue, she trotted up the drive. Thank God he'd been on Buck. She rallied against her brothers years ago for performing such a wicked trick, endangering their lives and Buck, but the gelding had been as wild as them and loved showing off. Tonight, he'd saved her life.

Outside the barn, she discovered Constable AJ Donaldson leaning against the bonnet of his paddy wagon patting Reggie. AJ was Gloria and Mayor Donaldson's son. They'd adopted him at the age of ten, after a hurricane hit his home of St Lucia in the Caribbean. Tightly curled black hair, honey-coloured skin and soft brown eyes, AJ was an outgoing cheeky twenty-two-year-old. And, his boss was Chelsea's brother, Riley. At least Abby hadn't been on call. As Senior Constable, she would definitely report to Riley. At least with AJ, Chelsea had a chance to smooth things over.

"Hey, Chelsea, where are the rustlers?"

"They went through the front fence. Your siren warned them of your approach, then you missed them by coming up the driveway."

"I didn't see them."

"Doesn't matter, I got a partial plate and glimpse of the driver." She swung down from the saddle. "I'll tell you everything, but first I've got to brush Muscat then ring Riley. Reid and Hunter Sullivan will give you a statement as they witnessed things too."

AJ's eyebrows rose. "The Sullivans are here?"

"Yes, they promised my father they'd keep an eye on me and the farm."

"Rightio." AJ accepted her statement without blinking. Everyone in Bindarra Creek knew Chelsea didn't lie. "You want for me to brush your mare while you ring Senior Sergeant Morgan?"

She hid a smile at his formality and how neatly he fell into her trap. "That would be great." She handed AJ the reins. It was common knowledge he loved horses and a little unfair to take advantage, but time was of the essence. "Her name's Muscat. Can you check her water too? I've worked her hard tonight."

"Yeah, no worries." He led Muscat into the barn.

"Come, girls." Chelsea jogged through the back-garden gate, filled two bowls with water then hurried into the house. Snatching up her phone from the dining table, she quickly keyed in Riley's number.

"Hey, Chelsea, what's up?"

"Hi, Riley, I'm just letting you know we had rustlers try to steal a bull tonight."

"Bloody hell. Are you okay?"

"I'm fine. Hunter and I saw lights so went to investigate. The rustlers made a run for it, but I got part of their number plate and AJ's taking our statements. The bastards cut a panel of the front fence, and I..."

"You what?" Riley's voice dropped. "What did you do?"

"I got a bit close and nearly got run down, but Hunter came to my rescue. Now he and Reid are fixing the fence."

"I'll drive back tomorrow."

"No, please don't. It will upset Samantha and Ali if you leave." Dealing that card was low, but her brothers adored their wives and would go to great lengths to keep them happy. "The rustlers are unlikely to come back and our neighbours will be watching over me like hawks. If it makes you happier, I'll sleep at your house, although I'll have to bring the dogs and a lamb with me."

"What if Harry were to stay with you?"

"No, he's looking forward to that camping trip with our cousins. Angus and Reid are only a phone call away."

"Okay, wait. What was Hunter doing there?"

"He's helping me paint the back verandah. Don't overreact. Dad knows about it."

"The wager, right? Tell AJ to ring me once you're done."

"Sure. Bye, Riley."

Ending the call with a wide grin, Chelsea turned to the table and her scattered array of markers, pencils and graph. Nothing was where she'd left it. Stalking back to the barn she found AJ in a stall, crooning as he brushed Muscat.

"So, you saw my dating graph?"

He looked at her blankly. "Your what?"

"The graph on the table in the dining room."

"I only went to the kitchen door. I didn't go inside your house." Truth and curiosity shone in his eyes.

She bit her lip. "I guess the wind must have blown my things about."

He looked through the barn door. Not a whiff of breeze stirred the air. "You want me to have a look around?"

"No." Hearing hoof beats, she paced across the barn and waited for Hunter by the door out of AJ's hearing. "What took you so long?"

"Missing me already." Hunter chuckled softly, dismounted then passed the reins over Buck's head.

"Reid is fixing the front fence. Tomorrow, I'll get some heavy-duty chains for your gates."

"Someone's been in the house." She hadn't thought she could get any more rattled. She'd been wrong. Little noises were making her jumpy.

He went very still. "What makes you think so?"

"Everything on the dining table has been moved. Someone must have come in while we were chasing the rustlers."

"Then why didn't we see them leave?"

"Maybe they arrived and left before we reached the front paddocks."

"I'll have a quick look around after I speak to AJ."

"Did Reid ring Riley?"

"Not yet, but he will. Sorry, sunshine, but it's the right thing to do. Sleep in town until your brothers get back. I'll help you do whatever's necessary here."

"I have everything under control."

"You're not staying here by yourself tonight."

This was her home. She refused to leave it and the animals unguarded. "Okay, I'll make up a spare bed for you." She sent up a silent prayer he'd stay.

"Chelsea?" By his tone, he wouldn't let her manipulate him, which didn't surprise her. She'd never been any good at it.

She shrugged. "Fine, go home, but I'm staying here." As she paced away, she heard an exasperated sigh, which said it all. He wouldn't leave her alone. Hunter Sullivan was his father's son. Thank God.

Chapter Eighteen

As far as Chelsea could see, nothing else in the house had been disturbed, so she made up a bed in her brothers' old room then fed Stanthorpe. Lola and Reggie were curled up in the barn with the lamb, so she left them to guard the other horses then, as an afterthought, watered her mother's roses which she'd forgotten to do earlier. Then she returned to the house via the front verandah. On a wicker chair, she found a small bouquet of purple pansies with a card attached.

"Happy New Year. From your greatest fan."

It had to be Craig Sanders. He'd asked her out several times over the last year. Or maybe the flowers were from Reece Nolan. The nice-looking farrier had been out three days ago to shoe Muscat. He'd lingered, making small talk until her father walked away then he'd asked her out.

Or, it could be Joe Rossiter or Shane Picton, both local shearers, who crashed her staff Christmas party at the bowling club a few weeks ago. Although a little tipsy, they'd livened things up, much to Craig's annoyance.

After closing the front door, she carried the pretty blooms through to the kitchen, where Hunter and AJ were going over the night's events. "I found these at the front door. There's no name, but they're from a secret fan."

Hunter's eyes narrowed. "A fan who entered your house uninvited."

"So, it would seem." Hiding her uneasiness, Chelsea filled a ceramic jug and arranged the flowers as she mulled over her newest dilemma. Whoever left the flowers knew about her dating agenda.

"I should inform Senior Constable Taylor." AJ pulled out his phone. "Dis is serious."

"No, don't. Abby has enough on her plate. It's probably my work colleague, Craig. He must have heard I was here alone and came to check on me. With all the doors open and no answer, he might come inside, out of worry. Afterall, it's quite late."

"Too late to be delivering flowers." Hunter scowled at her. "I'll call by Jon Johnson's tomorrow. If he sold the flowers, he'll have your admirer's name." Pulling out his phone, he took a photo of the pansies. "Who knows, it could have been an accomplice, hoping to keep you busy while the other rustler stole a bull."

Chelsea blinked at him. "That's hardly likely, Hunter." She couldn't hide the quiver in her voice. She slid onto a chair beside AJ. "Let's get this over, so I can go to bed."

AJ quickly read through Hunter's statement. When

she agreed with everything, he scratched his head. "How did you see the driver's face in the dark?"

"Good question." She closed her eyes, instantly recalling the scariest seconds of her life. The man's cruel countenance still gave her the creeps. "An interior light must have come on momentarily. He wore a beanie and a scarf round the bottom part of his face. And there was a dog in the cab, but I didn't see anyone else. It was too dark."

AJ rapidly scribbled in his notebook. "You'll need to come into the station tomorrow to sign your statement." After a quick word on the verandah with Hunter, he left.

Relieved, Chelsea followed Hunter through the entire house as he double-checked every room, window and all the French doors leading onto the wraparound verandah.

"I'm sure no one is planning to break into the house, Hunter."

"They'll get a surprise if they do." He winked. "Which room am I in?"

"The one opposite mine. It's Jake and Riley's old room. We should leave our doors open in case we hear something." Again, her voice wobbled.

Hunter clasped a hand over his heart. "Does that mean if I scream, you'll come running to my rescue, Miss Morgan?"

His attempt at humour eased her anxiety. "One good turn deserves another." She stretched up and kissed his cheek. "Thank you for saving my life tonight."

Concern and tenderness filled his eyes. "Promise me, you won't do anything like that again, Chelsea. You took years off my life."

"It took years off my life." Not sure what to do with her hands, she patted his biceps. Good lord, they were hard as rock. So were his shoulders and chest. Shocked to find her fingers spread over his wide chest, she raised her gaze to find his jaw locked and his eyes smouldering with desire. No one had ever looked at her like this. "Erm, I should go have that shower. I... I've left a towel on the...the bed for you."

Stepping away was harder than she thought. Her hands had a mind of their own and wanted to stay right where they were.

Hunter didn't say a word as she ran up the stairs, yet she could feel his eyes, like a laser, burning a path down her spine. It brought forth a yearning for everything she'd been missing. More kissing and touching, free of clothing. No wonder women chased him.

Chelsea showered then pulled on her primmest pyjamas. She would probably swelter, but it gave her an armour of sorts. As if she didn't have enough to worry about, there was an appreciation in Hunter's eyes that had her pulse racing. It only added to her growing awareness of him. As for the way he kissed and the strength of his arms...

Stop thinking about him.

With a huff, she climbed into bed and stared at the ceiling. Sleep would be a long way off, especially knowing Hunter stood under the shower next door, water streaming over his powerful body. She groaned, closed her eyes and pulled the sheet over her head.

Several minutes passed before the shower went quiet and Hunter left the bathroom. She strained to hear his movements but couldn't detect a sound, then the sheet lifted.

She screeched.

Hunter caught both her hands as she struck out. "Honey, it's me. You'll get all hot and bothered covering your head like that."

"I'm already hot and—good God." Her gaze devoured his magnificent naked chest then lowered, following a fine line of hair to the open button of his jeans. "What...what are you doing in my room?"

"Checking you're okay. Want me to tuck you in?" Without waiting for her answer, he folded back the sheet then kissed her forehead. "Sweet dreams." He hesitated, as if wanting to say something, but couldn't find the words.

"What is it?"

He shook his head. "I've never tucked a desirable woman into bed then left her with only a chaste kiss. Another first."

Her breath caught. "You...you desire me?"

"Yes, Chelsea, and it's damn inconvenient." He strode from her room, flicking the hall light off as he grumbled, "If this goes on much longer, the only way you'll be safe is if I lock you in a tower with a bloody chastity belt."

Tingles of delight rippled throughout Chelsea. "I assume I'm supposed to wear this primitive chastity belt?"

The springs on the spare bed squeaked. "Yes."

His gruff reply had her giggling. "But won't you have the keys?"

"Go to sleep, Chelsea, before I lose the thin thread of honour I'm clinging too."

"Good night, Hunter."

Her grin grew wider. There was so much more to Hunter than she'd ever appreciated. In fact, the past twenty-four hours had been more exciting than a single minute spent with any other man. That gave her a sobering jolt. The next three weeks promised to be anything but dull.

Chapter Nineteen

A shrill scream brought Hunter bolt upright. Another had him fumbling out of bed, so disorientated he slammed into a wall before realising he wasn't in his own house.

A woman shrieked his name over and over and it wasn't in the throes of ecstasy. He stumbled to the door, groping for the light switch. As the room exploded in light, so did his memory.

"Chelsea!" He dashed across the hall, fists clenched, a tornado of emotions detonating inside his brain. It was almost an anti-climax to find no opponent to take the brunt of his crazed imagination. With his heart pounding, he flicked on the bedside lamp.

Chelsea sobbed brokenly, her face drenched in sweat as she twisted back and forth, fighting to escape her tightly wrapped prison.

"Jesus." He dragged the offending quilt away then lifted her into his lap. Swiftly, he stripped off her saturated pyjamas then carried her to the bathroom, where he sat on the side of the bath, nursing her as he wiped a cool washer over her flaming face.

Frantic brown eyes blinked at him then she gasped and clung to his arm. "Hunter?"

"Shush, you had a nightmare." Grasping a towel, he covered her naked torso. It might hide the generous swells of her breasts and the all too feminine curves of her waist and hips, but once seen, never forgotten. Her bikini panties only fuelled his lust. He groaned.

She clung tighter. "The rustlers were chasing Reid. I tried to distract them, but they mowed him down, then backed over him."

"Reid's fine." Hunter couldn't hide his irritation. It was always bloody Reid.

"No, you don't understand." She straightened, clutching his face in hot little hands. "I ran to him, but his body...it was a cardboard cut-out."

Hunter coughed to mask the laugh he couldn't hold. She stared into his eyes, deadly serious. He'd never met a woman who could send his emotions soaring in different directions so fast. "Go on."

She drew in a shaky breath, her beautiful eyes filling with tears. "I flipped him over, only it wasn't Reid, it...it was you." A sob escaped and she buried her face against his neck. "It's the worst thing I've ever experienced."

"Honey, you were wearing flannelette pyjamas in summer then got twisted in your bedding. Overheating brought on a nightmare."

She lowered her hands to clutch the towel. As if realising her predicament, a ruddy blush bloomed over her face and upper chest. "I've never been in a pickle like this."

Neither had he. "I suggest you take a cool shower then try to get some sleep." He eased her off his lap then hightailed it to an ensuite off her parents' bedroom. He needed a cold shower more than she did.

It took longer than expected to cool his ardour. By the time he ducked his head into Chelsea's room, she had stripped her bed, remade it with clean sheets and was sitting on one edge yanking knots out of her wet hair.

She gave him shy smile. "You can come in, I won't bite."

"Pity." He didn't dare take up her invitation. "I'm only wearing jocks."

Her pretty lips twitched. "Hunter, I have two brothers and a father, who have no inhibitions about walking around in their underwear."

"I'm not your brother or your father." He should go back to bed instead of standing here captivated by a woman he couldn't have. That's what any sane man would do. Unfortunately, sanity had deserted him. "Can I help with those knots? At the rate you're attacking them, you'll be as bald as a badger in no time."

"Sure." She held out the wide-toothed comb. "Should I close my eyes to preserve your modesty?"

He glanced down at his constrained erection. "That would be appreciated." With her eyes closed, he was free to let his gaze roam over the pink singlet top and flowery boxers, neither of which dulled his memory. Taking the comb, he slid around behind her, confining her between his widespread thighs. The tremor that ran through her was small consolation to his arousal. What was he thinking?

Gently untangling her knots, he combed the lush

curls, surprised to find it soothed his raging lust, at least until she settled her palms on his thighs.

"You're very good at this, Hunter. I suppose you've had a lot of practice."

"Not unless your referring to my own hair. I've never done this for anyone else."

"Another first." She sighed. "You're *very* good."

He closed his eyes, battling the desire to roll her beneath him and draw pleasurable gasps from her pretty lips as he devoured every inch of her luscious body.

"Will you sleep with me?" Her whisper jerked him out of his fantasy.

"What?"

She jumped at his savage roar then twisted to glare at him. "I said sleep, Hunter, not have sizzling sex, you dolt." She elbowed his chest. "I don't want another nightmare."

He was still stuck on the idea of sizzling sex. With her passionate nature, under his tutorship, it *would* be sizzling. They'd both go up in a flaming inferno.

"Hunter, I don't want to be alone. You can sleep on top of the sheet and I'll stick a pillow between us to maintain proprieties."

He cleared his throat. "Just for tonight. Tomorrow you're moving into town. And, no touching me, there is only so much a man can withstand."

"Of course not." If ever there was an impish glow, it was plastered over her beaming face. He was definitely going to hell, one way or the other.

She deftly plaited her hair, wound a stretchy band around the bottom then padded around the double bed. "You can have that side."

A double bed. There was no way, they'd avoid bumping each other. Releasing a deep sigh, Hunter flicked the lamp switch, leaving a narrow strip of light from Riley and Jake's old room. They'd lynch him to the nearest tree if they got wind of this. As Chelsea rustled about arranging pillows, he stalked to the other room, turned off the light then felt his way back to her bed. The furthest thing from his mind being sleep.

Lying on the edge of the bed, fully aroused, with a pillow jammed against his back, and an extremely desirable woman within easy reach had to be some sort of karma. He wondered if things could get any worse.

They could.

A violent tug on his big toe woke him to the dim light of dawn. His contented state fled as he focussed on two irate men at the foot of the bed. *"Shit."*

Riley and Jake Morgan, although twins, had never looked more alike. Standing side by side, arms crossed, feet spread, their glares spewing retribution.

That's when he realised Chelsea lay tucked against his left side, her nose nestled against his shoulder, one limp arm draped across his naked torso, her fingertips an inch from his jocks and a morning erection that on any other day would do him proud. He groaned. "This is not what it looks like."

Chapter Twenty

The low rumble of male voices gradually induced Chelsea out of her dreamy snooze. She'd never been quick to wake, especially after a day at school followed by farm chores. It usually took a screeching alarm clock and a number of stretches before she could roll out of bed for her morning ride, unless it was raining then she'd curl up for another hour of sleep.

"You expect us to believe Chelsea had a nightmare and out of the goodness of your heart you gave her nothing but the plutonic comfort of your presence?" Riley's cold calmness sent a shiver through Chelsea.

"Something like that."

"Pull the other leg, Sullivan." Jake almost snarled. "You'd better have popped the question, otherwise I'm going to break every bone in your body."

Oh God, she wasn't dreaming. Riley and Jake were in her room and jumping to conclusions. She needed to handle them with extreme care.

She wriggled, pushing against the hard wall of muscle until she was leaning over Hunter, looking down on his magnificent chest. "Good morning." She yawned, sat back on her ankles and stretched, dropping her arms quickly when Hunter's arrested gaze fell to her breasts straining against the silk camisole. "Did you sleep well?"

"No." He jerked his head. "We have company. Your brothers believe I've taken advantage of you."

Keeping a cool countenance, she glanced over her shoulder at her posturing brothers. Indignation and fury radiated off them, yet if they truly believed he'd seduced her, they'd have hauled him out to the barn and beaten him to a pulp by now.

"Hi, Riley. Hi, Jake. It's the other way around. I took advantage of Hunter, although I did have to beg him to stay with me."

Hunter groaned. "You're not helping, sunshine."

"They won't hurt you, because you're an honourable man and you saved my life. And, you still owe me at least five hours."

Riley's lips twitched. He nudged Jake. "Chelsea *is* wearing pyjamas and Hunter *is* lying on top of the sheets."

Jake's unsettling gaze drifted over Chelsea. "You swear he hasn't touched you?"

"I would like to, but you know how I feel about lies." She ignored the groan below her. "Hunter saved my life last night by swooping me up while riding Buck, and last night held me after my nightmare."

"Bastard." Jake glared at Hunter. "You've coveted my horse for years."

"It was worth it. Buck faced down that cattle truck

without shying. Chelsea owes her life more to your horse than me."

"There he goes again, the reluctant hero." She hid her relief. If Jake was more put out over Hunter riding his horse than comforting her, he harboured no serious threat.

Riley caught her eye. "You've got ten minutes. Meet us in the kitchen. We want to know exactly what happened, including your unknown visitor and the flower delivery."

"Bloody AJ. I told him not to tell Abby." Chelsea huffed. "You should be swimming in the ocean and playing on the sand with your wives and daughters. I was handling things."

"Chelsea..."

"No, Riley. You listen to me. I'm sick of being mollycoddled and wrapped in cotton wool. I can run this farm just as well as any man."

"We know that, chickpea, but—"

"Don't 'chickpea' me." The nickname had always been her brother's way of soothing her ruffled feathers or gaining her silence after a teenage misdemeanour. It used to come with a bribe. "Go back to the coast and spend quality time with your wives and daughters. After last night, everyone will be on the lookout for the rustlers. It's only a matter of time before they're caught. Hunter will protect me, *if I need protection.*"

Her brothers' shrewd eyes shot to Hunter.

He shrugged. "The rules of her wager keep changing but having you two in my debt is an adequate upshot."

Riley and Jake exchange a cryptic glance before leaving her room.

"Ten minutes," called Riley.

"That's five minutes for you, Sullivan," snapped Jake. "I'm going out to the barn to check on Buck."

Turning back to Hunter, Chelsea's triumphant grin died on her lips. He was as still as a barn cat waiting to pounce on an unsuspecting mouse, the intensity in his eyes sending alarm bells clanging in her brain, warning her to tread carefully. "Is something wrong?"

"That's three minutes too long."

A sixth sense urged her not to ask, but she ignored it. "Why?"

"I can seduce you in one." He moved so fast she was on her back with her wrists imprisoned above her head in the blink of an eye, his heavy, hard body pressing her into the mattress.

"Hunter?" The shaky tremor in her voice sounded anything but alarmed. Her brothers' presence meant nothing, he was going to kiss her, and she'd wager her father's yet to be used golf clubs she'd never be the same again.

Hunter lowered his head, placing soft kisses on her eyelids and cheeks before moving his lips along her jaw, then catching her earlobe in a gentle bite. Every nerve in her body thrummed to life as he laid open-mouthed kisses down her throat, his warm breath tickling, making her squirm and arch under his hard body. She'd expected a ravishing kiss, but this...this tender seduction was unexpected. He wasn't conforming to his reputation at all and, God help her, she wanted to wrap her arms around him and get closer.

"Hunter." She gasped, straining against his hold. "More."

"Easy, darlin'." His deep voice vibrated against her throat. "Tell me what you want?"

"I... I don't know anymore. I can't think."

His deep chuckle brought tremors skittling across her collarbone. "I'll start with your mouth." He released her wrists then shifted his weight, no longer pinning her down, but pressed against her left side, leaning over her, the heat in his moss green eyes causing her breath to catch.

Callused fingers cupped her chin, holding her steady as he lowered his head. His lips moved restlessly over her own, before capturing her mouth and breath in an assault of the senses, demanding her full interaction. The few men she'd kissed had nothing on Hunter. He lured her deeper into the intimacy until she moaned and locked her arms around his neck, boldly meeting his tongue in a duel for supremacy.

She gasped as his hand closed possessively over her breast. Heat, desire and mortification exploded all at once. She wanted him to make love to her, but it came at too high a price and yet.... "Hunter."

Without removing his hand, he raised his head, watching her warily. Desire blazed briefly in his eyes before being replaced with guilt or maybe regret then a blasé expression.

She jerked as he rubbed his thumb over her sensitive nipple.

"Your first lesson in flirting, Chelsea. Invite me into your bed again and I promise you won't leave it a virgin."

Chapter Twenty-One

Sitting at a booth in the Cyprus Café, Chelsea traced the spotless tabletop with her finger. Over the years it had become a favourite haunt to meet Ali and then Samantha. With the Greek-style columns and small tables out front, she liked to imagine she was in Greece.

Today she'd chosen the privacy of being inside, surrounded by blue and white walls, and the smell of baking and coffee. Craig Sanders would arrive any minute but, for the life of her, she couldn't muster enthusiasm. Hunter's promise consumed every thought in her head. She only had herself to blame but, try as she had over the last few hours, she couldn't forget his one-minute seduction.

She barely remembered a word from the breakfast interrogation, other than her brothers' decision to resume their holiday and their insistence she stay in town tonight. At the moment, they were chaining gates and checking stock. As for Hunter, the arrogant seducer, had eaten a hearty breakfast while answering her brothers' questions then left with only the briefest glance in her direction. "Damn those bloody Sullivans."

Her mumbled curse drew Thea Levonis' attention.

"You okay, Chelsea?"

"I'm thinking about the mess I'm making of my life." The words tumbled out, making her cringe. Honesty wasn't always the best policy. Sometimes it made things much worse.

Thea left the counter and made her way around the middle tables. She and her husband, Stavros, and daughter, Thalia, had known Chelsea's family for years. They were hardworking and kind, not gossips.

"What mess? You have a good job and the kiddies love you. You win events on that horse of yours, and the parents appreciate that you teach their children to swim every summer."

Chelsea closed her eyes. "I want what I can't have."

"You mean Reid Sullivan?"

Good heavens, did everyone in town know of her obsession. "Thea, I want children. Is that so much to ask for?"

"It's what most women want, but you need to widen your horizon. You are attracted to the wrong man."

"I seem to be making a habit of it." Drawing in a deep breath, she smiled at Thea. "I'm meeting a male colleague for a coffee date, so who knows what will happen."

Thea rubbed Chelsea's shoulder. "There are many shells on the beach, *agapi mou*, but unique ones are hard to find. You might be lucky like my Thalitsa. She waited a long time for the man of her heart."

As Thea bustled back to the counter, Chelsea pondered the Greek woman's words. Thalia was a year older than Chelsea and recently she'd won the heart of one of Bindarra Creek's most eligible bachelors. "I'm not waiting another year."

Her phone buzzed. Seeing the ID, her mood lifted. "Hello, Harry, what's up?"

"You want to meet up for a milkshake in town?"

"Sure. How about one o'clock?"

"Cool. You want me to come over and watch a movie with you tonight?"

She laughed. "Not if my cousins come with you."

"Nah, Nicholas and Michael have to pack."

"You excited about your camping trip?"

"Yeah. Think about the movie. I'll catch ya later."

He hung up, leaving her wondering if Samantha's absence was behind Harry's need for feminine company. He might be a wizard at pool, but the carrot top, seventeen-year-old had a shy nature, and after losing both parents, tended to get a little anxious about his adopted sister. They might not be related by blood, but the siblings were incredibly close.

"Hi, Chelsea."

She jumped, vexed to be caught daydreaming.

Craig slid onto the seat opposite, his overly eager smile reminding her of a child on Christmas Day. The last thing she wanted was to encourage his infatuation, only to dismiss it and hurt him.

"Hello, Craig. I can't believe you're back in Bindarra. We still have a month before school goes back."

He shrugged. "My parents are into bowls and my sister is ten years younger, so wants to hang out with friends. I find it boring at home these days."

"What about your friends?"

"Since leaving school, we've grown apart. I hear your family are very close and they're all away. You must be lonely?"

His assumption made her uncomfortable. "They'll only be away a few weeks and I've got plenty to keep me occupied on the farm. My swimming class starts in two weeks."

"Do you need help?"

"The class grows every year. I'll take any help I can get. What would you like to drink? My shout."

"A flat white, thanks."

After ordering, Chelsea came back to the table to find Craig fidgeting with the menu. He moved it aside then met her eyes. "Did you have a nice Christmas?"

"I did. Shock of shocks, the Sullivans and Morgans spent the whole day together, eating, drinking and being very sociable. We started at Hickory Ridge with French Toast, pikelets and apple muffins then went to Tulachmhor for a game of cricket before the traditional Christmas lunch. Afterwards, we lounged around on the shady veranda with cool drinks, then competed over pool and darts, before eating leftovers for dinner. It was a good day." Even though Reid had avoided her like the plague.

Craig shifted forward then back before running his hand through his dark wavy hair. "I looked out for you at the New Year's Eve party in town."

"I didn't go. The Sullivans hosted a party in their barn." To her horror, heat invaded her face. "It was also a *bon voyage* party for our grans and parents."

"I guess you couldn't really miss it then."

"Craig, did you leave flowers at my front door last night?"

"No, I don't know how to get to your farm."

"Here you are." Thea placed a tray on the table. "One flat white, one café latte and some homecooked carrot cake. Enjoy."

"Thank you, Thea." Chelsea drew her latte closer then picked up her slice of cake. Her hand froze mid-air as Hunter strolled into the café, clean-shaven and wearing a powder blue, short-sleeved shirt and fitted cream moleskin pants. He called out a greeting to Thea then continued on, stopping at their booth.

Chelsea couldn't drag her eyes from the open V of his shirt where one button had been left undone, revealing a light dusting of dark springy hair. She knew it tapered down to a single line, disappearing below his jocks. With a hellion effort, she raised her gaze to lock with his amused eyes.

"Hello, Chelsea. Is that another new dress? Green suits you, but the red one is my favourite. Aren't you going to introduce me to your friend?"

"What? *No.* What are you doing here?"

"Collecting my morning coffee." He held out a hand to Craig, who looked as startled as a rabbit caught in headlights. "Hunter Sullivan. You must be Chelsea's colleague?"

"Yes. Craig Sanders. I teach year six. Chelsea was just telling me what a wonderful Christmas and New Year's Eve you had."

Hunter chuckled. "I certainly enjoyed New Year's Eve."

"Don't you have somewhere to be?" Chelsea waved her cake towards the door, hoping he'd take the hint. Instead he pushed in beside her then took a bite of her cake.

"No, sunshine." His hard thigh pressed intimately against hers. "At least nothing more important than getting to know your school friends." He made it sound like they were children. "So, Craig, have you got plans to stay in Bindarra, or will you move on?"

Chelsea kicked him. "There is no need to interrogate Craig."

"It's fine, Chelsea." Craig's smile appeared frozen. "If I were your boyfriend, I'd be interested to meet your work friends too."

She almost choked. "He's not my boyfriend. He's… he's…"

Hunter grabbed her fisted hand and brought it to his chest. "I'm more of a confidant, Craig. You're confusing me with my brother. Chelsea's been besotted with Reid for years."

She couldn't believe her ears. "What are you doing?" She kicked him again. "I'm finished with Reid and you are not my confidant."

"You're single?" Hope flared in Craig's blue eyes. "Would you like to—"

"One cappuccino." Thea clunked it down, the cup rattling in its saucer, her scowl making it clear she disapproved of Hunter hijacking Chelsea's date.

Hunter grinned, not in the least abashed. "Thanks, Thea." Idly stirring his cappuccino, he looked across the table. "You haven't answered my question, Craig. Do you have plans to settle in Bindarra Creek?"

The confusion on Craig's face was almost laughable. He cleared his throat. "I don't trust cows or horses, but I like the community spirit here, so who knows."

Chelsea swallowed. "When you say you don't trust cows or horses, does that mean you'd never consider living on a working property?"

"Never."

"What if you fell in love with a woman like…me, who regularly rounds up cattle on horseback and rides most mornings?"

"Surely when you're married you won't put yourself at such risk? I certainly wouldn't tolerate it if you were my wife, especially if you became pregnant." This was a side of Craig she hadn't foreseen. The stubborn tilt of his chin and determined eyes rendered her mute.

Hunter released her fist and slid his arm around her. "Crikey, Craig, you've done what no other man has achieved, taken her power of speech. If I were you, I'd leave now while you still have your hearing. Once she regains it, she'll blister your ears. It happened to me once and I've never forgotten it."

"Pardon?" Craig frowned. "I've never heard Chelsea raise her voice."

"It's extremely rare." Chelsea elbowed Hunter, taking great pleasure in his gasp of pain. She turned cool eyes on Craig. "I've been riding since the age of two when my father took me up on his horse. Hickory Ridge is the name of my family property. It's in my blood, as is working with cattle. Most mornings I go riding as the sun rises and the early morning mist clings to the dams. If I marry, it will be to someone who shares my passion for horses and cattle. I would sooner stay single than have a man try to take that away from me."

Craig recoiled as if she'd slapped him. "Chelsea, I only have your welfare at heart. They are such dangerous animals, and you're so lovely."

His remorse struck at her heart, dowsing her fury like a bucket of cold water. "I appreciate your concern, Craig, and value your friendship, but let's face it, outside of school, we have little in common."

"I guess so." He drained his coffee. "If you don't mind, I'll pass on the swimming classes. I think it's best I head back to Katoomba, maybe catch up with my old friends."

"That's a good idea."

"Thanks for the coffee." He nodded at Hunter then walked stiffly out of the café.

She groaned against Hunter's shoulder. "I handled that badly, didn't I?"

"Actually, I thought you were brilliant. The poor guy is crazy about you, and rather than rub salt into his wound, you backed off and left him pride enough to remain a friend."

"I hope so. It's a good thing you asked his intentions. I might not have discovered his true feelings for months. Forbid me to ride." She huffed. "The hide!"

"To be honest, Chelsea, if you were my wife, I wouldn't be comfortable with you working stock while pregnant, and certainly not riding past four or five months."

"You'd expect me to give up my morning rides?"

"Not at all. I'd compensate you with an early morning ride you'd thoroughly enjoy, and the biggest tumble you'd take is onto a soft mattress."

"Hunter!"

"Just saying." He drank his cappuccino then grinned. "Now that Sanders is out of the game, who is next on the list?"

"Shane Picton. At least he's a shearer."

Hunter chuckled. "Doesn't mean he likes horses and cattle."

"That will be my first question." Or it would be once she stopped thinking about morning tumbles on soft mattresses with Hunter bloody Sullivan. He wasn't making things easy. She'd spent her date with Craig, measuring him against Hunter's wit, physique, magnetism and wicked grin. It wouldn't do. Not at all.

Chapter Twenty-Two

On any working day, The Produce Store and Saddlery had a steady flow of customers, which often lead to enjoyable conversations. Today, however something was off.

After having five men in a row shake their head at him, Reid figured it was time to find out what was going on. He spotted Dodge Myers leaning idly against the counter talking to Dan Molyneaux, Kel Jones and Paddy Cullen. As the owner of the Riverside Pub, Dan heard all the juicy gossip whether he wanted it or not. As Captain of the local Fire Brigade, Kel Jones caught his fair share too. As for Paddy, the old timer loved gossip.

"Hey, fellas. Is there something going on I should know about?"

Paddy tipped his hat back to scratch his forehead. "Well, I don't know as you have any right to know, Reid, seeing as you've lost your marbles."

A slither of unease skittered down his spine. "I

have no idea what you're talking about, Paddy, but I'd be grateful if you let me in on the secret?"

"Dumping that darlin' girl after all the years she's waited as patient as a saint."

"Jesus Christ, not this again. I have never had a romantic relationship with Chelsea Morgan. We're neighbours, that's all. A schoolgirl crush has been blown out of proportion."

Dodge straightened. "So, it doesn't worry you that she's got a dating agenda and plans to have coffee with every unattached man in Bindarra Creek?"

"How the hell did you hear about that?" Reid swiped off his Akubra and wacked it against his thigh. "It's not real, just Chelsea's way of getting my attention."

"Oh, it's real," muttered Dan. "I heard it from Joe Rossiter who is hoping to get on the list. He heard it outside the post office this morning."

Dodge caught Reid's eye. "I called into the Cyprus Café for a takeaway coffee this morning and spotted her with Craig Sanders."

"Who the hell is Craig Sanders?"

Dan's lips twitched. "A young bloke who teaches at the primary school. Comes from the Blue Mountains. I also heard she's got a graph to rate her dates."

Reid's uneasiness grew. He'd spoken to Hunter and Riley about the mysterious admirer. Leaving flowers late at night was strange enough, entering the house uninvited then spreading rumours brought to mind a stalker. His blood ran cold. "We need to find out who started the rumour. In the meantime, I'll track Chelsea down."

Dodge grinned. "You might want to try the Cyprus Café."

"Thanks." Slamming his list on the counter, he grumbled. "I have more than enough to keep me busy without chasing bloody rustlers, stalkers and Chelsea Morgan. Ask the boys to fill my order. I'll drop by later and pick it up."

"No worries." Kel Jones caught the list under his palm before it could blow away. "There's a meeting at the Riverside Pub tonight regarding the rustlers."

"Yeah, I know."

Paddy held up a hand. "Sharing the load with a woman like Chelsea might improve your life, young fella. You wouldn't do any better."

"Maybe not, but she certainly could." Reid whistled to Gypsy then strode to his ute. Chelsea and her bloody dating agenda. She'd been let run wild for far too long. If her father and brothers couldn't rein her in, then he'd have to do it, before matters got worse or Hunter did something stupid.

Now that Christmas and New Year's Eve were out of the way, it seemed every man and his dog were in town. He drove past the Cyprus Café three times before finding a parking space. The instant he unclipped Gypsy, she leapt off the back of the ute to trot alongside him, as happy as a pig in mud at the intriguing smells around her.

Stavros and Thea Levonis owned the popular café, which rarely had an empty seat at lunch time, they also kept a dog bowl filled with water out the front by one of the elaborate Greek columns. Gypsy wasted no time quenching her thirst.

"Stay." Satisfied she wouldn't move, Reid stepped into the bright café, his gaze shooting to the blackboard and today's lunchtime special. Grilled fish with salad and chips. Breakfast had been hours ago. He checked his watch. A touch early for lunch, but at least he'd avoid the crowd.

Thea came through from the kitchen, her eyes flaring momentarily before her gaze shot to the last booth. She hurried forward to block his path. He could think of only one explanation for her strange behaviour. "Hello, Thea. Am I too early for lunch?"

"No, no, I give you a nice table outside, yes?"

"I'd prefer to sit inside. I'll have your special of the day and a lemon squash."

Stepping around her, he made for the back of the cafe where he could see Shane Picton sitting in the last booth in earnest conversation with someone. Although the shearer still had the mop of dreadlocks, his bushy beard had been shorn off to reveal a cleanly shaven pale face. His usual attire of T-shirt and faded stubby shorts had been replaced with an ironed, short-sleeve shirt and navy shorts. He was out to impress.

The second he noticed Reid's approach, a deep crimson flush mottled the shearer's entire face and neck. By his frantic blinking, he didn't know whether to make a run for it or dive under the table, which made it easy to guess who sat opposite.

"Morning, Shane, I hardly recognised you." Reid glanced at his nemesis. "Chelsea."

Colour bloomed in her cheeks. "What are you doing here?"

"I had thought to stop by for an early lunch. I'm glad I did. We need to talk."

Her breath caught then she cleared her throat. "You want to have a conversation with me? *Now?*"

"Yes, if I'm not interrupting anything important? There are things we need to resolve."

Her struggle was so visible he had to bite his tongue not to laugh. Good manners won out. "As a matter of fact, you are interrupting something important. If you can give me ten minutes, we can talk then?"

"Very well." With a nod to Shane, he walked back to the counter and Thea who stood with her arms crossed and eyes narrowed. "Can you put a ten-minute hold on my fish, Thea, I'll be joining Chelsea for lunch."

"What about her coffee date?"

"He definitely won't be joining us." With grim satisfaction, Reid sat at a table where Chelsea couldn't see him, but he could easily hear their conversation.

The next ten minutes were enlightening to say the least. Shane was quizzed and cross-examined as to his interests, hobbies, skills, future plans, habits, thoughts on women working with cattle and competing in horse events. If he liked farming, horses, dogs and children. If he'd be faithful to his wife, or object to her making major decisions. That one gave Shane pause.

"What sort of decisions?"

"Running cattle rather than sheep, putting in a new dam, buying new stock."

"Wouldn't she make those decision *with* her husband?" asked Shane.

"I would hope so, but some men think they know better than women." The injustice in her voice had Reid wondering if she referred to him.

"I'd confer with my wife on the big decisions." Shane replied quietly.

"I have one more question, Shane. If you were to marry a woman with a great deal of land, stock and machinery, would you be prepared to sign a prenuptial agreement not to make a claim on them, if the marriage didn't work out?"

"Far out, Chelsea, has anyone ever told you, you're a control freak?"

"I'm not normally, but I couldn't bear to lose Hickory Ridge."

"I don't have a problem with prenuptial agreements, but I like being a shearer and wouldn't know the first thing about running a cattle property. I'd be happy with thirty hectares, a couple of dogs and a pretty wife to welcome me home each day."

"That's sweet, Shane. I should introduce you to my cousin Lindsay. She's a bit of a hippy, but I think the two of you would get on like a house on fire."

"Is she as pretty as you?"

"Lindsay is lovely. She makes her own pottery. Here, I'll give you her number. Inquire about buying a platter for your mum, and if you click, ask her out. She likes Indian food."

"So do I."

"Excellent." Chelsea's tinkling laugh had Reid frowning. If this was an example of her proposed strategy, she'd end up marrying off all the contestants.

He waited until Shane left the café then slid into the booth opposite Chelsea. "How many contestants do you plan on interviewing?"

"That's my business." She flipped her notebook closed. "What do you want to talk about?"

"The rustlers, your admirer, this game you're playing to gain my attention."

Her eyes flared. "Stop right there. I'm not interested in you anymore. I've wasted enough time on a lost cause. You do not need to concern yourself with my safety. I promised my brothers I will stay in town until the rustlers are caught, and as for my admirer, I have no idea. Hunter's looking into it for me."

"Stay away from Hunter."

"You have no right to tell me who I can hang out with, Reid." She glared at him righteously, her chest rising and falling, her fingers clenched around the table edge.

Reining her in was going to be harder than he'd figured. "If I have to marry you, I will." Damn, he hadn't meant to say it aloud.

She gasped, clutching both hands to her chest. "What did you say?"

He couldn't very well back track now. "I'll marry you." A constrictive band tightened round his chest. She'd end up hating him, but he could see no other way to protect her from self-serving scoundrels who would take advantage. The silence was deafening, made worse when he realised Thea had stopped short of their booth, giving him a searching look.

As pale as a ghost, Chelsea slid along the seat, her hands shaking as she gathered up her notebook and handbag. "Your proposal leaves a lot to be desired, Reid. If you genuinely want to be considered in my matchmaking experiment, you will need to satisfy the same criteria as every other contestant. I need to feed Stanthorpe."

Dumbstruck, Reid watched the bane of his life stalk out of the café. Surely, she hadn't refused him. A quick glance at Thea's raised eyebrow confirmed the fact. Strangely, laughter bubbled up from his throat. "She actually knocked me back."

"I don't blame her." Thea snatched up the used cups. "That is not the way to ask a woman to marry you. We like romance and sincerity."

Exhaling Reid rubbed his jaw. "How do I get a coffee date?"

"Ring her." Thea shook her head and marched away.

He should be grateful Chelsea wasn't still chasing him. Yet, she had never looked so brittle. Had never thrown down such a damned objectional gauntlet.

Anger welled. For years Chelsea had worn her heart on her sleeve, making moon-eyes at him whenever they were within sight of each other. Turning a blind eye to all his faults and moods. He was fed up with busybodies asking him when he planned to marry her, convinced he'd been dating her secretly for years. They'd assumed he had an aversion to marriage because of his mother, which was partly true, but the main reason he'd kept Chelsea at arm's length was to protect her from the monster inside him.

Now she'd devised a dating game to get his attention and she'd conned Hunter into helping her. If that didn't spell disaster, he'd eat both boots. Every unattached man in Bindarra Creek would enter the contest. Chelsea was not only attractive and clever, she stood to inherit a large share of Hickory Ridge. What man wouldn't want her?

Rattled more than he cared to admit, Reid ran a hand through his hair. She was at risk of being hurt in any number of ways, and Hunter represented the biggest threat. The fool already possessed a soft spot for the damn woman. And, although he'd promised to protect her from gold-digging, lecherous or violent men, how did Hunter plan to protect her from himself?

Reid silently swore. Hunter would succumb and seduce her, which left Reid no choice. He couldn't allow his brother or any man to take advantage of Chelsea. Something needed to be done to keep them apart.

Chapter Twenty-Three

Dividing her time between bottle feeds, farm chores, coffee dates and running errands for her brothers was consuming every minute of Chelsea's day. To make life easier she'd brought Stanthorpe into town, along with Lola and Regina. The horses were in the house paddock. The hens were happy as long as they were let out in the morning and locked up at night.

Riley and Jake hadn't required her assistance, so she'd come into town for groceries and her first two dates. All being well, her brothers would be on their way back to Coffs Harbour by four, without being any the wiser to her agenda.

Pacing along Main Street, Chelsea suddenly became aware of curious glances. Paddy Cullen gave her a wink and a chuckle as he passed.

"Chelsea, wait up."

She spun on her heel to see a smartly dressed guy with gingery hair jogging towards her. He looked familiar.

"Hi, Chelsea, remember me? We were in the same year at school."

"Lewis Gantry. How are you?"

"Good thanks." He pulled at his earlobe. "I heard about your breakup with Reid Sullivan and wondered if I could throw my hat into the ring?"

"Pardon? Break up?" She blinked at him. "What ring?"

Colour crept into his checks. "Your dating agenda."

"You know about that?"

"Yeah, I heard three young fellas talking about it outside the post office."

Chelsea clenched her fists. "I'm going to kill Hunter Sullivan."

"What's my boss got to do with it? You're not including him, are you?"

"No, I am not. The double-crossing, bloody... You're the guy who works for Hunter?"

"Yeah." Lewis stuck out his thin chest. "I run the office when he's out, and I've almost finished my appraisal diploma." He cleared his throat. "So, can we go for a coffee, Chelsea?"

"Sure." If Hunter hadn't spilled the beans, she needed to find out who was spreading the rumour before it reached her brothers. The Cyprus Café was around the corner and across the street. "Are you free now?" She had half an hour before catching up with Harry and her two o'clock date with Jerry Eckford. Then if she had time, she'd drop by the Council Chambers and bank to ask Nigel Clemons and Leroy Murdoch out for coffee tomorrow.

Lewis rubbed his hands together. "Give me a few minutes to lock the office."

As he dashed around the corner, Chelsea's phone buzzed in her pocket. Seeing the caller ID, she cringed then took a deep breath. "Hello, Reid."

"Hello, Chelsea. When are you free for coffee?"

Frozen in place, she stared across the street without seeing a thing. "Why?"

"We need to talk, and unless you want me interrupting your interviews, it had better be soon. Are you free now?"

Of all the arrogant, conceited men in her life, he took the cake. "No, I'm meeting someone. What about eleven tomorrow at the Cyrus Café?"

"Done. I'll see you then."

What on earth did Reid want to talk about? His offer hadn't been intentional, so if he started lecturing her, she'd punch him in the eye.

The paddy wagon rolled to a stop beside her and AJ leaned out the window. "Hi, Chelsea, how's tings?" His shortened words always sounded so cute.

"Fine. My brothers came back and have chained all our gates."

"Great. Hey, I heard about your breakup with Reid Sullivan and your dating agenda. Can I take you for coffee later today?"

Words failed her. If AJ knew then she'd have to move up her schedule before her brothers scared off contenders. "AJ, I'm five years older than you."

"Come on, Chelsea. Jerry Eckford has to be in his mid-turties."

"How do you know I'm having coffee with Jerry?"

"He's on the list, isn't he?"

She gasped. "You swore you didn't see the graph."

"Graph?" Understanding dawned in his eyes. "The

graph you asked about. I didn't touch it or look at it. So, it's to do with your contest?"

So much for keeping a lid on things. I need some serious damage control. "It's a matchmaking experiment, AJ." Someone had definitely seen her graph. It was the only explanation. "Who told you about my dating agenda?"

"Paddy Cullen."

Chelsea cringed. The whole town knew. "Are you free at three?"

"I can be." With a wave he did a U-turn and drove back along Main Street.

Glancing across the street she noticed Nugget, an old Blue Heeler sitting outside the bakery. Nugget belonged to Paddy Cullen. She reached the bakery as he plodded out.

"Morning, Chelsea. Beautiful day, ain't it?"

"Sure is, Paddy. Can I ask you something?"

He chuckled. "I might be single, but ain't I a bit old for ya, luv?"

A giggle escaped. "I wasn't going to ask you out, Paddy. I was just wondering where you heard about my...matchmaking experiment?"

"Is that what you're calling it?" He chuckled again. "At the chemist. Would you consider having a drink with an old timer like me? Might improve my standing with the ladies in town." He chuckled. "Can't be too late though, I'm having dinner at the Riverside Pub so I can attend the meeting about those rustlers."

He was such a sweetie. "All right, but only if you let me pay?"

"Nah, that wouldn't be the gentlemanly thing, luv. I gotta pay."

"Very well. How's six o'clock at the Riverside Pub?"

He chuckled. "You've made an old man's day. Let's give those young bucks a run for their money?"

"Lets." She kissed his cheek then ran for her coffee date with Lewis Gantry.

Her footsteps slowed as she noticed him sitting at an outside table. The other three tables had been pushed together and were taken up with a group of much older ladies, all chatting avidly, sipping tea and eating cake at—she glanced at her watch. Twelve-forty, lunchtime. Her suspicion grew when Florence Miller directed a question at Lewis and he preened, puffing his chest out while nodding enthusiastically.

"Damn." It was too late to turn tail and run. Maureen Molyneaux and Beatrice Fukuka had seen her. There was no way to have a private conversation with six women sitting beside them. Then again, maybe she could turn this to her advantage and quell the rumours. "Hello, ladies. How fortunate you're here. I'm dabbling in a little matchmaking strategy and could use your assistance."

Lewis frowned. "Matchmaking? I thought we were having a coffee date."

"That's what I'm calling my initial interviews with prospective contestants. Once you've answered my questions, I will gain a better perspective of who you are and what you're looking for."

"But I thought you were looking for someone to replace Reid Sullivan?"

"Reid can't be replaced." She hadn't meant to raise her voice, but her patience was running thin. Taking a calming breath, she sat. "I haven't broken up with Reid."

"You haven't?"

"I can't break up with someone I've never dated."

"What about our graduation? He brought you."

"Yes, but only to keep an eye on his sister, who went with my brother."

"But Reid and Jake got into a big brawl over *you*. They wrecked our graduation arch."

Chelsea sighed; aware the ladies were hanging on every word. "The brawl was over Aleisha and turned out to be a huge misunderstanding. My aim is to assist single guys and girls in Bindarra to find compatible partners. If during my endeavours, I unearth a man who meets my stringent requirements and we're compatible..." She gave a light shrug. "Who knows what might happen."

Edwina Lette cackled. "This is priceless. Let the questions begin."

Chapter Twenty-Four

After showing a tight-fisted man and his finicky wife over three rural properties, Hunter had exhausted his tolerance. His least favourite clients were city slickers wanting a five-star residence at the price of a dump.

They sprouted words like tree-change and slower pace of life, when they really meant tax dodge and 'I want to play wealthy grazier'. In the end he'd informed them farming took blood, sweat and tears. Stock needed proper care and management. If they weren't prepared to hire a full-time manager, then they should rethink their tree-change and stop wasting his time.

On arriving back at the office, his mood improved at finding his brother waiting, only to sour when Reid confessed to messing up a marriage proposal to Chelsea. Needing to check on her, Hunter had driven out to Hickory Ridge, where he'd been warned off by her brothers.

In a black mood, he parked behind his office then stalked in through the rear door, surprised to find it empty and five messages queued on the answering machine. Unlocking the front slider, he stepped onto the footpath, his gaze shifting next door, to the lunchtime patrons seated outside the Cyprus Café.

"Bloody hell." Lewis was having coffee with Chelsea, surrounded by a group of women, who appeared to be heavily involved in the discussion, except... Hunter narrowed his eyes. He'd never seen Lewis, a conceited bastard if ever there was one, looking so desperate. A chuckle escaped. Only Chelsea could muster such formidable allies and turn a coffee date into an interrogation.

As if sensing his presence, she glanced over, her eyes lighting with devilment as she wiggled her fingers at him. He laughed, drawing the other ladies' attention. He didn't care. With one mischievous smile, she'd brightened his day. Sauntering over, he stopped by her chair. "Good afternoon, ladies, *Lewis.*" He made a show of looking at his watch. "Is this a late morning tea or an extremely early lunch break?"

Lewis jumped to his feet. "Hi, boss. I didn't expect you back until one."

"Hmm... There are five messages you might attend to before lunch."

"Yes, right. I'm on it. Afternoon, Chelsea, ladies." Red-faced and tense, he almost fell over his own feet in his rush to escape.

Hunter turned back to the ladies. "May I enquire what's going on?"

Edwina Lette chuckled. "Chelsea has started a matchmaking service and we've been giving our opinion on what a woman should look for in a husband. Sadly, your office manager falls abysmally short."

"Argh." A matchmaking service. It was a brilliant idea and would quell any rumours circulating about Chelsea's own search. He had to hand it to her, she'd neatly side-stepped the spotlight. "In that case, I will leave you ladies to your...matchmaking."

Chelsea caught his hand, halting his escape and intensifying an already heightened awareness of her. By the sparkle in her eyes, she was enjoying his discomfort. "Don't run away, Hunter. I'd like to put my questions to you, if you're game?"

Damn, but she loved to taunt him. Well, she'd met her match. "I'll answer your questions, Chelsea, but not here. I prefer our discussion to be in private. Shall we say my place, tonight at...ten?"

Several ladies gasped.

Edwina narrowed her eyes.

Chelsea laughed, releasing Hunter's hand to smack his arm. "You might have everyone else in town convinced you're shameless, but your innuendos won't work with me. I'll put you down for coffee tomorrow morning at nine."

"Sunshine, if you want to question me, it will be privately, but the very *last* thing I *want,* or *need* from *you,* is your matchmaking services."

Flexing his clenched fingers, he glanced from Chelsea to four outraged faces, before faltering on Edwina. She pinned him with an alert gaze. Bloody hell, she'd picked up on his underlying desire.

"Have a nice afternoon, ladies." Cursing his reputation and loss in judgement, Hunter forced himself to stroll inside the café then sit at a back booth to toy with Thea's homemade *pastitsio*.

What the hell was he going to do with Chelsea? She'd knocked back Reid's lousy proposal, but he'd soon make another. It spelt disaster. She deserved to be a man's everything, the centre of his universe, the mother of his children, the keeper of his heart. To foil Reid's plans would take underhanded and shrewd planning, calculated sabotage and clandestine seduction, traits Hunter had perfected over the years, all because he couldn't have Chelsea.

A smile spread across his face. "Let the contest begin." For the first time in his life, he'd go after what he'd always wanted. Nothing and nobody would stop him.

Shovelling a forkful of *pastitsio* into his mouth, he slowly chewed, appreciating the return of his appetite and the distinct flavours of mint and cinnamon.

"Okay, Sullivan, I agree to your terms." Chelsea slid onto the bench opposite. "And, don't think to renege. Your place tonight at ten. I have a list of questions and you will oblige me with honest answers. Be warned, I'm not leaving until I'm completely satisfied."

His pulse picked up, firing his imagination. "In that case, I promise you will have your satisfaction."

Her eyes narrowed, ripe with suspicion, but then lowered to his lunch. "That lasagne is too big for one person." She reached for the spoon beside his plate then neatly cut off a wedge, swiftly spooning it into her mouth. "Yum."

Grinning, he pushed the plate into the middle of the table. "It's *pastitsio*, the Greek form of lasagne."

"I love it." She hoed into his meal with gusto and

when they'd finished, she leaned closer to give him a detailed report of her coffee date with Shane Picton and her encounter with Reid. Surprisingly, she seemed rather blasé over Reid's proposal. It didn't escape Hunter's notice that several patrons had noted their presence. As such, he reached across and placed his hand over hers, elated at the slight tremor in her fingers.

"I assume you're going to the meeting tonight at Riverside Pub. Would you like me to pick you up?"

"Erm, no that's okay. I'm having a drink with Paddy Cullen before the meeting."

"Why?"

She motioned him closer, then whispered next to his ear. "He wants to improve his standing with the older ladies. He thinks a date with me might help."

Her breath tickled his neck, instantly spiking his desire. He brushed his lips against her ear, thrilled by a hitch in her breath. "I want you."

She lurched back, pulling her hand from his. "What?" Her yelp drew curious stares.

Where were his smooth moves? Nothing came to mind. He may as well have fallen off a ship without a life jacket when it came to Chelsea. Clearing his throat, he leaned back against the booth. "I want you...to make me a better person."

The tension left her shoulders and she reached for his hands, clasping them under hers. "Hunter, you are one of the best people I know. It's just your reputation that muddies the water. I can help you, but it means spending time with me and no flirting with other women. You have to honour our contract. You promised."

The alert trepidation in her eyes as she worried her bottom lip gave him pause. Chelsea wanted to be with him, but she was scared witless. Perhaps a little honesty would sooth her concerns. "Being with you has never been a hardship, Chelsea. Truth be known, if it hadn't been for your infatuation with Reid, you might have realised it years ago."

Her beautiful dark eyes widened at his revelation. "Hunter."

He'd confessed his true feelings, now he could either wait on her considered reaction and accept it gracefully or pull off the gloves and seduce her into wanting him.

Chapter Twenty-Five

Hunter enjoyed her company.

The truth of his words hit Chelsea like a soccer ball in the belly, rendering her speechless for the second time today. Memories flooded her mind.

The rivalry between their families went back generations. From her earliest memories, Riley and Jake had been competing against Reid and Hunter. As kids then teenagers, every weekend and holiday break, they'd set up races, whether it be on bike, horse or foot, trying to best each other.

On a sports field they'd always taken opposite sides. Their rivalry extended to breeding prime stock and horse eventing. If their grandfathers and fathers hadn't been so caught up in the past, the boys would have been best friends. And through it all, Aleisha Sullivan and Chelsea had tagged along, forging a close bond that had annoyed Reid, Riley and Jake. It had never bothered Hunter, who'd often accompanied Ali to see Chelsea safely to the boundary gate, when her own brothers and Reid had long since disappeared.

A shaky gasp escaped at the fleeting hurt she caught in Hunter's eyes before he looked away. *He liked my company.* She wanted to apologise for taking him for granted, but he might misinterpret it as pity. Hunter had too much pride to bare his heart, but what if he'd felt more, and because of her blind fascination with Reid, she'd never noticed?

His shoulders tensed. He was about to leave.

She clutched his hands tighter. "It was never a hardship being with you either. I can't even guess how many times you escorted me home in the dark. I did appreciate it, especially as you'd let me ramble on about anything. You still do. As a result, I know you better than most."

"Do you?" His amused smile and raised eyebrow gave her courage to continue.

"You show the world a smug, arrogant smile that doesn't reach your eyes, a bored smirk when you're irritated, an icy indifference when you're annoyed. Then there's your indulgent smile when I say something quirky. You raise one eyebrow and tilt your head slightly when something catches your attention, like you're doing now." She drew in a deep breath, recalling so many things she'd never given a second thought. "You have different laughs. I love your belly laugh, but it's rare. Then there's your flirtatious half-laugh when you're speaking to a woman. Your teasing chuckle when you pick on me, and your husky rumble when...when..."

His amused smile turned teasing. "When...?"

"When you're aroused." It was suddenly hard to breathe.

He turned his hands, catching her fingers. "What about my eyes, sunshine?"

"Your...eyes?" She bit her bottom lip. His green eyes were almost identical to Reid's, yet livelier and at the moment much, much darker.

"Yes, Chelsea. Can you read my eyes? They're a window into a person's soul." His fingers tightened, preventing her from pulling away. "A man could happily drown in your beautiful eyes. They're warm like flowing chocolate, most often brimming with kindness, intelligence and enthusiasm. Lately, there's been fire and passion."

This was a serious side of Hunter she'd never encountered. He wasn't using his teasing voice or smile. His heartfelt reflection had her pulse hammering so hard he must feel it.

She took a shaky breath. "Your eyes remind me of moss on river rocks. They have a tendency to dance with wickedness, dull with pain, cool with annoyance, and darken with anger or...arousal."

"Like now." He rubbed his thumbs back and forth over her palms.

"Yes." She swallowed, unable to drag her gaze from his.

"Interesting. I'm curious, do you notice these things in everyone?"

"Not everyone, just my family and Ali."

"What about Reid?"

"Reid?"

"Can you identify his faces, laughs and moods?"

She could definitely recognise Reid's cool disinterest and frustrated glare, but she'd never spent enough time alone with him to garner much else. Just another humiliating realisation where Reid was concerned, yet she'd always been honest. "No, I can't."

"Doesn't that tell you something?" His eyes softened with compassion.

"Yes, it tells me I've wasted years on a lost cause." She tugged her hands free, unable to think clearly with his intimate caresses. "Which is why I need you."

"I'm all yours." The inuendo in his voice sent her pulse racing again. This was dangerous territory, but God help her, she wanted more of his kisses.

Thwack.

Chelsea reared back as a bunch of lavender landed between her and Hunter.

"Hi." Harry frowned at Hunter. "You're not on a date with Chelsea, are you?"

"No. What's the lavender for?"

Harry flushed. "It's standard practise for a guy to give a girl flowers on their first date."

"What?" Chelsea's and Hunter's exclamations drew every eye in the cafe.

Harry's face mottled further as he squared his shoulders. "I'm Chelsea's one o'clock date and you're cutting into my time."

The shock on Hunter's face began to dissolve into amusement, which would shatter Harry's self-esteem. Chelsea kicked him under the table. "I enjoyed our chat, Hunter, but Harry's right. You need to leave. I'll see you later about those questions." After she gently let Harry down. She prayed Hunter read the appeal in her eyes.

He coughed into his hand. "My apologies, Harry. You're right about the flowers." He slid out of the booth then glanced at Chelsea. "Don't forget about the meeting tonight. The sooner we catch those rustlers the better."

"I won't." She gave Hunter a grateful smile then, fighting the temptation to watch him walk away, waved Harry into the seat opposite. Her mind and emotions were in turmoil. If she was swinging upside down from the ceiling, she couldn't be more disorientated.

"I know how to catch the rustlers."

"What?" Harry's assertion brought her back to earth with a jolt.

"If everyone's at the meeting tonight, the rustlers have an opportunity to steal stock. If me and my friends set up checkpoints, we could phone the cops if we sight the truck."

"It's a great idea, Harry, but these rustlers are dangerous. They tried to run me down. What if one of you got hurt or killed?"

"They wouldn't catch me or my friends on our bikes. We know off-road shortcuts."

"I suppose by friends you mean my cousins, Nicholas and Michael?"

"Yeah, plus Oliver McGregor, Drew and Eddie Taylor, and Kaylee Myers."

"Good heavens, Harry, if Abby finds out her boys are involved, she'll arrest the lot of you. As for Kaylee, she's only thirteen. Dodge and Tessa will have your head."

"Not if we ask Roman and Dodge to help organise the stakeout."

"Maybe." She chewed her thumbnail. Until his resignation a few years ago, Dodge Myers had been Bindarra Creek's Senior Constable. Roman Taylor had spent years as a specialist in mine rescues and now headed up Bindarra's Emergency Rescue Service. Both men would keep a tight rein on the teenagers. "If you can convince them to oversee the venture, I'll agree, but if they say no, you have to accept that."

A grin spread over Harry's face. "Did you find my other flowers?"

"*You* left the flowers on my front verandah?"

"Yeah, I knocked and called out, but you didn't answer, so I went around the back and saw your ute and Hunter's Landcruiser. When I checked the barn, I found Muscat and Buck missing, so figured you were checking on something. Now I know it was the rustlers."

"You found my dating graph, didn't you?"

He blushed. "No, that was Nicholas and Michael. They were worried when you didn't answer the door."

"My cousins were with you." She groaned. "That explains the leak."

"We didn't tell anyone, at least not on purpose." His face reddened. "We got into an argument about you outside the post office and there were a few people about."

"What's done is done. Now explain why you brought flowers to the farm."

"They were a reward for beating Hunter at pool. I planned to ride over by myself, but Michael and Nicholas insisted on coming with me."

"You rode your bikes in the dark? That's so dangerous, Harry."

"We wore head torches and took a shortcut along the river."

"Okay, so why are you bringing me more flowers and telling Hunter we're on a date? I'm too old for you."

"That's why I was arguing with your cousins. They dared me to ask you out for coffee then the movies. Michael said they were the first two dates on your graph. I told them we're just friends, but they said I was gutless, and you wouldn't go out with me anyway."

"Harry, they were winding you up. We *are* friends and any time you want a milkshake or game of pool, I'm your girl." She smiled to soften the blow, just in case he did have a crush on her. "You're a great guy, Harry. Trust me, it won't be long before you're fending off wannabe girlfriends."

"I'm going to be a vet. I don't have time for girlfriends."

His vow made her smile. "Believe me, you will. Buy me that milkshake and I'll tell you the difference between a person who takes you for granted and a person who really cares."

"You're talking about Reid and Hunter."

For the third time in one day, Chelsea lost the power of speech.

Chapter Twenty-Six

Having moved to a chair by the front window, Hunter dealt with his emails and messages, while keeping an eye on the customers next door. He adored Chelsea's reactions to his inuendoes, and he treasured the interaction between them. Their hot conversation had left him floundering until he realised she really did know him better than anyone.

Harry had long since left, a swagger in his step as he high-fived Chelsea's twin cousins on the footpath. Oddly, Harry's grin appeared genuine. Chelsea had a soft heart and would have let him down gently.

Jerry Eckford arrived at the café spot on two o'clock, cleanly shaven and dressed in his Sunday best. The farmer was a nice guy, but he wasn't outgoing, and the eleven-year age gap bothered Hunter. Jerry would bore Chelsea to death, or his overbearing mother would drive her crazy.

Chelsea dashed out at two-fifteen, which eased Hunter's concern somewhat. Hopefully her questions scared Jerry off. When he left, a few minutes later, he certainly looked stunned. Assuming Chelsea had rushed off to feed Stanthorpe, Hunter took the opportunity to return a few calls.

She arrived back at two-fifty-five and waited by the kerb as AJ pulled up in the paddy wagon. The way the young constable was grinning left Hunter in no doubt who her next date was. AJ left the café at three-fifteen, still smiling.

Hunter stiffened with alarm when Reece Nolan turned up at three-thirty, along with a small contingent of Bindarra's CWA ladies. The café had to be bursting at the seams. Surprisingly, Riley and Jake hadn't intervened. They either supported their sister's venture or more likely, hadn't heard the rumours.

It was useless trying to concentrate on work. Reece Nolan was a serious contender. At thirty-one, he might well be looking to settle down. He was the farrier for most of the horses in the district. Clean-cut, physically fit, friendly, a good sense of humour. A charmer around women. He well knew how to use his blue eyes, smooth tongue and good looks to attract the ladies, and keep them hanging.

Swearing under his breath, Hunter threw down his pen and closed his laptop. "Lewis, I'm going next door for a coffee then out to Tulachmhor to help Reid move some cattle. Ring me if there's an emergency."

"Sure, boss."

Every table inside the café had customers chattering away. Thea, Stavros and Thalia were running between the kitchen, tables and counter. The volume of voices was enough to give a man a headache. Chelsea and Reece were seated at the back booth with a plate of scones between them. Thea had to be cheering with the extra customers. She most likely had the booth reserved for Chelsea and her potential dates.

Hunter silently cursed as Reece leaned forward, the interest in his eyes unmistakable. Why wouldn't he be attracted to a beautiful, vibrant woman like Chelsea? It was a no-brainer. Frustration ate at Hunter. There was nowhere to sit, except...

May the best man win.

"How ya doing, Reece? Haven't seen you around in a while." Hunter slid in beside Chelsea, taking more seat than his fair share when she scooted across the bench. He had her nicely confined between his thigh and the wall.

Chelsea's eyes flared momentarily then turn suspicious. "What are you doing?"

"I've come up with a couple more questions for your clients."

"What?"

"You can thank me later." He grinned at Reece, who didn't look amused. "I'm helping Chelsea get her matchmaking service off the ground."

The café fell silent. He imagined every pair of eyes were boring into his shoulders.

"Matchmaking service?" Reece glanced at Chelsea. "I thought this was a coffee date?"

Hunter laughed. "For a tea drinker, Chelsea must be well and truly sick of coffee. This is her sixth interview today."

She elbowed him hard in the side. "I was doing fine on my own, Hunter."

"I'm sure you were, but it might be wise to ask your potential clients if they're dating anyone. Take Reece for example. The Gillespie triplets could well turn volatile if they find out he's having coffee with another woman."

"You bastard." Reece glowered. "My personal life is none of your business, Sullivan."

Chelsea frowned. "You're dating triplets, *at the same time*?"

"We have an open relationship, no commitment, no ties."

"I see." By the confusion in her lovely eyes, she didn't see at all.

Hunter closed his hand over her knee and gently squeezed. "These scones look tempting. Mind if I have one?" Without waiting for an answer, he removed his hand and took one, smothering it in strawberry jam and cream then sank his teeth into it. "Hmm, these are delicious, sunshine, nearly as good as yours."

"I'm so glad you think so." She kicked his ankle. "Don't you have a business to run?"

"No, I'm good. I might marry you myself, just for your cooking."

She scowled at him. "You'd better want me for more than my cooking, Sullivan." Taking a scone, she dolloped cream on it then squashed it into his nose. "Have another."

A gasp went around the café.

Trying not to laugh, Hunter wiped the cream away with a serviette then calmly reached for a second scone, lathered it in cream then squashed it against her nose to more gasps. "You're right, Chelsea. I want you for more than your cooking skills. Our morning ride yesterday is something I'd be happy to repeat on a regular basis."

Reece's mouth dropped open. "What the hell...?"

Horror filled Chelsea's eyes as she wiped cream away with a serviette. "You...you..." She kicked his shin. "I thought you preferred staying in bed, to checking boundary fences *early in the morning*?"

"I do." He bent, reaching under the table to make a big thing of rubbing his shin. "But a mutual love of riding *early in the morning* is invigorating, wouldn't you say?"

She jumped as he ran his fingers up her calf, a tremor rippling under her skin. A soft blush blossomed in her face then she surprised him by bursting into laughter. "Hunter, you are wicked. Stop with the double meanings and admit you'd rather stay in bed than ride *a horse* early in the morning."

"That would depend if I'm with you." In bed or on horseback he left hanging in the air.

Chelsea's stunning eyes flared. "Me?"

He winked. "A man can dream, sunshine." He slid out of the booth, only then realising Reece had left the café. Every patron *and* all three Levonis' stared at him and Chelsea in astonishment. Assuming his standard amused if slightly bored expression, Hunter held his arms wide. "She's right. I'm very wicked, but it's such fun teasing her."

Pamela Brown, an uptight, elderly lady, rose to her feet. "You should be ashamed of yourself, young man. Your innuendos would ruin Chelsea's reputation if we didn't know she has far too much intelligence to dilly-dally with the likes of you."

"That's so true, Mrs. Brown, and yet I live in hope."

"That's enough, Hunter." Chelsea glared daggers at him. "Stop pretending to be someone you're not. You're kind and funny and dependable. I won't tolerate you or anyone saying otherwise."

"Is that so?" Her valiant defence humbled him. He had no right taking advantage of her innocence when there were far better men out there. Men who wouldn't sully her reputation. "Mrs. Brown is right, Chelsea. You're too respectable for the likes of me."

She shook her head. "Hunter, don't do this."

Ignoring the tears in her eyes, he strode out of the café.

Chapter Twenty-Seven

Sweat stung Reid's eyes and the flies were driving him mad. The paddock they'd just moved cattle from resembled a dust bowl. It would need a month of rest and a good shower of rain to rejuvenate the grass. Thank God they had enough land to move stock about.

The current drought had gone on four years, with only occasional thunderstorms to relieve things. It was a major worry. Depression and a sense of failure contributed to the high rate of suicides among farmers. Others were selling off land dirt cheap, or in some cases, walking away. Men and women who spent their lives providing meat, wool and crops to the nation, were desperate for support and financial aid to see them through.

He wiped the sweat off his forehead, whistled to Gypsy then urged Jock into a canter. His father's horse was a cantankerous old brute and unhappy about working in the heat, but as his horse had thrown a shoe and Ali's was heavily in foal, Reid didn't have much choice.

Hunter and Monty waited by the gate, both covered in sweat and dust. Without their help, he wouldn't have moved the heifers and calves so efficiently. To establish a serious cattle and sheep stud, he needed Hunter, otherwise they'd have to take on extra labour.

He gave Hunter a nod. "Thanks for your help."

"No worries." Hunter closed the gate then walked Monty alongside. "Do you need me for anything else before I rub Monty down and grab a shower?"

"No. You go ahead. Reece Nolan will be here any minute to shoe Zeus."

"Reece had coffee with Chelsea earlier."

"Did he?" Reid frowned. The farrier was a decent guy and a hard worker, but the idea of him and Chelsea didn't sit right for some reason.

"Bloody hell, Reid, is that all you can say?" Hunter glared at him. "Nolan's been in a relationship with the Gillespie triplets for years."

"What, all three of them?"

"Yes, they have an open relationship that allows him to date other women. I don't want him anywhere near Chelsea."

"I didn't know."

"You would if you listened to gossip and got out more." Hunter sounded pissed off.

"If you've got something to say, Hunter, just say it."

"I know you date plenty of women from Armidale and Moree, but I'm the one with the disreputable reputation, and it's been blown out of proportion. I'm not the bastard you think I am, and I've never been a cruel sod."

"This is about our mother, isn't it?" Reid grimaced. The woman might have long left town, but she kept coming between them.

Hunter sighed. "Have you ever kicked or beaten one of our dogs or horses?"

"You know I haven't."

"Not even Gypsy? I heard she chewed some of the chess pieces Grandpa made you."

"I was angrier with myself for leaving them out. She didn't know any better."

"Okay, what about when our mother thrashed us black and blue with a tennis racket for calling her a witch, did you hit back?"

"No."

"Did you strike her when she locked us in the woodshed, or hosed us with cold water for soiling our undies because we were terrified a snake or rat might bite us?"

"No. After the first time, I loosened a few boards so we could break out and run to Antonia or hide on Eagle Rock. You and Ali always came with me. What is this, Hunter?"

"When she couldn't intimidate or bully you anymore, but delighted in caustic remarks, did you ever retaliate?"

"No, I ignored her and walked away."

"Exactly. Neither of us is capable of hurting a woman or a child. It took Chelsea to make me see things clearly. She knows me better than I know myself. I don't have a nasty streak and neither do you. I've been thinking about it a lot over the last few days. We deserve to be loved, like Antonia loves Dad, and Jake and Riley love our sisters. We deserve the chance to raise our own families."

"Hell, Hunter, I never expected this from—" A plume of dust caught Reid's attention. "That must be Reece. Let's leave this conversation for another time?"

"Sure." Hunter narrowed his eyes. "Delay Nolan while I put Zeus in the lunging yard. He and I need some distance at the moment."

"By that, I assume you sabotaged his coffee date with Chelsea?"

"You could say that."

"I'm glad. I wouldn't want a guy like that near a soft-hearted girl like Chelsea."

"I'll see you at the pub." Hunter sprang Monty into a gallop, taking a wide course behind a line of trees to the barn and stables.

Shaking his head, Reid cantered Jock across the hard-packed earth. To head Reece off, he'd need to intercept the van, before it reached the fork in the drive. He kept Jock to a steady stride, even though Hunter's revelations and questions had him in a spin.

For years he'd imagined his brother enjoyed his reputation as a prolific flirt. Whenever it came up in conversation, Hunter looked bored or amused, yet he'd never boasted of conquests.

The van pulled off to the verge then Reece opened his door. Steve Eckford climbed out the passenger side and they ambled to the gate to wait for Reid.

"How ya doing, fellas." He stayed astride Jock and leaned on the pommel.

Steve shrugged. "Bloody hot. I'll be better after a beer or five."

Reid gave a non-committal nod. He didn't know Steve Eckford well as he'd been in Hunter's year, which made him thirty-one, yet he appeared older and was fast developing a beer gut. At school he'd been a bully, although to Reid's knowledge he'd only ever picked on Hunter once, cornering him in the sports shed with another thug. They'd got a few punches in before Jake Morgan came to the rescue. They might have been fierce competitors in every arena, but the Morgans hated bullies.

Reece scowled. "It was a good day until your brother ruined it."

Suppressing a groan, Reid looked askance. "What's he done now?"

"I was having coffee with Chelsea Morgan at the Cyprus Café, doing rather well I might add, until Hunter swanned in to monopolise her attention. The bastard exposed my relationship with the Gillespie triplets. I'm not sure what Whitney, Britney and Courtney will do when they hear, but my name is rubbish with all the old ladies in town. What I don't understand is why would Hunter care what I do with Chelsea?

Reid stiffened. "Hunter wouldn't want to see her hurt." He reigned in his temper. Best not to piss Reece off before he shod Zeus.

"I knew *you* wouldn't care." Reece waved his hand at Reid. "You've been stringing her along for years while you sow your oats."

Reid hackles rose. "I've never been in a relationship with Chelsea. I took her to her year twelve dance, got into a fight with her brother then the police threw me in a cell for the night. End of story. Now that we're related by marriage, Hunter and I have an obligation to see Chelsea doesn't get hurt."

Reece shook his head. "Then you'd better keep an eye on her. Hunter implied they're in a relationship. She refuted it of course, but mud sticks. If you don't believe me, ask anyone who was in the café this afternoon. It was packed."

Inwardly groaning, Reid shrugged. "They're not in a relationship." *At least not yet.* "Hunter is helping her with this bloody dating game. If he was in a relationship with her, he wouldn't announce it to the world. Have you ever heard him boast of his conquests?"

Reece rubbed his jaw. "I can't say I have." He looked about. "Where's your old man? You two are usually joined at the hip."

"He's on a cruise with my stepmother. They took my Gran and Kathleen Sullivan with them." He sighed, still baffled by the turn of events. "James and Hannah Morgan went too."

Reece shook his head. "I knew your half-sister turned up a few years ago and then married Riley Morgan, and that Aleisha married Jake Morgan, but I never would have believed your fathers would go on a cruise together."

"You and me both." Reid shrugged. "It all started when Samantha arrived in town. Now, the only thing Dad and James argue over is who gets to teach their granddaughters to ride when they're old enough."

"That takes the cake." Reece swatted a fly away. "Where's Zeus, I'd better get him shod so I can have a beer."

"I'll be in that." Steve sneered. "This horse shoeing business is hard yakka, especially when the bastard is a nasty tempered mongrel."

Reid figured Hunter should have Monty rubbed down by now, so he leaned down and opened the gate. "I thought you drove trucks, Steve?"

"Used to. I got done drink-driving by Riley Morgan. Lost my licence and my job. Reece gives me a bit of casual work. You don't have anything going, do ya?"

"Not at the moment. What experience do you have working cattle and sheep?"

"A fair bit and I'm handy on a tractor."

Reece patted Jock's neck. "It must be tough with your dad away. I don't imagine you get any help from Hunter."

"He does his fair share. You haven't heard anything about the rustlers, have you?"

"There's talk they've moved on. With all the interest, they'd be fools to hang around."

"I hope you're right. There's a meeting at the Riverside Pub tonight at seven. It should give us a better idea of who's been hit and what the rustlers are after."

Reece nodded. "Let's get Zeus shod, so we're not late. It's only the one shoe, right?"

"Yep, I've got him in the lunging yard. Come on through and I'll close the gate."

"Thanks." Reece gave a wave then followed Steve back to the van.

Chapter Twenty-Eight

Disturbed over Hunter's retreat and a bone-deep loneliness, Chelsea had a mind to pack her bags and drive to Coffs Harbour. Alas, she had a lamb, two dogs, a cattle farm, eighteen hens and five horses to look after. Aside from her responsibilities, she couldn't let Paddy down or miss the meeting.

"Always dependable and well-behaved, that's me. One day, I'm going to do something really outrageous."

A giggle rose in her throat. *Something more outrageous than snuggling up to Hunter Sullivan all night or creating a dating agenda.* She eyed her dusty old ute, parked between two equally filthy vehicles. A good downpour would clean them up. What on earth was she doing? If she dawdled in the Riverside Pub's car park much longer, people would begin to question her sanity.

Drawing a calming breath, she adjusted the strap of her shoulder bag then marched towards the pub's welcoming verandah and the curiosity she would most likely meet inside.

Due to four phone calls from concerned patrons, Riley had been given an almost word-perfect account of her coffee date with Reece Nolan and Hunter's intrusion. Foreseeing such an outcome, Chelsea had enlisted the aid of her brother's wives, apprising Aleisha and Samantha of her dating agenda, Hunter's involvement and everything that had passed between them. Sam and Ali were her best friends and could be counted on for support.

Ali hadn't been the least surprised by Hunter's confession or behaviour, claiming he'd always had a soft spot for Chelsea. Honesty had proven the best policy. Sam and Ali promised to phone their respective husbands and make it plain they were to back off and let Chelsea manage her own life. And, if they didn't return to Coffs Harbour immediately, they needn't bother coming back at all.

When she'd driven home, her brothers were waiting in the kitchen. They'd checked on the bulls and cattle, shut the hens in their coop and the horses in their stalls in the barn. While she fed Stanthorpe, they warily voiced their concerns then asked for her promise not to stay at the farm alone. It was an easy promise to make. After hugging her, they drove away, leaving her surprisingly lonely. She missed having her noisy family around and cuddling her nieces.

"Here's my date." Paddy yelled, waving her over. "I've got the best table in the house." He winked. "You're looking very fetching, my dear. Blue suits you."

"Thanks, Paddy." She glanced down at her sleeveless silk blouse and denim mini skirt. She hadn't worn them since a holiday to Fiji, four years ago with her cousins, Emma and Lindsay. Her normal attire in summer consisted of long-sleeved cotton shirts, jeans, riding boots and Akubra, or when at school, long shorts or pants, T-shirts and sandals. Dresses weren't suitable when she spent so much time on the carpet with her kindy kids.

She smiled at Paddy, taking in his checkered shirt and flowery tie. They clashed terribly. His short beard looked to have been combed and he'd pulled his salt and pepper hair into a ponytail. "Sorry I'm late. My brothers heard about my matchmaking venture and wanted some assurances before they returned to Coffs Harbour." Taking a seat opposite him, she relaxed into the chair. "I would love a glass of Chardonnay."

"Right you are." He waved the waiter over. "The lady will have a Chardonnay and I'll have a beer. Thanks, mate."

"No worries, Paddy."

Chelsea glanced about the crowded dining room, giving a quick wave to Antonia's elderly parents sitting at a table with Mary Moonie. "It's busy for a Thursday night."

He leaned forward. "The rustlers have got folks worried. A lot have come out in support of the farmers, but word also got out about your dating agenda. Bet you didn't know Dan's got a book under the counter. Most folks are placing bets on Reid Sullivan."

She lowered her voice conspiratorially. "Who do they think he'll make a match with?"

"You, of course." Paddy chuckled. "I reckon your decision to look around gave him the push he needed."

A knot formed in Chelsea's stomach. "Is that what everyone thinks?" She'd waited so long for Reid to notice her, and in doing so had missed years of dating and kisses. Reid's pathetic proposal still hurt, but surprisingly not as much as Hunter's desertion.

She tapped the side of her nose. "If I were you, Paddy, I wouldn't put money on anyone just yet. I have more contenders to interview tomorrow."

"Thanks for the heads-up, luv." He waggled a bushy eyebrow at her. "Our date is doing wonders for my image. I've had three dames glare at me since you arrived."

"Isn't glaring bad?" Chelsea caught Mrs Eckford scowling at her. Poor Jerry, he really was under his mother's thumb, while Steve got to do as he pleased.

Paddy shrugged. "No, it's a huge improvement. Now they'll see me as an eligible seventy-year-old, not an old man to be taken for granted."

His words made her wince. Where was Hunter? Would he even turn up for the meeting? "No one should ever be taken for granted, Paddy."

"That's true, luv. I imagine you're a mite lonely with the family away. Let me buy you dinner? I'd appreciate the company, and it'll show the ladies I'm a generous bloke."

"I would love to have dinner with you, Paddy." She was still smiling when Reece Nolan ambled over to their table.

"Hello, Chelsea. Look, I'm sorry Hunter ruined our coffee date. I don't know what came over him. My relationship with the Gillespie triplets has never been serious, and to be honest, I've had an eye on you for years. How about dinner tomorrow night?"

His rude disregard for Paddy and cavalier attitude annoyed Chelsea to such an extent, she bristled with contempt. "No, thanks. I believe in monogamous relationships and expect any man I date to have the same values."

"Exactly. Off you go." Paddy winked. "You're interrupting our date."

"I see." Reece's lips thinned. "If you change your mind, Chelsea, give me a call." He strode out of the pub.

To Paddy's amusement, Steve Eckford stopped by the table, insisting on a coffee date. She politely refused then suggested he try an online dating company. With Hunter's desertion, her heart wasn't in it. She almost changed her mind after spying Reid and Emma having dinner at a corner table, but by then her potential date had left the pub.

An hour later, Chelsea left Paddy entertaining two ladies from the retirement village and found a post to lean on in the beer garden.

Overhead, a wisteria's heavy foliage blocked the night sky, its soft fragrance wafting in the still air. Several bees hovered amongst late blooms, searching for that last nip of nectar for their queen.

The beer garden had been slowly filling with farmers and concerned residents. Her only bright spot had been running into Hannah McKenna, who trained racehorses and was fast becoming a force to be reckoned with. Having several million-dollar horses under her care, she was also concerned about the rustlers.

"Why so sad, Miss Morgan?"

"Hunter." She straightened. His jaw had the five o'clock shadow happening, and his normally neat russet waves were an unruly mess, as if he'd been dragging his hands through it. "Are you, okay?"

"I received a call from your brothers. They apologised for any misunderstandings and asked me to keep an eye on you. I told them I have a business to run and I'm not your babysitter."

"Are you reneging on our deal?"

"I should. It's like asking a starving fox to watch over a plucky little hen, who thinks she can talk him into becoming a vegetarian."

Relief and elation bloomed in her heart. Hunter desired her but sought to be chivalrous. She was twenty-seven, what would it hurt to gain a little experience? Yet if they became lovers it would sound the death knell to any future with Reid.

Who was she kidding? Reid had shown more interest in Emma than he'd ever shown in her. A romantic liaison with Hunter was a risk, especially if it ended in heartbreak, but what if it blossomed into something more?

Looking up, she found him watching her warily. "I want us to be friends, Hunter."

He ran a hand through his hair. "I have friends, Chelsea. You belong in a different category. One that's driving me insane."

"Well then you should— *Oh.*" Something dropped down her cleavage. A sharp sting had her gasping. "Ouch, something stung me." She looked up. "Bees." Another sharp sting had her flinching. "Hunter, I've got bees in my bra."

"Shit. Show me." He snatched her blouse and looked down her cleavage.

"Stop it." She smacked his hand away.

"Let me see."

"No." Another sting had her flinching. "Ow, maybe it's a spider."

"Damn it, Chelsea, let me see." He flicked the buttons open, exposing her crimson bra for all and sundry.

"Hunter, behave yourself."

"Not until I know what's stinging you." His gaze searched her barely covered breasts as heat consumed her.

"Be still." His fingers brushed under the lace edge of her bra. "Got it."

"Got...what?" She choked out the words, mortified by his scandalous actions.

"A green ant. You might want to step away from that post before the rest of his buddies decide to take a bite out of you."

"Hunter, what have you done?"

He buttoned her blouse, his eyes locked on her lips. "My intention wasn't to embarrass you, honey. Consider it a strategic declaration. With my reputation, only a true admirer would dare win your heart. I've done you a big favour. You should reward me."

His words were barely a whisper, yet his attempt at humour only heightened her humiliation and awareness, whirling her into a vortex of vulnerability. Everyone knew his Uncle Jack had died from a bee sting, but Hunter's reaction risked mangling her reputation. Her brothers would assume he'd taken liberties and the town hadn't had a scandal like this since the last Sullivan-Morgan fiasco between Jake and Ali.

"Sullivan, you're dead meat."

He smiled. "Then I should make love to you and die a happy man." With a wink, he strolled back to the bar, leaving her spluttering like a fledgling salmon leaping upstream only to land on a scorching rock.

"Damage control, that's what you need, my girl."

Chelsea swung around, coming face to face with Edwina Lette. The elderly hippy chuckled. "Unless you'd rather see him skinned alive?"

"*No.*" She gulped. "A green ant fell down my blouse and stung me. We thought it was a bee. Hunter overreacted."

"Understandable, after what happened to his uncle." Edwina nodded. "That young man has a reputation, Chelsea. Best to avoid him or you'll have your heart broken by another Sullivan."

Annoyance had Chelsea stiffening. "Hunter respects me and would never hurt me. He's a good man and my friend. I won't have anyone criticise him."

"Hm." Edwina sniffed. "Be that as it may, he's a handsome devil, hot-blooded with eyes in his head. He'd have to be dead not to notice you. Even if you *are* a Morgan." She chortled, her gaze turning crafty. "It's unnatural, not having your family feuding with the Sullivans. It's high time a woman upset the apple cart."

"I beg your pardon?"

Edwina snatched Chelsea's right hand and peered at her palm so long a nervous tremor ran through Chelsea. A quick look about confirmed her worst fear, conversation in the beer garden had lowered to excited murmurs and everyone was watching her and Edwina with open interest. It was well known Edwina's predictions weren't to be ignored and following Hunter's actions everyone wanted to hear the outcome. She groaned. "What do you see, Edwina?"

"Twisted paths. You need to choose wisely. Be very sure you know what you want then go after it, no matter what barriers are put in your way." She chuckled. "See here, you have three children in your future."

"Who is he, Edwina?"

"Now that would be telling. Half the fun is finding out for yourself." With a cackle and flick of her long braid, Edwina made for the bar and Hunter, who had been deep in conversation with Dan and Angus. They were quickly joined by a bustling Florence.

"Poor Hunter." She'd wager Hickory Ridge, Florence and Edwina were reading him the riot act. Pulling out her phone, Chelsea composed a group text to her sisters-in-law, her mother and Antonia Sullivan. They could deliver the true version of this latest incident to their husbands before any others reached them. The last thing she needed was her brothers storming back to defend her honour and making things much worse.

She glanced at the bar. Edwina appeared to be reading Hunter's palm. He was tolerating it with mild amusement, until she said something that knocked the grin off his face.

Edwina held up three fingers then winked, just as a man stepped in front of Chelsea, blocking her view.

"Reid?"

"We need to speak in private." He clasped her hand and towed her towards the rear of the beer garden.

Chapter Twenty-Nine

"Reid, stop manhandling me. For a guy who hates being centre stage, your behaviour is drawing everyone's attention."

"What I have to say is for your ears only."

"It had better not be another back-handed marriage proposal. I'm well and truly over you Sullivans and your insipid offers."

He spun around and she ran into him. "Hunter proposed to you?"

"He inferred he might have to marry me for my cooking and my..." She bit her lip. Best not to voice the rest of his innuendos. "He was teasing."

"Are you sure?" Reid backed her into a corner, blocking everyone's view of her with his body. "I need to ask you something important."

"No." She pushed his hard chest. He barely moved an inch. "You can't do this, Reid. It's not fair. I've accepted we don't suit or know each other at all. Go back and talk to Emma, she's obviously more to your taste."

"Leave Emma out of this, Chelsea. I'm a first-class idiot. Hunter's been proclaiming your virtues for years and warning me I'd lose you. I know you'd make a good wife and mother. You have what it takes to face year after year of drought. You're kind to kids and animals. You have a big heart and you've been raised on a large property. I've always known these things. In my defence, I feared I'd make a bastard of a husband and father. You deserve better than that."

"I know I do, which is why—"

"Let me finish, please?" He rubbed his forehead. "Earlier, Hunter berated me for how badly I've treated you, and he's right. He also drove home some hard facts, about him and me. Our mother was a cruel and vindictive bitch, who made our childhood hell."

She swallowed. "I know that, Reid, but—"

"You perceive a different side of Hunter to most of us. You've made him realise he's not like our mother. Neither of us are and I now accept we wouldn't physically hurt a woman or child. We deserve the chance to raise our own families."

"Exactly, but as I was trying to say—"

"No, don't say anything. I would like you to do me a favour."

"I kissed Hunter. Three times."

"What?" Reid's eyes narrowed. "When?"

Anyone would think he had the right to question her. Still, if she wanted to end this conversation, she'd best give him the truth. "The first time was by mistake, because I thought it was you in the woodshed on New Year's Eve. The other two times, he caught *me* by surprise, but I didn't stop him, because I liked it. So, there." She crossed her arms.

"Thank you for acknowledging my virtues, but the man I marry has to be in love with me. I need him to place me before six damn rams. So, unless you can offer me your heart, it's a waste of time even speaking of marriage."

His lips twitched. "That wasn't what I wanted to ask you, Chelsea."

"Oh." Heat rushed into her face. "What then?"

"Three things. Your forgiveness for the years I've ignored and avoided you. If I hadn't been such an ox-head, we'd probably be married with three kids by now."

Chelsea reared back. "Why three?"

"Your family do have a tendency for producing twins and Edwina Lette believes I have three children in my future."

"Oh dear."

He exhaled. "The next thing I would ask is, please drop your dating agenda. It's stirring up too much interest and I don't want you or Hunter hurt."

"How will Hunter get hurt?"

"He's always been protective where you're concerned, Chelsea. According to several sources, he's ambushing your dates and being a real bastard. He'll either end up in a fight, or his innuendos will land you both in hot water. He's got a reputation—whether it's been blown out of proportion or not—and people talk."

"Yes, they do." She studied his handsome features, so like Hunter's, yet missing some vital ingredient. "I forgive you, Reid, and I will consider your second request carefully. What's the third thing?"

"Will you have dinner with me tomorrow night?"

"Dinner… We haven't had a coffee date yet."

He grinned. "We can have coffee later…at my place."

She gasped. Over the years she'd fantasized this exact scenario. Reid waylaying her then issuing just such an invitation, and now that he had, she felt ill. "I can't go home with you, it's…it's in the rules."

"Who's rules?"

"Hunter's. It's to safeguard me against men who might take advantage."

Reid laughed. "My brother is the last person to abide by such a rule, and I'm sure he wouldn't apply it to me. If you prefer, we can eat at my place. I'm not a bad cook when it comes to steak and salad, or eggs and bacon…if you decide to stay the night."

"Like hell!" Hunter pushed in beside Reid, towering over her, blocking her in completely. He stood as rigid as a rottweiler, aggression pouring off him in waves, eyes flashing with fury as he confronted Reid. "Chelsea's not interested in your proposals or propositions."

Could this night get any more humiliating? Vibrating with fury, she directed her ire at Hunter first. "Damn you, I can speak for myself. Stand aside."

Surprisingly he did, giving her room to slip between them. She took a step then spun to face them, well aware of the crowd's interest. "What is it with you Sullivans?" She stabbed a finger into Reid's chest. "For twelve years you've ignored me, now suddenly you're interested, even *prepared* to marry me, if necessary?"

"Yes."

She waited, yet he didn't elaborate. "That's it?" She shook her head. "In the romance stakes you really suck, Reid. It makes me wonder if your real aim is to destroy my friendship with Hunter. Whatever you're up to, it's not good enough. I deserve better."

"I agree." Reid's eyes flicked to Hunter. "You warrant a man who can and will commit to you. I'm offering what you've always wanted."

"You have no idea what she wants, Reid, so back off. Chelsea belongs to me." Hunter's feral growl drew gasps along with a few cheers and whistles.

Chelsea blinked at the predatory glint in his eyes then his words hit home and anger consumed her. She stabbed her finger into his chest repeatedly. "You must really get a kick out of embarrassing me with your innuendos and caveman mentality."

"That's not what this is, Chelsea." He took a step closer, his eye imploring. "I care about you. Everything Reid said is true, but he doesn't deserve you. He doesn't love you."

"Do you think I don't know that?" She held back her tears, determined to thrash this out. "I thought we were friends, Hunter, but you're a...a big phoney. I do not belong to you...or you." She jammed a finger into Reid's chest again then glared from one to the other. "I am so over you Sullivans. If I never see either of you again, it will be too soon."

"Way to go, luv." The yell from behind her was followed by clapping.

She swung around and strode through the parting crowd, surprised by the cheerful grins and thumbs up. They were all on her side. A soothing thought amid her embarrassment, but she couldn't stay. She needed to escape, find somewhere to lie low and lick her wounds.

"Chelsea, no one knows you like me." The booming declaration added to her humiliation and effectively silenced the crowd.

Would this torture ever end?

"I've loved you in silence for fourteen years. It stops tonight." Hunter's voice shook slightly, slowing her steps. He cleared his throat. "You *are* mine, sunshine, so get used to it." His masculine drawl, now steady and resolute, brought her to a grinding halt.

She turned, her pulse beating a rapid tattoo in her ears. The steely intent in Hunter's eyes sent elation shooting through her. She'd waited years for Reid to claim her in such a way, only to find it wasn't Reid she wanted.

Hunter had stepped out of his comfort zone, onto a precarious limb to voice a truth he'd hidden from her and the world. *He loves me.* What might he do to prove it?

"Make me." She crossed her arms, hiding her shaking hands. "If you dare?"

One eyebrow rose, a wicked grin spreading across his handsome face. "Oh, I dare, honey." He moved so fast, she didn't have time to do more than squeak, before he caught her in his arms and kissed her senseless, amid cheering and clapping.

She didn't have any idea what Reid thought, and cared even less.

"Chelsea!" Harry burst into the beer garden gasping for air.

Floating in a haze of euphoria, Chelsea clung to Hunter's arms as Harry pushed through the crowd.

"Where's Chelsea?"

"What's happened?" Reid calmly stepped forward,

no outward sign of annoyance, jealousy or fury to be seen. She couldn't help thinking if it had been the other way around, Hunter would have torn Reid to shreds then probably kidnapped her. The thought both thrilled her and filled her with sadness. Reid would have made a terrible husband.

Harry bent over trying to catch his breath. "The rustlers took the horses."

"Whose horses?" Chelsea met Harry's distressed gaze and fell against Hunter, dreading the answer as a fist closed around her heart.

"I recognised Buck, Tucker and Muscat. There were others, but I didn't have time to identify them. The cattle truck was heading west along Reservoir Road."

"No!" Her legs gave out.

Chapter Thirty

So be it. A calm acceptance settled over Reid as he leaned against the bar. He'd taken a major gamble and now must accept the outcome. Three days ago, he would have used dirty tactics and his fists if needed, to keep his brother away from Chelsea, yet the long-term effects on all three of them would have been disastrous.

His focus shifted to the uproar that had broken out with Harry's revelation. The rustlers were dangerous and threatened livelihoods. Hunter looked fit to strangle someone, his warning glare and protective hold on Chelsea spoke volumes. As soon as things calmed down, Reid would need to rebuild his relationship with them.

Dan's wife Alice handed Chelsea a small glass of amber liquid then encouraged her to drink it. Shock and disbelief had knocked Chelsea sideways, but once she rallied, there'd be no holding her back.

Senior Constable Abby Taylor blew a shrill

whistle, drawing everyone's attention. "Settle down, folks. We need to work together to catch these thieves." She did a slow perusal of the beer garden, as if cataloguing every face. "I want you all to keep your eyes open for the cattle truck and check on your livestock first thing in the morning. Report back to the station if you have news. Do not, under any circumstances, approach the rustlers."

The hum of voices rose as conversations broke out amongst the crowd.

Holding up a hand, she waited until she had everyone's attention again. "My husband, Roman, is coordinating SES members to check on outlying farms and any abandoned buildings. More volunteers would be appreciated. I've requested police assistance from Boggabri, Tamworth, Moree and Armidale. They're sending out local patrols right now and setting up roadblocks, so if the rustlers have left our district, they will be intercepted."

She grimaced. "We've received a report from Moree police of a stolen truck that matches the partial plate Chelsea Morgan gave us. Tyre prints taken from Tulachmhor, Hickory Ridge and Craigellachie properties match tyres used by the truck company. We've passed word on to sale yards within a couple of hundred miles, notifying them of the Sullivan's missing sheep and McGregor's cattle. If the stock turns up, they will be identified by their electronic ear tags. Unfortunately, horses are a different story, most are not branded or microchipped unless they belong to a racing stable or compete in overseas equestrian events."

"Morgan's horses are microchipped." Reid felt a

little of his anger ebb as he met Abby's surprised gaze. "Aleisha insisted on doing all our horses after her mare was almost stolen at Armidale show last year."

"That good news. Anyone interested in joining the search parties, please see Roman."

As Abby made her way out of the beer garden, Reid glanced around the crowd. He knew everyone. Most farmers had attended without their wives. Angus and Dodge gave him a nod. Hannah McKenna stood between Ryan Rossiter and Daniel Stone; their attention focused on Roman as he organised people into search parties.

A shiver of apprehension slid down Reid's spine. With the other members of his family away, Tulachmhor was vulnerable. He needed to get home. Reid's gaze connected with Edwina Lette. She glanced from him to Emma Fahey then narrowed her eyes. Apprehension prickled. The elderly woman had an uncanny ability to read people.

"I don't know whether to slap your face or kick you." Emma edged in beside him. For any observing them, it would appear nothing more than polite conversation. "You want to explain, before I ditch you?"

He sighed. "Hunter is a good guy, losing Chelsea would have turned him into the man we've all wrongly labelled him."

"So that's what tonight's performance was about? You deliberately provoked Chelsea into despising you, and Hunter into making his confession?"

"Yeah, but it could easily have gone differently."

Emma's eyes widened. "You love Chelsea." She hadn't raised her voice, but they were now attracting attention.

"Not exactly." He realised he needed to explain before she went through with her threat or walked away. "I've never considered Chelsea in a romantic light. I took her to her year-twelve formal so I could keep an eye on my sister and Jake Morgan, who I got into a brawl with. Chelsea went off to university for four years. When she came back, I kept a healthy distance. A twist of fate on New Year's Eve changed everything."

"Do you regret taking me home?" The hurt in Emma's eyes cut him deep.

"No, sweetheart. I took you home because after one kiss, I wanted so much more. I don't regret one minute of what we've shared. You're intelligent, graceful, sexy as hell, and I can't get enough of you. Neither of us wanted marriage or kids, but we definitely have something special. If I can change my mind, maybe you can too."

A soft blush rose in her cheeks, along with a sultry smile. "I might change my mind, with the right encouragement." She raised a delicate eyebrow. "If you dare?"

He laughed at the words Chelsea had thrown at Hunter. "Oh, I dare, sweetheart." Leaning forward, he kissed her enticing lips, then with a groan, pulled her into his arms and deepened the kiss. Some things were worth raising a few eyebrows.

A gasp sounded behind him then several throats were cleared. Finally, someone tapped him on the shoulder, bringing the sensual joining to an end.

"Interesting tactics, Reid Sullivan." Edwina Lette chuckled. "I'm sure your grandmother and Antonia would appreciate the show, but your father might not be pleased." She tapped his arm. "You did a good deed tonight. Your brother and Chelsea are much better suited."

Edging him aside, Edwina took Emma's hand, studying her palm carefully. "I know your past holds painful memories, my dear, but your future is rosy. Three children and a long life. Most importantly, you'll be happy. Sullivan men make loyal husbands, given half a chance." She winked at Reid then wandered off to join Dodge and Tessa Myers.

Dodge held his hands wide and called out. "What can I say? My grandmother is never wrong." He laughed then followed Edwina and Tessa out of the beer garden. Most of the crowd had left or moved inside. Alice shook her head at Reid then urged Harry into the kitchen.

"Come." Reid captured Emma's hand then drew her with him to where Hunter and Chelsea were sitting, shocked along with everyone else by Reid's impulsive out-of-character behaviour. He needed to clear the air, make things right. At least he wouldn't be doing it in front of an audience. Hunter stood, waiting in stony silence.

Reid exhaled. "I apologise for what happened earlier. Blame it on a moment of reckless courage." He met Hunter's eyes. "You might not believe this, but I never wanted to hurt Chelsea."

"At the moment, I'm not sure what to believe." Hunter's gaze flicked to Emma and their joined hands. "You'd better have a bloody good explanation or the Morgans are going to string you up by your balls."

Emma tried to detangle their hands.

Reid held fast, needing her close. His best bet lay in being totally honest. The horses would have to wait. "Spending time with Emma has opened my eyes to a lot of things I've been blind to. And, I've been mulling over what you said. You're right, we both deserve happiness and families of our own."

Chelsea came to her feet. Reid wasn't surprised to find her gaze frosty and unwelcome. Hunter's arms tightened around her protectively.

Reid grimaced. "Chelsea, you're intelligent and kind. With your upbringing, stock experience and knowledge, you'd be an asset to me, but after talking to you this morning, I realised two vital elements. I never considered your feelings. Yet, with Emma, it's different."

He hesitated, shifting from foot to foot. "Hunter loves you. There isn't anything he wouldn't do to for you, which is why he agreed to assist in your dating agenda." His lips twitched. "It was destined to fail, as no man would measure up in Hunter's opinion. I care about you, Chelsea, but more like a sister. You deserve a man who will put you first, love you unconditionally and walk through fire for you."

Chelsea's dabbed at her tear-filled eyes. "I know, but I can't think about that now."

Hunter held his hand out to Reid. "Thank you, bro. I owe you big time. I'll take you up on that equal partnership in Tulachmhor, once I'm satisfied Lewis can manage the agency. We'll make a good team."

"We always have." They shook hands.

Chelsea straightened her shoulders and looked at Hunter. "I need to find Harry. You should check your horses."

A chill ran down Reid's spine. As with the Morgan horses; Jock, Monty, Zeus and Blossom were an integral part of their lives. Aleisha would be frantic as her mare was heavily pregnant.

He ran a hand through his hair. "Chelsea, would you drop Emma back to her granny flat, and then Harry at your uncle's house? We'll check on our horses then swing by your farm. It would be best if you stay in town."

"Okay." She gave Hunter at worried glance. "See you tomorrow."

As Emma and Chelsea walked away, arm in arm, heads together, Reid frowned. "She's only just holding together, isn't she?"

"Yeah." Hunter pulled out his phone. "I'll ring Riley and Jake. Let them know about the horses. I dare say Riley will check in with Abby the minute I hang up."

"You'd better fess up about tonight before he hears it from Abby. Tell him you'll watch over Chelsea twenty-four-seven."

Hunter rolled his eyes. "I intend to, but another night in the same house without making love to Chelsea could well kill me."

Reid raised an eyebrow. "I'm beginning to think your reputation *is* all talk."

"When it comes to Chelsea, I want to do things properly. She deserves wooing and flowers and seduction. Until the rustlers are caught and the horses retrieved, we'll need to keep her occupied, and tucked away somewhere safe, like Edwina's guesthouse."

Reid nodded. It was the perfect solution, if Hunter had the strength to implement it.

Chapter Thirty-One

Parked under a streetlight on Wattle Drive, Chelsea returned Emma's wave. The ute idled a touch roughly, reminding her it was due for a service and oil change. Once Emma disappeared down the side of the house, Chelsea turned to Harry, fidgeting beside her.

"As you saw the rustlers on Reservoir Road, I assume you went ahead with the stakeout tonight?"

"We did." He was almost jumping out of his skin with excitement.

"So, Roman and Dodge agreed to help you?"

"No, they said it was too dangerous and we should leave the rustlers to the police."

"Damn, Harry. Where are Oliver, Abby's boys and my cousins?"

"They're watching the roads out of town. Kaylee and two friends are hiding in Lette Park. If the rustlers drive through town, or leave town, they have to pass one of our checkpoints."

It was a brilliant plan, but risky and the kids'

parents wouldn't be happy. "You need to send them home, Harry. The rustlers are dangerous."

"We know, that's why we agreed to stay hidden and alert each other by text."

"Okay, so why were you on Reservoir Road?"

He grinned. "Because you, Hunter and Reid were at the meeting tonight. It stands to reason, with your families away, the rustlers would realise Tulachmhor and Hickory Ridge were unprotected."

She put the ute into gear and drove along Wattle Drive. "I assume you've been in contact with your friends. Which way did the rustlers go after they passed you?"

"That's the weird bit. They only had two choices. Turn left into town or right towards Moree, but Michael reckons no truck came out of Reservoir Road, and none of my other friends spotted it either."

Chelsea made a right turn onto Mount Ingalls Road. "So, the rustlers turned off before the intersection, which means they live or are hiding out on one of the properties along that stretch of road."

Harry grinned. "Yes, and there's only four properties to choose from."

She made another right onto Main Street. "Good work, Harry. Text your spies to go home. I'll drop you at Uncle Ron's place, then call by the police station. You did good."

"Thanks. I can back out of the camping trip, if you need me to stay with you." He met her gaze, looking torn.

"No, go camping. As sure as hens lay eggs, Riley and Jake will be back tomorrow, and I've got Hunter and Reid, if I need them."

Harry sniggered. "While I was in the pub's kitchen, I heard what happed in the beer garden. Reid and Hunter are in so much trouble. Your brothers are going to hit the roof. It's worth staying to see the fireworks."

"It won't come to that." She concentrated on the road ahead as they drove the three kilometres out of town to her uncle's poultry farm.

"Drop me at the front gate." Harry undid his seat belt. "That way I can text everyone then sneak in undetected."

"Okay. Ring me or Senior Constable Taylor, if there's any problems?"

"I will. See ya in a couple of weeks, Chelsea." He jumped out, slammed the door then ran up the dirt drive.

She sent Hunter a text, informing him of Harry's suspicions then did a U-turn and drove back into town. The bee incident, Reid's behaviour, and Hunter's declaration kept flashing through her mind, tormenting her. They would be the talk of town tomorrow. She desired Hunter, enjoyed his sense of humour and company. Craved his kisses and worried about him, but was that love? He was offering her everything she'd ever wanted, but could she really switch her affection from one brother to the other that quickly?

"Yes, but am I in love with Hunter?"

She longed to thrash it out with Ali and Sam, yet on second thoughts it was Hunter she should talk it through with, once their horses were retrieved and the rustlers behind bars. In the meantime, she could do what she always did when needing to think. Go to her favourite rock on the ridge and meditate to the sounds of nature. Although, it wouldn't be the same without Muscat. A tear rolled down her cheek.

"Where are you, sweet?"

She turned into Church street and then Willow Tree Drive. Hopefully Abby could fast track roadblocks and request search warrants for the interlaying farms.

Chelsea grimaced. She'd have to inform Ali and Sam of the latest incidents with Hunter and Reid Sullivan. Hopefully they'd convince Riley and Jake to stay in Coffs Harbour, but she doubted it.

Her phone chimed as she parked between Riley's patrol car and the paddy wagon.

The message was from Hunter. *Jock and Blossom here. Zeus and Monty missing.*

Fifteen minutes after Chelsea walked into the police station, Harry sent a text, informing her Roman and Dodge had picked up the other teenagers and taken them home. A fact she already knew as Abby had rung the two men the minute Chelsea told her about the juvenile spies. As a result, Kaylee had been grounded and Abby's boys were now Stanthorpe's foster carers. By the delight in Eddie's voice, looking after the lamb wasn't a punishment.

It was after midnight when Abby persuaded Chelsea to go home. She'd stayed on at the police station to man the phones while Abby and AJ paid informal visits to the four farms on Reservoir Road. Not that it did any good. No one had seen the rustlers.

Word of the Morgan and Sullivan thefts had spread like wildfire and calls had been coming in all night. Cattle and sheep were missing from all over the district. Unfortunately, with the Christmas break, their absence hadn't been noted.

The SES were manning roadblocks either end of Reservoir Road. Only residents were allowed in or out. So far all had been quiet.

It was only as Chelsea turned into Samantha and Riley's drive that a blinding realisation hit her. Wallaby Flats Road ran off Reservoir Road, which meant Tulachmhor offered the rustlers an escape route into Akuna National Park. Or, they could cross through the back of Hickory Ridge then enter Tulachmhor and the National Park. It would be almost impossible to find them on the vast network of fire trails and off-road tracks.

"Not on my watch." She tried ringing Hunter, but went straight to message bank, so she left a message explaining her theory and asking him to meet her at Hickory Ridge. "What if he doesn't check his messages?" She worried her bottom lip then sent a lengthy text.

Opening the garage door, she was immediately barraged by Regina and Lola, whining with excitement, licking her toes and knees. Roman and the boys had collected Stanthorpe earlier. "Come on, girls, we're going home."

Both dogs leapt into the back of the ute, tails thumping wildly as she clipped them to their short leads. Going anywhere always thrilled them, but tonight she needed their company and protection. The rustlers had to be laying low on one of the farms along Reservoir Road, with or without the owners' permission. If they were to make their escape, it would be in the early hours and she would see them from the top of Hickory Ridge.

Hunter hadn't replied, so she sent him another text. *I need you.*

Chapter Thirty-Two

Steaming hot water beat down on Hunter's shoulders and back, relieving the aches and knots. A bone-weary tiredness made it necessary to lean against the tiles, close his eyes and do nothing more than enjoy the relaxing heat, releasing his pent-up tension. He and Reid had checked every paddock, gate and boundary fence on Hickory Ridge and Tulachmhor. None of the chains had been cut or fences tampered with, yet the rustlers had hit both properties under cover of darkness. Reid hadn't thought to put a camera on the stables.

The rustlers had taken Tucker, Buck and Muscat from their stalls, yet left an older mare and gelding in the house paddock. The only horses missing from Tulachmhor were Zeus and Monty. Hunter suspected the rustlers had driven straight up the drives of both properties, backed their truck up to the barn or stables then loaded the horses as bold as brass. It had to be someone with local knowledge.

"Bastards."

They hadn't bothered stealing old Jock, left to graze in the paddock, so he either wasn't worth the effort to catch, or they were after younger, more valuable horses. Reid's stallion would net them thousands of dollars. The rustlers had also left Blossom in her stable with the door wide open, maybe because she was heavily pregnant and easily agitated. He could only hope she'd taken a bite or two before they backed off.

He needed a good night's sleep in a large bed, without erotic dreams involving Chelsea in all her naked glory, which left him frustrated and randy. Lack of sleep over the previous two nights had taken their toll. He could lay the blame for that solely at Chelsea's feet.

Reid knocked on the bathroom door. "I'm heading over to my cottage to catch a few hours' sleep. I assume you're sleeping here?"

"No, I'm heading back into town." If he couldn't sleep with Chelsea, he'd do the next best thing and have breakfast with her.

"Don't forget your phone, it was dead, so I've recharged it for you. And stop wasting water, you've been in there long enough."

"Yeah, yeah." Hunter pressed the lever, shutting off his soothing massage. Maybe he should sleep at Tulachmhor tonight. Driving wasn't wise when he could barely function.

Grabbing a towel, he dried off then padded down the hall to his old room. He pulled on a pair of jocks and looked longingly at the bed. It was almost two o'clock. He really should get some sleep then drive into town later, yet a niggling apprehension took root and wouldn't abate. He grabbed clean jeans, a T-shirt and socks then headed down the hall.

With his grandmother, father, and Antonia away, the house lacked its usual baking smells and lived-in vibe. The kitchen benches were too tidy, the floor tiles too clean, the fruit bowl on the dining table empty. Not a newspaper, shopping list or rural magazine to be seen. His thoughts shifted to the Morgan's kitchen. It projected a very much lived in vibe too, even with only one head-strong female ruling the roost.

Muscat, Buck and Tucker had been stolen, so Chelsea had to be hurting. She wouldn't rest until they were found. A shiver of unease ran down his spine. It was too late to check on her, but if he didn't make sure she was safe, he wouldn't sleep a wink. He reached for his phone, stilling as he saw a backlog of messages, missed calls and texts, all from Chelsea.

"Shit."

He listened to the first message, swearing as he scrambled into his boots. Her theory had hit him and Reid as well, so they'd dug a deep, wide trench preventing any vehicle from accessing the fire trail through Tulachmhor's back gate.

The next message urged him to call her immediately. Her last message threatened to band his testicles if he didn't ring back. He couldn't decide if the wobble in her voice was due to worry for him or her own safety.

"Hell." He tied his laces, pulled on his jacket then brought up her text messages.

The first he dismissed. It was a repeat of her

theory and asking him to meet her. The rest of her texts showed her growing concern.

I need you.

Where are you?

Has something happened?

Are you all right? Please ring me. I'm worried.

I refuse to be ignored, Sullivan.

Bloody hell, Hunter, please talk to me.

I'm coming over.

As if on cue, an engine roared in the distance. Shrugging off his jacket, Hunter threw it over a chair then paced across the kitchen. He stood on the back verandah, his heart thumping wildly as he watched a pair of headlights bouncing about as the vehicle sped up the drive. Relief flooded him when he recognised Chelsea's old ute. At least he now knew where she was and where she would stay for the rest of the night.

She crunched gears then braked hard, sending dirt flying as the ute slid in the gravel, missing the garden gate by inches. Lola and Regina leapt out of the cabin the moment Chelsea opened her door then jumped the fence and bounded up to him, their tails wagging furiously. He gave them each a pat then leaned against a post to wait for their mistress.

He could almost feel the animosity bouncing off her as she slammed the ute's door then marched up the garden path. She still wore the sexy blouse, short skirt and sandals, but by her pursed lips, death stare and jerky movements, she wasn't in a forgiving mood. The last time he'd seen her so worked up, she been fourteen. Her fury back then had been the catalyst which sparked his interest, now all these years later, she resembled an Amazon warrior, about to launch an all-out attack.

"Hello, sunshine."

"Don't you *'Hello sunshine'* me, Sullivan. I've been worried sick about you. Where the hell have you been for the last two hours?"

"Checking Tulachmhor's and Hickory Ridge's gates, fences and stock. Then digging a ditch deep enough to stop the rustlers escaping into Akuna National Park."

"Oh." She halted at the bottom step. "Why didn't you answer my texts? I was terrified something had happened to you."

"My phone ran out of charge, and we only finished fifteen minutes ago."

Her animosity deflated instantly, replaced by something close to defeated acceptance. Had she really been itching for a fight, or was there something more to her sagging shoulders and downcast eyes?

"Chelsea?" She raised her face and he went cold at the profound sadness spilling from her lovely eyes. "What is it, honey?"

"I can see you've been busy." Her lips trembled. "With everything that's happening, I overreacted. I was worried something might have happened to you."

"Honey, I love you, that's why I wanted you safe in town. Abby told me you were at the station, so I asked her to keep you busy. I rang twice, but you were on other calls, and AJ assured me you were holding up well. I planned to stop by the station myself, once we finished digging the trench, but time got away and my phone died. I was caked in dirt and sweat. I stopped here for a shower and clean cloths then I swear I would have come to you."

"Really?" Her eyes welled with tears.

He nodded and opened his arms. "It's been a hectic night, honey, but you never left my thoughts. Come here."

With a sob, she stepped into his arms, her head falling against his chest as she clung to his T-shirt. "I must be in love with you too, because I've never been so tied in knots with worry for anyone else."

He hid his grin. "You'll feel better in the morning. We're both exhausted. Come on inside. You can sleep in Ali's old room."

"I want to sleep with you."

A groan escaped. "Not a good idea, sunshine. I'm in desperate need of sleep. If you're in the same bed, I'll toss and turn in aroused torment and neither of us will get any sleep."

"Hmm." She exhaled, her warm breath feathering across his chest. "What are your plans for tomorrow?"

Her easy acceptance piqued his pride. *She's tired.* His attempt at reason didn't help. *She's an innocent. Once she's sensually awakened, it will be a different matter.* "I've got Antonia's parents coming out to Tulachmhor. Anthony and Sarah Luchetti have become de facto grandparents since Antonia married my dad. They've agreed to stay here during the day and keep an eye on things, while we paint your house. Paddy, Harry, Edwina and Tessa Myers have spent the evening procuring a team of volunteers to help us later today and tomorrow. We kick off at nine o'clock."

"That's so kind. I don't know what to say." She drew back so their eyes met. "We should put a barbecue on Saturday evening, then they can watch our rematch."

"Rematch? What about the gossip it will generate?"

"I've come to the realisation that curiosity and gossip are a natural part of life. We're all guilty of it occasionally. As long as it's not malicious or harmful then why worry? I also think most people mean well and, gauging from the cheers in the pub tonight, the crowd were happy with the outcome. Now, if you don't mind, I'd like to grab a shower and go to bed."

Shower. Bed. His brain and body might be exhausted but imagining Chelsea in either place had the power to stir one particular muscle. He cleared his throat, dragging his gaze from her enticing lips. "You go up, I'll put Lola and Regina in the laundry then lock up."

"Okay." She stretched up and feathered the lightest of kisses on his lips. It barely rated as a kiss yet left him desperate for more. At the kitchen door, she glanced over her shoulder, sending him a sultry smile before continuing inside. Had it been any other woman, he would have taken it as an invitation to join her.

With a groan, he turned to the two dogs sitting at his feet. "Come on, girls." They trotted along behind him to the laundry, where he filled a bucket with water then left them to enjoy more sleep than he was destined to get.

Leaving his boots and socks at the back door, he turned off the kitchen light then walked down the hall and past the bathroom. Hearing the shower had him hesitating, playing with the idea of joining Chelsea. He forced himself to walk on to his bedroom, drag off his T-shirt and jeans, pull the doona back and fall on the bed. Amazingly, he began to drift into semi-consciousness immediately.

As usual, it wasn't long before she entered his dreams, sliding in beside him, kissing his shoulder, stroking his back, rubbing her foot along his calf, wrapping an arm around him then snuggling against his side. Nothing like his usual dreams, yet so much more enthralling.

Chapter Thirty-Three

A crowing rooster impinged on Chelsea's delightful daydream. She'd have to leave her cosy bed soon, but not yet. Since New Year's Eve, her fantasies had featured Hunter, usually in his boxers or without a shirt, each fantasy becoming more and more erotic. His fingers skimmed her ribs before gliding down over her hip to stroke her naked bottom in sensual circles. Tingling goose bumps erupted under his fingertips, bringing every nerve in her body alive, along with a yearning for more. It was like a feather tickling her skin, or a desperate itch that needed scratching.

She squirmed, stretched, pushed against the warm body behind her and froze. Her eyes flew open and memory flooded back. Hunter's declaration in the beer garden, then that kiss. Harry's arrival and her heartbreak on learning the rustlers had taken Muscat. Her panic when she couldn't reach Hunter last night. Coming to Tulachmhor then crawling into his bed stark naked. Heat instantly washed over her. Where was the sheet and doona?

His hand stilled on her hip. "Morning, sunshine."

Wriggling her toes, she found the rumpled bedding at the bottom of the bed. What did one say after being discovered naked in a man's bed? "Morning."

Taking a fortifying breath, she rolled over to face him. He lay on his side, watching her, his naked chest inches away. The blatant desire in his eyes chased away her embarrassment and nerves. She reached up and spread her fingers over the broad expanse of his chest. "As I'm here and you're here, I'm hoping you will make love to me."

His lips curved. "I figured that might be the case when I woke up to find you in my bed, without a stitch of clothing on, but you did stipulate—"

"Forget our wager. I'm willing to overlook that you've made love to other women, after all we can't change the past. It's the future that interests me."

He raised a hand and stroked her face. "I may have had sex with other women, but *you* are the only woman I will *ever* make love to." He leaned in and kissed her.

An hour later, Chelsea lay cradled in Hunter's arms, her head on his chest, their legs entangled. His heartbeat had resumed a regular rhythm, yet he still held her possessively, his fingertips caressing her gently. The reality of what she'd been missing miffed her no end, although it would be exhilarating making up for lost time.

Her grin widened, much like a cat discovering an Olympic size swimming pool full of whipped cream. She would dive back in once her muscles recovered. Making love with Hunter had definitely been worth waiting for. He'd been considerate and gentle, concentrating on bringing her insurmountable pleasure, although they'd soon been consumed by flames and he hadn't held back, ravishing her thoroughly, much to her appreciation. She loved him. The realisation filled her with wonder and joy.

He kissed her forehead. "I must have imagined holding you like this a thousand times, but the reality is far better than any dream, especially as I know you love me, sunshine."

"Oh?" She wriggled up then crossed her arms on his chest and raised an eyebrow "What makes you so sure, Sullivan?"

He chuckled. "You never would have crawled naked into bed with me otherwise."

"Hmm." She traced a fingertip back and forth across chest. "Maybe it's because I'm becoming a reckless wanton, and craved being ravished by the man who professes to know me better than anyone else."

"That's true too, but you *do* love me, and I'll make you admit it." He rolled her onto her back and tickled her, drawing screeches of laughter, until she had to beg for mercy.

"Please stop. Okay, I admit it. I love you, Hunter. Stop!"

"Say it again?" He leaned over her, unthreatening, yet so powerful and magnificent.

"I love you. I love you."

His green eyes darkened with desire. "Marry me?"

"What?" She hadn't seen that coming. It was too much, too soon. "Are you mad? We need time to get to know each other. To see if we gel, or...something."

"We've known each other for years, and we gel very nicely, sunshine, in and out of bed." He pressed closer, proving his point.

"Your smug grin and arrogance aside, someone in this relationship has to keep a level head. What about your rules, Hunter? We haven't even had a coffee date." She tried to don an unamused air, except his heated gaze dropped to her lips and she began to melt.

"I had coffee with you yesterday." He nudged her chin aside to nuzzle her neck.

"Oh, that's...." She lost her train of thought for a moment. "I'm trying to have a serious conversation with you, Sullivan. We haven't been on a dinner date."

He chuckled, his deep rumble vibrating against her sensitive skin. "We had dinner together two nights ago at your house, and you ate most of my lunch yesterday." He feathered kisses across her collarbone, igniting an ache deep in her core.

A soft moan escaped. "You're twisting your own rules, Hunter. What about being seen together at an event in Bindarra Creek."

"What would you call the meeting at Riverside Pub last night, and our very public kiss?" His mouth closed over her nipple.

"Um, oh, a...an embarrassment I'll never live down."

He moved lower and all resistance fled. His heady diversional tactics were so much more pleasurable than talking or thinking.

A car horn blasted several times, interrupting her pleasure and sending Lola and Regina into a barking frenzy.

Hunter cursed then rolled off the bed to stalk to the window. "Shit. It's Reid and...your brother's patrol car is parked behind him."

"What?" She leapt out of bed and ran to his side. "Oh, it's only Abby. Reid must have seen my car and wanted to alert us." She groaned, her gaze raking Hunter's magnificent broad back and taut butt. "Damn, another thirty minutes would have been nice."

"Grab a shower in my grandmother's ensuite, I'll take the main bathroom. Reid can hold Senior Constable Taylor off for five minutes."

"Can I get a raincheck on what we were about to do?"

"Are you going to marry me?"

"Maybe, probably, I need some time to think. For me, marriage is the biggest commitment I'll ever make. I want my husband to be my best friend, partner and...and lover. We need to trust and respect each other. It has to last until death do us part."

He kissed the tip of her nose. "You have the promise of my love and fidelity, Chelsea. I won't rush your decision, but I'll do everything in my power to persuade you we are meant for each other. Edwina is right. We will have a long and happy marriage, with several kids, and I'm guessing lots of orphaned animals."

The truth of everything he professed was there in his eyes. His usual amusement nowhere to be seen. He meant every word. They would be happy together.

He would make sure of it. Her heart overflowed with so much love, a sob caught in her throat.

"Hey, I didn't mean to upset you." He caught her to him and hugged her tight. At least she had the answer to her biggest worry. She'd switched her idolisation from one brother to the other due to several mind-blowing kisses, yet the intensity of her love and desire for Hunter far outweighed the schoolgirl crush she'd had on Reid.

"I do love you." She sniffed against his chest. "It's actually a bit overwhelming."

"Tell me about it." He grabbed a throw rug and wrapped it around her shoulders. "Now, move that sweet arse before Senior Constable Taylor catches us naked. We have rustlers to catch, horses to rescue and a house to paint."

"One more kiss." She wrapped her arms around his shoulders then stretched up and kissed him. She really didn't care if the whole of Bindarra Creek walked in on them at that moment. Hunter's kisses were so damn addictive.

Chapter Thirty-Four

Freshly showered and shaven, Hunter strolled into the kitchen, an aloof guise in place. His body and mind might be consumed with Chelsea, but he'd mastered the art of concealing all signs of outward emotion years ago. His desperate act in the pub last night had raised plenty of eyebrows, yet not one person stepped forward to rescue Chelsea, or berate him for claiming her in such a public way. As if they'd decided to overlook his notorious reputation, or maybe they'd accepted the truth behind his declaration.

Whatever the case, he wouldn't allow any harm to come to Chelsea or her reputation. The announcement of their marriage would see to that, and in the meantime, he would show her nothing but respect.

Reid opened the kitchen door, glanced about swiftly then sent Hunter a probing stare. So much could be said without uttering a single word. Seemingly satisfied, he stood back for Abby Taylor to enter then set a cardboard box on the counter. "Have a seat, Senior Constable, I'll whip up some eggs and bacon."

"Thanks, Reid, but I can't stay long." She smiled at Hunter. "Good morning. As Chelsea's ute is outside, I assume she's about *somewhere*?" Abby's eyes lasered him.

Hunter played dumb. "She turned up before dawn, worried about the rustlers." He opened the fridge, frowning at the empty shelves. "I heard the shower running in my grandmother's ensuite, so I assume she's awake. Any news on our horses?"

"That's why I'm here." By the sharp edge to Abby's voice, she hadn't believed his vague theory any more than Reid had, who chose that moment to have a coughing fit.

"Here." Reid handed Hunter a packet of bacon. "It's no good hiding your guilty arse in the empty fridge. Bread's in the freezer, make yourself useful and fry up that bacon. I'll cook the eggs and tomatoes."

So much for protecting Chelsea. "I intend to marry Chelsea."

"That's good to know." Abby flipped open a notebook. "Emergency Services personnel are still manning the roadblocks, but there's been no sighting of the cattle truck. Police patrols from Moree, Armidale, Tamworth and Boggabri have also reported no sightings. I felt it only right to inform Riley the rustlers must have turned around and escaped via the eastern end of Reservoir Road before we set up the roadblocks. He advised me to speak to Arnold Delaney, an old timer who lives that end and spends most of his day on his verandah, weaving bullwhips. If a cattle truck passed, he would notice."

"That's true." Hunter pulled out a couple of frying pans and the toaster. "Arnold must be eighty now, but he's as sharp as a tack."

"You're right. I called in this morning. He was on his verandah until late, mainly due to excitement after speaking to Emergency Services. No truck passed, which means it's on one of the properties along Reservoir Road or Wallaby Flats Road."

"It's not on Hickory Ridge." Chelsea sailed into the kitchen, as fresh and bright as a sunbeam after rain. "Hi, Abby. I sat on top of our ridge for almost two hours last night, waiting for the cretins. Then I chained the front gates and came here." She glared at Reid. "I've already told Hunter off for leaving me to worry over your worthless butts. Next time you go off to check a potentially dangerous situation, I suggest you send a text to those who might be worried."

"Sorry. I assume Hunter reassured you."

"He did, eventually." She flounced over to the kettle, flipped the switch then pulled four mugs out of the drawer. "I'd wager every acre of Tulachmhor and Hickory Ridge, the rustlers have gone into hiding. They'll wait a couple of days, until the roadblocks are lifted, then make their escape in the early hours of the morning."

"That's what Riley suspects." Abby tapped her notebook. "He suggests leaving the roadblocks in place. It might push the rustlers to escape through the Akuna National Park, which means they'd need to come through Tulachmhor. He suggested we set up a trap."

"Reid and I had the same thought, which is why we dug a deep trench our side of the fire trail."

Hunter popped four slices of bread in the toaster then flipped the bacon. He lowered the gas then moved aside so Reid could cook the eggs and tomato.

Chelsea frowned at him. "Tulachmhor is too open. The rustlers are more likely to come onto Hickory Ridge then cut through the back gate to Tulachmhor." Her lovely eyes widened in horror. "If they panic, they might shoot the horses."

Hunter pulled her into his arms. "It won't come to that, honey. We make it known you and the dogs are staying here. The rustlers won't risk coming through Hickory Ridge during the day as we will be painting the house. Then we organise a watch on top of Hickory Ridge, day and night. When the rustlers appear, we alert Abby so she can arrest them."

"It's sounds good in theory, Hunter." Abby looked from him to Chelsea. "But how do we bait the rustlers?"

Chelsea smiled at Hunter. "The Bindarra Creek grapevine of course."

Chapter Thirty-Five

Soon after Abby left, Emma arrived with three bags of groceries, followed by Sarah and Anthony Luchetti. Chelsea had become very fond of the elderly couple over the last few years and would have liked to stay and chat over a cuppa, except the morning was racing away and there was much to do.

With a hug for each of them, she ran down the steps to her ute. Hunter had already secured Lola and Reggie in the back and climbed in the cab, so with a final wave, she jumped in and started the engine. It coughed and spluttered before settling into a rough idle. "I must get that looked at next week, it's definitely getting worse."

"You need a new ute. It can be your wedding present."

"Attempting to bribe me will get you nowhere, Sullivan."

They left Anthony, Sarah and Emma to their morning tea. Reid gave them a wave from the tractor.

He planned to spend most of the day ploughing the front paddock, so if the rustlers thought to make a daylight escape through Tulachmhor, they'd soon change their minds. Chelsea could only pray the grapevine would do its job and the rustlers would enter the trap before any harm came to the horses.

She wasn't sure what to expect when she pulled up at Hickory Ridge's front gate, but it certainly wasn't a line of cars along both sides of the road, or the crowd of people gathered around a water tanker. "What's going on?"

Hunter chuckled. "I did warn you volunteers were being gathered for a nine o'clock kick-off. They're here to help paint the house."

"What, all of them?" She turned to him in stunned disbelief. "There must be forty people here. Why would so many want to help paint? There are even parents from school and ladies my grandmother's age."

"Sunshine, you've had a positive impact over the years and you're always involved in fundraising projects. You're a well-loved member of the community, as are your family. It's only natural these people want to do something for you in return."

In a daze, she turned off the engine then opened the door. Lola and Regina were yapping madly, fit to bust with excitement. She shushed them then turned to the eager faces. "I'm blown away. Thank you."

Alice pointed to a trailer. "We've got morning tea, lunch and afternoon tea. The boys down at the hardware store supplied the brushes, overalls, undercoat and paint, which has been put on your father's account. We have everything but the kitchen sink. Dan and Roman borrowed a few ladders and a water tanker from the fire station. They've filled it with river water, so they can wash the house down. Tessa and Dodge brought a barbecue to cook our sausages and steak for dinner tonight."

Tears blurred Chelsea's vision. She sniffed back the wad of emotion that threatened to erupt. "It's so generous of you to give up your time like this."

"Fiddlesticks. That's not the case at all." Edwina waved a bangled wrist about. "Half of us are here to discover the outcome of Hunter's declaration last night. The rest are curious to see how you intend extracting your five hours of service from him, unless you've *done* it already." She gave an exaggerated wink and raucous laughter broke out.

Chelsea's face heated at the flagrant inuendo. Edwina might make light of why everyone had come, yet they were all good people with hearts of gold. They'd definitely be curious, but first and foremost, they were here to help.

"Actually, Hunter has worked off the wager, much to my enjoyment." Chelsea sent him a teasing grin. "He got very hot and sweaty painting the back verandah."

More laughter broke out.

He touched a finger to the brim of his Akubra. "Ah yes, but what a pleasure it was to work alongside you, sunshine. And, we do have our rematch tomorrow night, which I intend to win, so I'm not complaining." His deep rumble warmed her heart.

"Don't count your chickens before they've hatched, Sullivan. I intend to win, then keep you busy for hours at my beck and call."

"We will see, sunshine."

Blowing him a kiss, she paced to the gate, unlocked the chain then opened it wide. The rustlers might have disappeared, but she wouldn't rest until all the horses were home, safe and sound.

For the next three hours, Chelsea and Hunter worked alongside a team of men and women washing down the front and sides of the house then sanding down facia boards, verandah posts and window frames.

The older children spent their time chasing each other, playing with a batch of new chickens, or throwing sticks for Lola and Reggie. The tiny tots splashed in a toddlers' blow up pool, under the supervision of Edwina and Florence. Pretty little Tilly Myers might only be ten months old, but she had the elderly ladies wrapped around her tiny fingers.

The CWA ladies were out in force, manning a trestle table laden with cakes, slices and biscuits. Coffee, tea and water were dispersed with jovial efficiency. Dan had donated two large water barrels to quench everyone's thirst and a keg of beer as reward at the end of the day.

A halt was called for lunch, which was laid out on trestle tables. The spread of cold meats, salads, bread rolls and fruit drew everyone like flies.

Sitting beside Hunter, Chelsea couldn't help but wish her family were here to join in the laughter and chatter along the tables, to appreciate the kindness of their friends and neighbours. She made a mental note to thank them all in a nice way.

Hunter placed his hand over hers. "You okay?"

"Yes, I'm just trying to decide how to thank everyone properly."

"Invite them to our wedding." He winked. "The sooner the better."

She met his not-at-all innocent eyes. "If I agree to marry you, it won't be some flash in the pan, quickie affair. I want the whole kit and caboodle, flowers, dress, bridesmaids, and at least a two-week honeymoon."

"Say yes, sunshine, and I'll give you anything you want."

"I'd want a plain rose gold wedding band, as I'm not into extravagant jewellery."

"Noted. Anything else I can do for you?"

"Hmm, maybe you should convince me of your merits, tonight."

His chuckle sent goose bumps skating down her arm. "It will be my pleasure, sunshine." Their murmurs had drawn Paddy's interest from across the table, so they turned away from each other to speak to their neighbouring diners.

Talk eventually got around to the rustlers, the missing horses and stock numbers. It soon became evident the rustlers must have been working the area for some weeks. Thanks to the grapevine, every farm in the district had been advised to check their stock. Incoming losses had the grapevine swinging with contempt and anger. Some farms were missing as many as twenty cattle, goats or sheep, while others had discovered a bull or ram missing. It seemed to Chelsea most farms had been hit.

Emma's sister, Lindsay, and their parents dropped in with several dishes of baked custard and a tub of ice cream. They stayed for dessert and coffee then volunteered to help undercoat the railings on the front verandah. As the afternoon wore on and each assigned job was completed, people began to leave or gather in small groups to chat over tea, coffee or a beer. Chelsea had given up trying to hide her awareness of Hunter. Whether he was washing down walls, cleaning out gutters, sanding, painting or chatting, she found her gaze returning to him again and again, anchored in fascination.

Jerry Eckford waved a hand in front of her face. "Earth to Chelsea."

"Oh, sorry, Jerry, I was wool-gathering."

"No guessing over who." He glanced to where Hunter stood talking to Angus, Dan, Roman and Dodge. "Any word on your horses?"

"No, although..." She wanted to tell him the plan, but Hunter insisted the less who knew, the better. He and Reid planned to draft a trusted few to lay the groundwork then sit back, watch and wait for the grapevine to do its work. She imagined that's what Hunter was explaining to the four men.

Realising Jerry was waiting for her to continue, she sighed. "I hope we get the horses back soon. We're a close community and everyone is on the lookout for the rustlers. Why would anyone take our horses?"

"Maybe they're out to prove a point or are desperate for money. Be careful, Chelsea."

"I will."

"I hear Reid and Hunter got into a brawl over you last night?"

"Not true." She frowned. "You were at the pub. Didn't you see what happened?"

"No, I left after dinner. Mum was in a bad mood and wanted to go home."

"Right. Well, to cut a long story short, Reid pushed Hunter into confessing he loved me, then Hunter kissed me in front of everyone."

"Wow, I hope you're not falling for him, Chelsea. Hunter ain't interested in marriage."

She raised an eyebrow. "Apparently, you don't know Hunter as well as you think. Catch you later, Jerry."

With a grin, Chelsea jogged across to her uncle, aunt and cousin Lindsay. She spent a few minutes assuring them everything was under control then waved them off. A few tears escaped when her gaze fell on the house paddock, where Muscat, Tucker and Buck should be grazing. They were microchipped, which might or might not come to light if the rustlers tried to sell them. She prayed they didn't know about the microchips, otherwise they'd likely shoot each horse. Her vision blurred with tears.

"Chelsea." Hunter put his arm around her shoulders. "What's up?"

"I want Muscat back." She wrapped her arms around his waist. "I want...my sweet girl home."

"I know, honey. I'll do everything in my power to find her, I promise." He held her tightly against his chest, rocking her gently. It wasn't until she wiped her eyes and looked around that she realised Emma had arrived and was hovering close by.

"I'm okay, Emma."

"It's been a hot day." She touched a palm to Chelsea's forehead. "You're certainly warm. Take her inside, Hunter, and place an icepack under her neck for ten minutes, that should do the trick."

"I'm fine, honestly."

Emma raised an eyebrow. "Drink a litre of water over the next hour. That should help. Are you staying at Tulachmhor tonight?"

"Yes."

"Good, I'll be at Reid's cottage if you need me." She lowered her voice. "I've decided to move in with him."

The cool aloofness that had been in Emma's eyes and voice for the last two years had vanished, replaced by a sparkling vivacity that warmed Chelsea. It seemed her lovely cousin had recovered from her broken heart and fallen in love again. This time with a man who would never betray her.

"Delightful." Edwina handed Chelsea a glass of water then rubbed her hands together. "Nothing like a little romance in the air to cheer us all up. Anyone else hungry?"

As if on cue, a loud clanging drew their attention. "Dinner is cooked, folks."

Chelsea finished her water then accepted Hunter's hand. They walked over to the barn. Dave Buckley stood beside the barbecue, wearing her grandmother's frilly apron as he beckoned them with a pair of tongs. "We have plenty of sausages and steak for everyone."

Hunter squeezed Chelsea's fingers. "How do you feel?"

"Angry. I want the horses back unharmed and without anyone getting hurt." She bit her lip. The rustlers had the whole town stirred up. It wouldn't take much to ignite tempers.

Chapter Thirty-Six

Hunter hung up the last roller to dry then gave the house a nod of approval. Thanks to thirty-odd volunteers, they'd achieved more than he'd envisaged. Tomorrow they'd do the topcoat, and maybe finish the gutters, windows and railings.

Dinner had been a much smaller affair than lunch, as several families, along with most of the elderly helpers had departed. Dan, Angus, Roman and Dodge, along with their wives and children had stayed. Each couple willingly taking on the task of spiking the grapevine. With luck, by tomorrow the rustlers would have heard Hickory Ridge was unguarded and use it to make their escape into Akuna National Park.

After hearing the plan, Dodge, Angus and Roman volunteered to help keep watch over the next few nights. All being well, the rustlers would be in police custody by Monday and the horses back in their stables.

Then I'll reel in my girl.

"Hey, Hunter, what's this I hear about you kissing Chelsea last night?" Jerry Eckford's quiet question came with a scowl. He kicked a stone. "I heard other stuff that...well, can't be true, otherwise Riley and Jake would have high-tailed it home to skin you alive."

"It's all true." Hunter shrugged. "In my defence, I plan to marry her, if she'll have me."

"You reckon you can stay faithful?"

"I'd stake my life on it." He was well and truly over his fickle reputation. Glancing across to where Chelsea, Claire and Tessa were clearing away the leftover food, he sighed. "I'd never do anything to hurt her."

"Hell, that's one for the books." Jerry cleared his throat. "I know you've got a lot on your plate at the moment. Do you want me to keep an eye on things here?"

"Thanks, mate, but we've got it under control. Reid or I will drive around every morning to check the stock and fences, while Chelsea lets the chooks out and waters the vegetable garden, then we'll come back in the afternoon to do another run and put the chooks in their coop. Roman lent us a drone to check on things through the day. I don't want Chelsea here alone, so she's staying at Tulachmhor. I'll hang around tonight, so we can get an early start in the morning. I want the house finished tomorrow as I'm going away for a few days."

"I'm really sorry about your horses. That's gotta fricken' hurt."

"Yeah, you got that right. I'd like to rip the mongrels' throats out. Hopefully the police catch them soon and we'll get our horses back."

"Don't hold your breath. Talk around town is the rustlers are gone." Jerry kicked another stone. "It's really weird, but the only horses reported missing are yours and Morgan's. It's almost like they were specifically targeted."

"It wouldn't be anyone within camp drafting circles. Our horses compete often enough to be easily identified. No, I reckon the rustlers saw an opportunity and took it. Maybe they heard our folks were on a cruise."

"That, or you've messed with the wrong woman and some guy is out for revenge, or to hurt those you care about."

Hunter shrugged off the comment. "I've never dated women already in a relationship, and until Samantha married Riley, my only adversaries were the Morgans. Now I'm bloody related to them twice over. Nope, I don't have enemies."

"I heard the Gillespie triplets dumped Reece Nolan and are moving to Melbourne. They've been the talk of the town since you exposed their arrangement with Reece, so there's three ladies who want your guts for garters. Reece ain't happy either. Every female in town is giving him a wide berth. You've also sabotaged Chelsea's other coffee dates, either in person, or by supplying her with a list of questions to scare off contenders, me included."

"That because none of you have a clue how to make her happy. Chelsea requires a man who will treat her with respect and value her opinion. Someone with common interests and a love of the land. She needs a man who will always put her first and be faithful."

"And that's you?"

"It certainly is, mate." He hadn't meant to rabbit on, yet he'd meant every word.

Jerry gave him a thoughtful look. "I believe you will."

"Thanks, mate. I see Reid trying to get my attention. It must be time to check the fences and stock. Are you coming over tomorrow?"

"Nah, I've got cattle to drench. Think about what I said. If someone wants to hurt you, they may go after Chelsea." He gave a nod then sauntered away.

Hunter mulled over Jerry's words as his gaze drifted to Chelsea. Keeping her safe had been his priority since discovering the rustlers. Keeping her busy so she didn't dwell on the missing horses had been harder, which is why he'd left her to manage the workers and coordinate each task. In her quiet moments he'd sought her opinion on who they could trust to be part of a surveillance team and the best place to set a trap. Now they just needed the rustlers to take the bait.

As the last of the volunteers drove away, Reid and Emma joined Hunter by the barn.

"Does Chelsea know you're staying here alone tonight?" Emma glanced at the house where Chelsea had gone to pack an overnight bag.

"Not yet. I'm determined to send her back to Tulachmhor in case the rustlers make a move tonight. Our lookouts will be in place by nine, although it's doubtful anything will happen until Saturday or Sunday night."

"I suggest you let Chelsea decide where she stays, otherwise you'll put her nose out of joint." Emma's lips twitched. "This is not the time to go all macho and protective. Chelsea will not appreciate it."

"I know, but if anything happens to her..."

Chelsea threw a duffle bag in the ute's tray then marched across the yard. "I know a conspiracy when I see it. What's going on?"

Hunter sighed, accepting the foregone conclusion and bowing to a higher power. "I was telling Emma and Reid I'm sleeping here tonight. I'd prefer you at Tulachmhor, but it's totally your decision."

"What's to decide? Of course, I'm staying with you."

Emma rolled her eyes. "I need to see a neurologist. I could have sworn you said you were determined Chelsea would stay at Tulachmhor."

"Never!" Chelsea clutched her hands over her heart, the embellished shock on her face worthy of an Oscar. "You wouldn't dream of doing such a thing, would you, darling?"

Darling? The endearment filled him with a warm fuzziness. She'd only ever called him by his first or last name. *Darling.* He liked it.

"Of course, I wouldn't, honey." He raised an eyebrow at Emma. "I must remember never to divulge any secrets in your presence."

Reid laughed. "You should know women stick together, Hunter. Need I remind you that Ali has shared our every secret with Chelsea, or that they both took great delight in apprising Samantha of our misdeeds over the years."

"How could I forget. I assume they'll take Emma into the fold now."

"Of course." Chelsea nudged him. "Women need to stick together, or men will try to lord it over us." She grinned at Emma. "Did I ever tell you about the time these two were caught stark naked by a bus full of elderly nuns?"

"No." Emma's eyes sparkled. "Do tell."

"It was another competition of courage and strength with my brothers of course." Chelsea linked arms with Emma as they strolled towards the house. "They were to swim across Akuna River and back. Riley and Jake went first then got dressed and stole Reid and Hunter's clothes. These two climbed out of the river naked, just as the busload of nuns pulled into the picnic area."

"Bastards didn't let us live it down for years. I was twelve at the time." Reid's aggrieved tone had Hunter chuckling as they tagged along behind Chelsea and Emma.

"I don't know who was more mortified when we streaked across the picnic grounds. The nuns or us." Hunter grinned at Reid. "It was all over town the next day and Therese Morgan made Jake and Riley chop a winter's worth of firewood."

"Did *you* get even with them?" Emma's delight was infectious.

"We did. The next weekend we challenged Riley and Jake to a trailbike race along one of the four-wheel drive tracks in the National Park. Then we let the air out of their tyres, so they had to walk ten kilometres home. Then our grandmother made us chop a winter's worth of firewood."

Chelsea and Emma dissolved into fits of laughter. It was nice to hear. Hunter hated to spoil the light-hearted moment, but he and Reid had an important rendezvous.

"We'll leave you ladies to lock up the chooks and feed the dogs. We're off to check the fences and stock."

"Okay." Chelsea jogged back and gave him a quick kiss. "Ring me if there are any developments. Don't think to hide anything from me, Sullivan."

"You know if I get my way, you'll be a Sullivan, sunshine." He winked.

"Not if you don't involve me. Trust is a major factor in any relationship. I might need a two-year engagement to be sure of you."

"Holy shit, you can't be serious?"

"Try me." With a flick of her high ponytail, she swanned off, arm in arm with Emma, leaving him and Reid looking at each other in horror.

"Hell, Morgan women are worse to deal with than the men." Reid scratched his head.

"Yeah, but our lives will never be dull." Hunter followed his brother to the barn. "What's the go with you and Emma?"

"I'm crazy about her, but we're taking it slowly. She left a four-year relationship after the guy cheated on her and hasn't dated in over two years. I'm hoping she'll eventually marry me, but for the moment she's moving into the cottage."

"That's great news. I've asked Chelsea to marry me. She hasn't said yes, but I'm confident she will, eventually."

Reid whacked Hunter's shoulder. "It's a foregone conclusion. You two have always gelled well, and since you kissed Chelsea on New Year's Eve, it's impossible to miss your chemistry. I'm only sorry you took so long to make a move, and that I misjudged you."

"Forget it, Reid. All worked out in the end."

"Yeah. Let's do a quick run around the fences then check in with Riley and Jake. You got everything we need?"

Hunter pointed at the two loaded quad bikes in the back of the barn. "Everything."

There was a lot to organise in a short time, and the fewer people who knew the better.

Chapter Thirty-Seven

While Emma made a pot of tea, Chelsea checked her phone for missed calls or messages. It was really weird Riley and Jake hadn't been in contact. She'd sent a couple of texts during the afternoon, keeping them in the loop, and assuring them Abby had things under control. The fact they were putting their wives and daughters first was to be commended, yet she couldn't see them relaxing on a beach or building sandcastles while knowing Buck, Tucker and Muscat were missing.

"They're going to pop up any minute."

"Pardon?" Emma set the teapot on the table. "Who?"

"Riley and Jake. They know what Muscat means to me and would be going through the same torment over their own horses."

"Exactly. I caught Reid standing in Zeus' stable today. He looked wretched."

They drank their tea then Emma watered the

vegetable garden, while Chelsea put the chooks away and fed the dogs. Chores still needed to be done and certainly beat standing around fretting.

As darkness fell, Hunter and Reid returned on the quad bikes. They parked inside the barn, closed the doors then sauntered up the garden path to where Chelsea and Emma sat on the top step with Lola and Regina.

Emma stood. "How's things looking out there?"

Reid put his arm around her shoulders. "All good. Let's hope the rustlers have gone to ground and try to make a run for it tomorrow night."

"Hi." Hunter pulled Chelsea to her feet and into his arms, surrounding her in his heat and a minty pine scent.

"You smell like eucalyptus leaves." She sniffed his neck and detected the now familiar scent of citrus, cinnamon and patchouli. His subtle aftershave and deodorant had a hypnotic effect. She must be more tired than she thought, but it was nice to rest her head against his shoulder and cuddle in close. "I take it the others approved of my idea."

He chuckled. "We all smell of eucalyptus leaves, but the camouflaged hide-outs were a brilliant idea. We built one near the trench and one beside the bridge to McGregor's. Painting the house is a great ruse to explain all the people coming and going."

"We're heading home." Reid smiled at Chelsea. "Tomorrow will be another busy day, followed by a long night, so get some sleep."

"I will. Goodnight." She stayed wrapped in Hunter's arms as Reid and Emma strolled hand in hand to Reid's ute. "They suite each other, don't they?"

"Hmm." He nuzzled her neck. "Your brothers will be here tomorrow."

"I figured as much." She met his gaze. "What else have they kept from me?"

He lowered them both to the step then pulled her across his lap. "Riley's been in contact with the army base at Singleton. They're deploying personnel along the fire trail in the National park, in case the rustlers try to escape on foot. He's also requested extra police to monitor every road out of Bindarra Creek."

"I'm scared the rustlers will harm our horses?"

Hunter exhaled. "Not if we act fast. With so many of us on hand, it should be fine."

"At least you let me be part of the stakeout."

"I would prefer you safely tucked up in bed at my house, but I realise that's asking *too* much."

"Yes, it is, darling. I'm quite capable of keeping watch on the ridge. As soon as I see headlights or hear the truck, I'll warn you." She frowned. "If Riley and Jake are coming home, I think Sam and Ali will insist on coming with them?"

"That make sense." Hunter chuckled. "Riley grumbled something about stubborn women and having to book two rooms at Fig Tree Lodge. I thought it strange as he and Jake are on the stakeout, and the fewer people who know they're in town the better."

"Don't worry, Ali and Sam will keep a low profile. They need to be here too."

"I guess so. In the meantime, I have an amazing therapy for a good night's sleep. It's guaranteed to give you great pleasure then knock you out for at least seven hours."

"Just what I need, after a shower."

He grinned. "Water restrictions are in force, sunshine. We really should shower together. I'll try not to ravish you until we reach your bed." The desire in his eyes said otherwise, but she didn't care, this wanton business was addictive.

"As you've promised me a great deal of pleasure and a good night's sleep, I will concede to your request, Sullivan."

Chapter Thirty-Eight

Bacon sizzled under the grill, tomatoes, eggs and mushrooms were frying in a large pan and the golden hash browns were almost ready to come out of the oven. Hunter smiled to himself. After their nocturnal activities and morning ride, Chelsea would need a good breakfast to get through the day.

His grin widened. Since New Year's Eve, life had taken on a whole new meaning. All was good in his world and getting better each day.

"Ouch." He rubbed at his bare chest where the pan had spat fat at him. Another sting hit his belly, urging him to seek cover. A frilly pink pinafore apron hung on a peg beside the pantry. Just the thing to protect the important bits of his anatomy, which should be lying dormant after its morning workout. Impossible when his mind kept drifting to the delicious, wanton ray of sunshine upstairs.

"Christ almighty."

"What the fuck?"

Hunter flinched, swinging around, tongs in one hand, egg lifter in the other. Not that they'd be much protection against Chelsea's irate brothers. "Hi, fellas, you're early. Can I interest you in breakfast?"

"No," they chorused, simultaneously taking a step forward.

"You'd better have a bloody good reason for looking like that, and Chelsea better not be part of it." Jake glowered at him.

Hunter sighed. "There you go again, jumping to conclusions."

Riley's hand rested over his side holster. "Your butt is naked, Sullivan. You're wearing our grandmother's apron, and you're cooking breakfast in our family kitchen."

"Obviously that part *is* what it looks like. However, in my defence, your sister wouldn't want her future husband pockmarked by flying fat or buried by her brothers under a ton of cow shit."

"Brother-in-law?" Jake quietly closed the back door. "So, everything you've been reported to have said at the pub is true?"

"It certainly is." Hunter turned to check on the eggs, grinning when both Jake and Riley swore again, promising bodily harm if he didn't cover his butt. Hunter tucked a tea towel under the apron bow. "You two have seen my butt before, I don't know why it should upset you now." He turned off the gas and dished up two plates.

Riley pulled out a stool and sat, never taking his eyes off Hunter. "You've got a death wish, or a hell of a nerve going after Chelsea. She's too soft-hearted for a guy like you. Walk away before you break her heart."

"No." Hunter placed both hands on the counter and glared at Riley. "I have loved Chelsea for years. There isn't anything I wouldn't do for her, except stand by and watch her marry a guy who won't make her happy, or is unworthy of her trust. I might have a reputation, but it was gained because I didn't think I stood a chance with Chelsea. New Year's Eve changed everything."

Jake and Riley looked at each other, then spoke at once. "The kiss in the woodshed." It was uncanny how often they said the same thing.

"I didn't realise you knew about that." Hunter rubbed his chin. "Who told you?"

Jake shrugged. "Chelsea had a heart-to-heart with Ali and Samantha. They broke it to us after we got back to Coffs Harbour, then demanded we leave Chelsea to live her life the way she wants."

"However..." Riley narrowed his eyes. "We keep hearing disturbing reports of your very public interactions and decided an intervention might be necessary. We want your word that you won't hurt or betray Chelsea in *any* way for as long as you live."

"You have it." Hunter looked beyond them to where Chelsea now stood in the doorway, dressed but looking tousled, beautiful and wary. "Morning, sunshine. Breakfast is ready, and your brothers have arrived just in time to make coffee."

"Smart arse." Jake sauntered the long way around the counter to the coffee percolator and set about filling it with water.

"Hello, chickpea." Riley strolled over and kissed Chelsea's cheek. "You're looking wide awake for so early on a Saturday morning."

"I've had a great night's sleep. What's going on?" She gave each of her brothers a pointed stare. "I hope you're weren't trying to intimidate Hunter or warn him off, because if you were, I would be very disappointed."

"Just looking out for our little sister." Riley tousled her dishevelled hair further. "Hunter reckons he's going to be our brother-in-law."

"He is your brother-in-law. You two are married to his sisters?"

"That's not what Riley means, and you know it, chickpea." Jake set four cups out on the counter. "Our question is, are you seriously considering marrying a Sullivan, and if so, have you lost your flaming marbles?"

"Yes...no...and I'm going to tell your wives what you said. As Sullivan blood runs thick in their veins, they won't be at all pleased with you."

Jake groaned. "What will it take for you to forget I said that?"

"Shake Hunter's hand, and don't interfere in my love life."

"Done." Riley reached across the bench and shook Hunter's hand. "Welcome to the family, Sullivan."

"Thanks, mate." Hunter turned to Jake. "I can't remember a weekend or school break, where we didn't spend most of it in each other's company. Even during school hours, or sport, we've been within slanging range, or on opposing teams. I think it's time we admitted to a friendship that's always been there, only we've been too stubborn to see it. What do you say, Jake?" He extended his hand. "Friends?"

"Bloody hell. First you show us your butt and now you want to go all touchy feely." His lips twitched.

"Yeah, all right, but no hugging." He shook Hunter's hand then punched him in the shoulder. "That's for seducing our little sister, *mate*."

Hunter grinned. "Your little sister seduced me, but I'm not complaining."

Where had the day gone? Chelsea brushed her hair, contemplating all they'd achieved. She'd expected breakfast with her brothers and Hunter to be awkward, but once he threw on clothes, they discussed the stakeout in detail, going over every little detail.

Her brothers had stayed at Craigellachie last night then set out on foot this morning. After coffee, Riley and Jake changed clothes, packed supplies then hiked to the hide-outs. Their presence in Bindarra Creek a secret.

With her brothers accounted for, Chelsea turned her attention to the team of volunteers who arrived right on eight o'clock. It took twenty adults four hours to apply the first coat of paint to the house, windows, verandah posts and railings. They stopped for a lunch of cold meats and salad then completed the final coats in three hours. The end result declared fresh and inviting as everyone partook in caramel slice, tea and beer.

Maintaining a façade of normality, hour after hour, while the fate of the horses couldn't be determined, left Chelsea emotionally drained. It came as a great relief to finally send everyone home to change for the barbecue.

While Hunter cleaned the rollers and brushes, she prepared a feast then fled for a well-earned bath. Soaking in the warm, soapy water had been so therapeutic, she wanted to stay there forever, but Hunter's threat to join her had the power to shift her butt. She'd wager her father's secret stash of chocolate paddle pops a bath with Hunter would leave her in need of another eight hours sleep.

She brushed her hair once more then stood back to view her reflection. She wasn't big on makeup, normally only applying moisturiser, lip balm and sunblock when working about the farm. For school, she added a touch of mascara and lip gloss. Tonight, was a special occasion so she'd left her hair down, enhanced her eyes with liner, eyeshadow and a thicker mascara. The effect pleased her.

She stood side-on to check out her butt in the tight jeans. Her soft, blue silk camisole top—also new— was hidden by her hair which almost reached her waist. How had it grown so long without her noticing?

A nervous tension strummed throughout her body. With the barbecue to thank volunteers, followed by a rematch with Hunter, and then the stakeout, she had plenty to keep her mind busy, yet she couldn't shake an ominous sense of impending disaster.

If anything happened to Hunter, or her brothers, or Reid, it would haunt her for life. At least they hadn't excluded her from the stakeout.

Her other torment was that the rustlers were local, and their arrests would shame their families, who were more than likely already suffering under the effects of the drought. What would push anyone to steal from hardworking people they've known for years?

Major financial debt. Hungry children. A sense of failure. Desperation.

She could forgive any of those reasons as long as no one got hurt and the horses were returned unharmed. If, on the other hand they shot the horses, or were stealing stock as some sort of lark, she hoped they were dealt with severely. Dishonest financial reward off the backs of struggling farmers was a low and vile act.

A car engine drew her to the window. It couldn't be six-thirty yet. She glanced at her alarm clock. "Yes, it can."

Tossing her brush on the bed, she quickly touched her favourite perfume to her wrists and under each earlobe then slipped on the rose gold bangle and hoop earrings her grandparents had gifted her on her twenty-first birthday. She didn't wear rings but couldn't help glancing at her left hand. A wedding band would be a nice touch.

"Sunshine, you ready?" Hunter called up from below.

"Coming." She crossed her fingers for luck then ran downstairs to join him.

"Wow." His eyes lit as he held out a hand. "You look stunning." He took her hand and kissed it.

"Thank you." She ran her gaze over his crisply ironed, shirt and denim jeans. "You're looking very handsome." She stretched up, lingering to breathe in his sexy cologne, before raising her face for a kiss.

He didn't disappoint, drawing her closer then parting her lips to deepen the kiss.

"Come on you two, there's a convoy of cars coming up the drive." Emma smacked Chelsea's backside as she passed. "Kissing can wait. It's time to feed your guests."

"Spoilsport." Hunter's murmur tickled Chelsea's throat as he searched and found the spot that made her bones melt. He ran a soothing hand over her backside, not that Emma's tap had hurt, but why halt a good thing?

"Let's go, love birds. Doctor's orders." Emma stood at the kitchen bench, hands on hips and tapping her pointed shoe. "The food isn't going to walk out to the barn on its own."

"Yes, Doctor." Chelsea gave Hunter a quick hug then pushed away. "Duty calls."

"Unfortunately." He strode to the bench and lifted the large tray loaded with steak, sliced onions, marinated chicken thighs and sausages.

Chelsea handed Emma the glass dish of potato salad and a saucepan full of corn cobs wrapped in foil. She took the Mediterranean and pasta salads then followed them out to the barn, where she was greeted with smiles and cheers. The glow of satisfaction on each face warming her heart.

"Hi, everyone, help yourselves to a glass of wine, or a beer or my homemade punch. It's non-alcoholic, but I can't guarantee it will stay that way."

The next hour passed in a friendly laid-back atmosphere with plenty of speculation about the rustlers. She appreciated everyone's concern, but it only added to her apprehension.

Once the tables were cleared and dishes washed, everyone ambled into the large family room where the rematch would take place. She hadn't had time to make dessert, so she raided the laundry freezer for her father's stash of chocolate paddle pops, which she planned to replace before he came home. He'd definitely notice three boxes missing.

"Ready to rack 'em up, sunshine." Hunter winked. "I'm taking you down."

Haunted by Muscat's beautiful brown eyes, a game of pool was the last thing she felt like, but it would kill time, and everyone looked so enthused, so she played along.

"In your dreams, Sullivan. Your arse is mine." She sashayed over to him then skimmed her fingers over his belly as she passed, delighting in the spasm it caused. Touching him gave her immense pleasure, although he'd assume it a tactic to put him off his game. So much the better as it guaranteed her victory. She lowered her eyelids slightly and sent him what she hoped was a sultry smile. "Want to break, or shall I?" She repeated his exact words from their New Year's Eve game.

He narrowed his eyes, watching her warily. "Let's toss for it."

A laugh escaped. She loved being wanton and wicked. She loved Hunter, and she loved that for once he couldn't read her.

Chapter Thirty-Nine

Damn it, what the devil is she up too? Hunter knew exactly what Chelsea was doing, and so did most of their spectators, much to their amusement. She was paying him back for teasing her with light touches and whispered promises during their first match. Concentrating on sinking pool balls was the furthest thing from his mind.

The adults along with Abby and Roman's two boys, Angus' lad, and young Kaylee had divided into two camps. The females cheering Chelsea on and the males sympathising with him. His supporters were clearly wondering if he'd even get another go, after screwing up two easy shots.

"Nine in the corner pocket." Chelsea bent forward, her hair falling like a silk veil over her back, drawing his eyes to the band of golden skin on her lower back and her shapely backside. Clapping and whistles snapped his attention back to the table.

She grinned at him. "Fourteen in the side pocket."

She bent again, this time touching her tongue to her top lip and sending him another of those take-me-to-bed looks. Bloody hell, if she kept it up, he'd be forced to send everyone home and haul her upstairs.

More whistles heralded her success.

"Twelve in the corner." She leaned in, hands steady as she stared down the cue then drew it back nice and smoothly, giving her complete attention to the task as she always did.

There were no half measures with this gorgeous woman. It was all or nothing.

"Way to go, Chelsea." Kaylee's excited squeal brought Hunter to his senses as she sank the black, winning the first game. He used the break to enlist a little protection from Dodge and Angus. It might be cowardly, but to have any chance of winning the match, he needed to keep Chelsea and her dainty little hands well away.

The second game was a landslide in his favour, thanks to his amused protectors and several major fouls on Chelsea's part. The spectators followed their interactions and teasing with laughter and fascination.

Hunter watched silently as Chelsea made the break shot on their third game, instantly sinking the striped red. He could only pray for a miracle as he feared a repeat performance of their New Year's Eve match.

"Blue in the corner." She lined up for the easy shot, drew back the cue and missed it completely. "Damn." She straightened and frowned. "How did that happen?"

"I've no idea, sunshine, but I won't look a gift horse in the mouth." He made sure she was leaning against the far wall before he studied the table. "Green, middle pocket." He sank five balls before fouling.

Chelsea strolled around the table twice, considering each ball carefully before sinking one after another.

Harry and Samantha had taught her well. He must remember in future games to make a new rule. Wives had to team up with their husbands. He had mentally accepted his loss when the unimaginable happened. Chelsea missed the green and struck the black eight ball, knocking it off the table.

Everyone stared at her in shocked disbelief.

She frowned. "That wasn't what I intended. If anyone tells Harry or Samantha about this, I'll track you down and make you very, very sorry."

"I win." Hunter could hardly believe his luck. "I win." He laughed then strode around the table and hugged her. "You're mine for two whole days, sunshine. Hooray for me."

She laughed. "Don't let it go to your head, Sullivan. My rules still apply. What are we going to do, that you've never done with any other woman?"

Laughter, suggestions and cheering drowned out his words. Once everyone quietened, he lifted her hand to his mouth and kissed it. "Get married."

"What?" Her eyes widened along with their spectators'. "I have to say yes first."

"You will." He wrapped an arm around her shoulders. "In the meantime, there's this special place I want to take you once we catch the rustlers and get our horses back."

"Red Gum Gully, where the family of ducks live?" The excitement in her voice gave him pause.

"You remember what I said on New Year's Eve?"

She squinted towards the ceiling. "Race our horses across Tully Flats, and up through Red Gum Gully to a special dam. Ride through Akuna National Park and take our horses swimming in a deep watering hole. Lie side-by-side under the stars on a clear summer night to search out the constellations...and...erm... I forget the rest."

Make out under the stars and fall asleep in each other's arms. He smiled at the soft blush in her cheeks. As well as being an excellent rider, cook and pool player, she had a memory like an elephant. He glanced at the pool table then back into her expectant eyes. "You took a dive."

"A Morgan conceding to a Sullivan. Never." She turned to their friends. "Thank you for giving your valuable time to help paint the house. It looks stunning, and my parents and grandmother will love it."

Paddy stepped forward and squeezed her hand. "It's a pleasure, luv. We haven't enjoyed ourselves so much in years, have we Edwina?"

"Speak for yourself, Patrick Cullen." Edwina came over and kissed Chelsea's cheek. "I wouldn't let this Sullivan get away, dear." With a wink she turned to the crowd. "It's been a lovely night, but Chelsea needs to lock up, so she can head back to town with her cousin."

Emma gave the thumbs up. "We're actually staying at Tulachmhor with my parents. Reid asked us to keep an eye on the sheep and cattle while he and Hunter are in Goulburn."

"Whatcha doing in Goulburn?" Paddy's innocent query brought a smile to Chelsea's face. Paddy offered

Hunter the perfect opportunity to lay down one more lure.

"We're attending a liquidation sale. If we leave by eleven and drive all night, we should be there well before it starts, and can make an offer on an almost new harvester then check out the other equipment."

"It's a long way to go," called Dodge. "When will you be back?"

"Monday." Hunter grimaced. "Timings not great, but there's some huge bargains." He put an arm around Chelsea. "You'll be safe at Tulachmhor over the next two nights."

"I know." She leaned into him, praying their plan worked. Dan and Alice hadn't come tonight as Saturday evenings were always busy and they would bandy the same story about the pub. Roman and Kel had dropped into the bowling club earlier on the same errand, while Angus stopped by the Royal Hotel on his way out.

Thalia Levonis gave Chelsea a hug. "If you need us to check on things here, just shout. Kel and I are happy to come for a drive."

"Thanks, Thalia, but all I do is let the chooks out in the morning and put them to bed in the evening. Emma and Lindsay will be with me. I don't even have my lamb as Eddie Taylor is now Stanthorpe's temporary foster carer."

"Okay, on that note, we will say our goodbyes."

With murmurs of agreement, everyone made for the front verandah then after more hugs, and farewells, headed to their vehicles.

As the last car drove away, Hunter caught Chelsea's hand then turned to Emma and Lindsay.

"You drive my Cruiser back to Tulachmhor. If anyone is watching, they'll assume it's me and Chelsea."

"Sure." Emma bit her lip. "You two be careful tonight, and don't let Reid do anything heroic. I know there's a mob of you, but...just be careful."

"We will." Chelsea pulled her hand free and gave Emma and then Lindsay a hug. "It's more likely the rustlers will strike tomorrow night, but keep the dogs in the house with you, and padlock the front gate."

"We will." Lindsay gave her another hug. "Thanks for sending Shane Picton my way. He's a real sweetie."

Chelsea chuckled. "I thought you two might hit it off."

"We do. Good luck, cuz." She shot a quick glance at Hunter. "With everything."

"Thanks, Lindsay. Goodnight."

As they drove away, Chelsea leaned into Hunter again. "I have a bad feeling."

"We've still got your ute. I can run you over to Tulachmhor."

"No, I'm staying here. It's just that something Jerry Eckford said is bothering me."

"What?"

"The rustlers could be out to prove a point. I keep thinking about the man who tried to run me down. He looked furious and he's obviously dangerous."

"He is." Hunter frowned. "Jerry said a similar thing to me. He thinks we've been specifically targeted, or I have an enemy set on revenge."

"That's ridiculous." She cuddled closer, wrapping her arms around his neck. "How long before we take up our positions?"

He grinned. "An hour. Let's lock the house then take advantage of your hay loft."

"You're full of good ideas, Sullivan." She stole a quick kiss. "I do love you."

"I know you do, sunshine." He claimed her lips and mouth in a voracious kiss, rendering her boneless.

The hay loft ended up being too far away.

Chapter Forty

Other than a soft rustle in the overhanging branches, possibly from a possum, and the occasional warble or bird call, all remained quiet. Reid leaned back against the tree trunk and crossed his ankles. "Are we doing the right thing asking Emma and her family to stay at Tulachmhor tonight?"

Hunter shrugged. "I think so. Her father's on hand if need be and they have the dogs. Emma or Lindsay will text me and Abby if they see or hear anything."

"I wish Chelsea had gone with them."

"This is too personal. She should be safe on the ridge." His lips twitched.

Reid narrowed his eyes. "What's so funny?"

"She's pitched a tent up on the ridge. If nothing happens soon, I plan to join her."

"James Morgan isn't going to be happy when he finds out you're involved with Chelsea. I hope you've been careful. You'd want to be engaged, if not married before there are more grandchildren on the way."

"I'm always careful. What about you and Emma?"

"We got a little carried away New Year's Eve, but she assures me she wasn't ovulating, and she'd know, being a gynaecologist." He looked out through their leafy window, contemplating his complete trust in Emma. Knowing his father had been forced to marry his first wife, because of two vile lies, Reid had always assumed responsibility for birth control, until now. He'd fallen for Emma and one day planned to marry her and start a family. If it happened sooner than expected, he wouldn't grumble. The thought cheered him. "I don't think the rustlers are coming tonight."

Hunter shifted. "I need to stretch my legs. We made these shelters too small."

"Tell me about it." Reid leaned his head back against the tree. "I had an interesting conversation with Reece Nolan after you took off today. He's really pissed at you for exposing his relationship with the Gillespie triplets."

"No wonder. Jerry Eckford told me they've dumped him and are leaving town. He also said, I must have an enemy or we're being specifically targeted, maybe because I sabotaged Chelsea's coffee dates."

"Can't see it." Reid frowned. "Reece Nolan was under the impression I've been stringing Chelsea along for years, and he warned me you were sniffing about her. He also asked about Dad. He said he'd catch up with me at the pub, but he left early. You don't reckon he's holding a grudge, do you?"

"No way. He might not be into monogamous relationships, and he'd know the value of our horses, but rustling is a serious offence. It would end his career, not to mention jail time."

"Exactly. Reid rubbed his jaw. "And yet, Reece brought up the feud between us and the Morgans. Did you know he's got Steve Eckford working for him?"

"No." Hunter sat up; his attention suddenly very focused. "Steve's a truck driver."

"Not anymore. He got charged with drink-driving. Lost his license and job. He asked if we had any work going. He's nothing like his brother, is he?"

"No. Jerry's an honest, hardworking bloke, but Steve could well be a rustler. He's local and working with Nolan, he'd be calling at farms in the district. If he's out of work, he could need money—" Hunter groaned. "Steve could be the one with a grudge. Chelsea's knocked him back several times over the years, and I'll bet it was Riley who caught him driving while drunk. Hell, remember that time he trapped me in the school sports shed?"

"Yeah, I was only thinking about that a couple of days ago."

"Jake and I taught the bastards a lesson they'd never forget."

Reid glanced out again. "Chelsea only sighted the driver, so our rustler could be working on his own. If it is Steve, why take Zeus? I've never upset the guy."

"I don't know, but I'm going to alert Riley and Abby." He crawled out of the hide-out.

Reid sent a text to Emma then stared out over the dark paddock. Eagle Rock lay to his left, steep, rocky and thick with bush. A dangerous route on foot in the dark. Akuna National Park was east, behind him, and army personnel were stationed along the fire trail. The river ran along the south side of the paddock, impossible to cross unless using the bridge. The SES were manning roadblocks either end of Reservoir Road. To escape Bindarra Creek, the rustlers had no choice but to come through Hickory Ridge or Tulachmhor.

AJ had positioned the paddy wagon behind bushy scrub at the corner of Wallaby Flats Lane. He would make the first sighting and text Abby. Chelsea would be watching over Hickory Ridge. Reid checked his watch. It showed almost four. The rustlers hadn't showed.

Hunter crawled in, excitement brimming from his eyes. "Riley was about to call it quits when Abby got a text from AJ. A cattle truck loaded with horses passed him. It turned into Hickory Ridge."

"*Yes.*" Reid flexed his fingers, willing himself to relax, but their cramped quarters and his excitement made it impossible as he eagerly stared out their window. As the minutes ticked by his tension grew. "Where are they?"

Hunter's phone pinged. "It's Chelsea. Hello, sunshine. What's happening?"

"A truck came up the drive and it's stopped in front of the barn. I can't see what they're doing. Do you want me to get closer?

"No, stay where you are for now."

"Okay. Do you miss me?"

"Yeah, I'd tell you how much, except Reid's here and you're on speaker."

"Hi, Reid."

"Chelsea."

Hunter held the phone to his chest. "I don't like this, Reid. I'll let Riley know about the truck then I'm joining Chelsea." He switched off speaker, mumbling into his phone as he crawled out of the shelter, leaving Reid staring into the darkness.

Why would the rustlers stop at the barn? To knock off tools or steal the tractor. If they were out for revenge, what else might they do?

He surged out of the shelter, colliding with Jake.

"Hell, Reid. Get out of my way." Jake scrambled to his feet then took off running. Ahead of him Riley and Hunter streaked across the paddock.

"Damn it." He took off after them.

Abby yelled for him to come back, but he ignored her. Chelsea could be in danger.

Chapter Forty-One

Chelsea squinted at the barn's black silhouette. The truck remained hidden from sight. What were they doing? She felt so antsy, she may as well have been sitting on a hornet's nest.

Hunter had answered her call with his usual drawling tenor, asked her a question, then turned serious. He suspected something. She ran across the track to the other side of the ridge, searching the dark arena before her. Eagle Rock stood like a fortress, high and mighty to the east, a fabulous sanctuary for the eagles and other wildlife that called it home. To her right the river snaked past Hickory Ridge's south boundary and on through Tulachmhor. Below she could make out the bulky shapes of bulls and four people sprinting towards the ridge.

Her phone vibrated.

"Hunter, what's wrong?"

"Don't…leave…the…ridge." His rugged breathing made the rest of his words incomprehensible.

"I said I wouldn't. What's happened?"

"Wait...for...me." He hung up.

"Okay." Something was definitely wrong. She ran back to her vantage point on the other side of the ridge. The rear doors of the barn had been opened and light flickered from inside. Not light... "Fire." She fumbled for her phone and rang the fire station.

"Bindarra Rural Fire Brigade, Kel Jones speaking."

"Kel, it's Chelsea Morgan. Our barn's been set alight."

"Where are you?"

"I'm up on the ridge."

"I'll notify my crew. We're on our way."

"Thanks." She hung up and rang Riley. "The barn's on fire. I've rung Kel Jones."

"Good. Stay...on...the...ridge."

"Argh." She hit Hunter's contact. "The barn's on fire."

"Stay where you are."

"Stay, stay, stay, that's all I hear. Hurry up." She hung up and looked down on the growing flames. An horrific scream made her jump, followed by another and another. Horses screaming in terror. *"No."*

She took off down the side of the ridge, slipping, sliding and falling hard a couple of times before she reached level ground. The horrific screams tore sobs from her throat. Tears streamed down her face. She dropped her phone but didn't stop to retrieve it.

Her brothers and Hunter wouldn't be far behind, but they'd never make it in time. She had no choice but to run into the burning barn.

Intense heat smacked her in the face and chest. Flames licked along the beams above and raced down one wall engulfing the dart board. The hay loft over the stables was fully alight. Thick grey smoke billowed in the rafters.

She ran to the first stall, yanked the bolt back then swung the door open.

Tucker leapt out, missing her by inches, his eyes rolling back in his head as he galloped for the open doors.

Sweat drenched her as she ran to the next stall. The bolt wouldn't budge. Whichever horse was inside screamed and kicked, splintering a panel of wood. She worked the bolt loose as the horse kicked again, the swinging door flinging her to the ground. She curled into a ball, covering her head as the huge grey horse reared, pawing the air above her.

Zeus.

His hooves slammed into the ground by her ear, yanking her plait so hard she cried out. With a horrendous scream, he tossed his head and surged for freedom.

She crawled to her knees. It was becoming hard to see, her chest tightened as she gasped for air and her eyes stung, but she forged on as the alternative was to leave her beloved Muscat to burn.

Reaching the next stall, she released the bolt and swung to door wide, coughing hard as she held out her hand to get some sense of a horse rushing past. It didn't come. Edging around the wall, she squinted through blurry eyes.

"Oh no." Muscat's lead rope had been secured to the hitching ring, but whoever returned her hadn't unclipped it from the halter. Muscat threw her head back and forth and whinnied, attempting to rear.

"Chelsea." Reece Nolan gripped her arm, scaring the crap out of her. "I saw the flames from the road. What happened?"

"The rustlers put the horses in the barn then torched it. We have to save them."

"I'll check the next two stalls. Once you get that horse out don't come back in."

"Okay." The smoke had thickened so much she couldn't see three feet in front of her, let alone the other side of the barn. Thank goodness the stables hadn't caught light yet. Covering her mouth, she inched forward. "Muscat, calm down, sweet."

Chelsea's voice crackled, but it must have reached her mare. Muscat swung round, eyes rolling, her sweat-caked coat quivered as she backed against the wall. Chelsea stumbled forward and unclipped the lead rope. Muscat surged forward, shouldering Chelsea off her feet and against a wall.

Bruises were the least of her worries. She crawled to her knees amid another coughing fit. It was getting hard to breath and she barely had the energy to stand.

The flames behind her cast a glow over a man, lying face down in the straw, almost under the feed trough.

"Oh my God." She hurried forward, falling to her knees.

The door slammed shut, cutting off all light, then came the clang of the bolt sliding into place.

"*No.*" Blindly, she shuffled forward and hammered on the door. A coughing fit brought her to her knees. She didn't want to die. "Please help me."

She could hear someone shouting her name. "I'm

in here." She stood again, tears rolling down her face. "Please." On that strangled plea, the door flew open and she fell into wonderfully strong, familiar arms.

"Chelsea, love." Hunter sounded distraught. He lifted her off the ground and ran.

"Buck and Monty?"

"Reece got them out." He kept running. A loud crack above had her cringing, terrified a burning beam would crush them. "There's a man." She buried her face against Hunter's neck and clung to him, praying for a miracle.

It came faster than she expected. Fresh, cool air cloaked her in its heavenly sheath, making breathing easier. Hunter sank to the ground, cradling her across his thighs, holding her so tight it hurt.

"I thought I'd lost you." He made a choking sound, his chest and shoulders quaking. "I couldn't find you. I searched, but I couldn't find you."

"It's okay." She rubbed his back, her own tears flowing freely. "There's a man."

Jake and Riley fell to their knees, both speaking at once. "Are you hurt?"

"I'm...fine, but there's a man in one of the stalls. He's unconscious or...dead."

"Which stall?" Riley jumped to his feet.

"Third...from this end."

"I'll come with you." Jake raced off after Riley into the inferno.

Chelsea clung to Hunter, her heart in her mouth as she stared at the barn, willing her brothers to appear. If the rustler was dead, they couldn't do anything for him. She didn't want her brothers to die too.

Flames leapt in the air, the whole roof ablaze. If

the house hadn't been so far away, it could have gone up too.

Riley and Jake stumbled out of the barn, carrying the man between them. They laid him on the ground, then while Jake examined him, Riley rang for an ambulance.

Hunter squeezed her fingers. "What happened?"

"I'd just found Muscat when Reece Nolan grabbed my arm. He told me to get Muscat out and not to come back in, then he went to check the other stalls. Muscat knocked me down. I saw the man lying under the feed trough then someone shut me in. Everything went black. I called out and banged on the door but..."

Riley grabbed her shoulders. "Are you sure it was locked, not just stuck."

"I... I guess it could have been stuck. I thought I heard the bolt slam across, but..."

"The bolt *was* across." Hunter scowled at the burning barn. "Someone deliberately locked Chelsea in that stall along with whoever he is."

"It's Jerry Eckford." Riley rubbed his forehead. "What was Nolan doing in the barn?"

"He said he saw the flames from the road and came to help."

Riley looked about them. "Where is he now?"

Jake pointed into the darkness. "Helping Reid catch the horses."

An almighty explosion blasted behind them. Hunter pushed Chelsea onto the grass then covered her with his body.

"Dad's barn." She turned into Hunter's shoulder unable to hold the sobs any longer.

"It can be replaced, Chelsea. You can't. I told you to stay on the ridge."

"If I had, our horses would have burnt alive."

"*You* almost burnt alive. Two more minutes and the roof would have collapsed."

"Thank you for saving me, darling."

"Don't *darling* me. This is the second time you've taken years off a life I had planned to share with you."

She gave him a teary smile. "I'll make it up to you."

He looked slightly less aggrieved as he climbed to his feet and glanced at Jake. "Is Jerry alive?"

"Yes, but he's got a nasty head wound. Muscat must have kicked him. His partner probably didn't even know he was in the stable."

Chelsea shivered. "He was under the trough and Muscat wasn't as agitated as the other horses." She shook her head. "Why put our horses in the stables then set fire to the barn? What sort of monsters do a thing like that?"

"I assume we'll find out when Jerry regains consciousness." Hunter eased back to look at her. "I want you inside, out of sight."

A siren wailed in the distance. She frowned at the inferno before them. "The fire was started in the loft. What exploded?"

"Probably the tractor's fuel tank. Thankfully, the bastards didn't have time to set the house alight. The other one must have heard us coming and taken off."

Riley glanced about. "Let's keep your rescue quiet for now. I want you inside the house with a guard."

Hunter nodded. "I'll stay with Chelsea."

"And I'll keep an eye on Jerry." Jake looked into the darkness. "Let's get him inside."

Chelsea looked about in confusion. "What about the other rustler?"

"He won't be far away, chickpea." Riley bent to lift Jerry's legs. "I'll tell Abby to leave our watchers in place and come here." He gave Hunter a pointed look. "Don't leave Chelsea alone."

"I won't." He swung her into his arms then followed her brothers. "The ambos can assess you both then take you to hospital if need be."

Chelsea lay her head against his shoulder. "Are we good?"

"This is not over, Chelsea. I want your promise you'll never again put your life at risk."

"That's impossible, Hunter. I would do whatever it takes to rescue someone I love."

"Not the answer I need."

She snuggled closer. "It's the only one you'll get, Sullivan."

Chapter Forty-Two

Hunter sat Chelsea on the kitchen bench then filled a glass with water. "Drink."

"Thank you." She skulled the lot.

He locked the back door then closed all the blinds before turning on the light. "Hopefully the person who locked you in the stable believes you perished in the fire."

"Why?"

"Because he knows you were close enough to rescue the horses, so he must believe you can identify him." He refilled her glass.

She drank the water then frowned. "Reece Nolan can't be a rustler, surely."

Hunter rubbed the bristly fuzz on his chin. "I hear Reece is mortgaged to the hilt."

"Even so, he wouldn't lock me in a burning barn. As for Jerry... I can't believe he'd steal our horses. He must have had another reason for being here."

Hunter lifted her down. "Until we know more, you stay with me."

"Deal. Can we check on Jerry?"

"Sure." He followed Chelsea into the family room where Jerry lay on his side, unconscious with a towel under his head.

Riley stood with his hands on his hips. "I'll talk to Reece then have a look around."

Chelsea kicked off her runners and padded to the window to peep through the curtains. "I see flashing lights at the front gate."

"Let's get you upstairs, sunshine." Hunter ignored her half-hearted protest and swung her into his arms. "A shower then bed. *You* are grounded."

Although grimy, scratched, scruffy and exhausted, she was alive. He didn't think he'd ever forget the terror of seeing her run into the burning barn then not being able find her.

He needed to check every inch of her for his own peace of mind. He deposited her in the bathroom then cleaned her cuts and scratches. As he was just as scratched and dirty, he stripped off and joined her in the shower. Her sleepy moan brought a smile to his face. He held her in his arms as warm water sluiced over them, washing away the soap and his tension. She was almost asleep on her feet.

Figuring they'd used enough water, he wrapped her in towel then carried her to her room, where he dried her hair as best he could. Leaving her to dress, he crossed the hall to borrow clothes from her brothers' room, then returned as Emma came up the stairs.

"Reid phoned me. I can't believe someone burned

down the barn." She examined Chelsea then seemingly satisfied, left her dozing and joined Hunter by the door. "She's lucky. The tiredness is due to sleep deprivation, shock and exhaustion. Once this is over, I want you to take her to the hospital for a thorough check up."

"No worries." He looked at the love of his life. "Can you stay with her, while I have a word with the ambos and Kel Jones?"

"Of course. Is everything all right?"

"It will be. Don't leave her alone. I'll be back in a flash."

With Chelsea in Emma's care, Hunter raced downstairs.

The ambos were loading Jerry onto a trolley. He groaned, opened his eyes and fixed on Hunter. "Where's Chelsea?"

"Why?"

"Steve's lost his mind. He's always had a thing for Chelsea, so he hates Reid. He hates you and Jake Morgan for destroying his tough guy status at school, and he hates Riley for charging him with drink-driving. He came home Wednesday night in a filthy mood threatening to get even with all of you."

"The night someone tried to steal a bull from here and run Chelsea down."

Sharon Bennett, one of the paramedics held up a hand. "We need to get this guy to hospital."

"Wait." Jerry caught Hunter's shirt. "Chelsea's in danger."

"What were you doing in the barn, Jerry?"

"Bringing your horses back, but I swear I didn't take them."

"Who did?" asked Jake.

"Steve. I didn't know for sure until last night. I was suspicious he might be rustling, so I confronted him. He said it was just a few sheep and cattle. Then I found your horses in one of our hay sheds. I insisted he return them and hand himself into police. Mum demanded I keep my mouth shut and shoot the horses. Nothing I do has ever been good enough, yet Steve can do no wrong. I told them to go to hell, loaded the horses then brought them back myself." He gingerly touched his head. "The last thing I remember was putting the mare in a stall. She must have kicked me."

"Doubtful," muttered Jake. "You were found under the feed trough in a locked stall and the barn was on fire. We couldn't save it."

"What?" Jerry blinked. "The horses?"

"We got them out," muttered Hunter. "Everything else is gone. Tractor, motorbikes, quads, saddles, tools, fencing, everything."

"I'm sorry." He touched his head again. "Steve must have followed me." His eyes widened. "He meant to kill me. Where's Chelsea?"

"Safe. She's the one who found you."

"Then I owe her my life."

"You can thank her later. Right now, you need that head checked." Hunter glanced at Sharon Bennett. "Nothing you've heard can be repeated to anyone but the police."

She nodded. "Senior Sergeant Morgan has already spoken to me and Colm, and Constable Donaldson will be accompanying us to the hospital to guard this guy."

"Great. If possible, we need to keep Jerry's identity hidden."

"It's too late." Jerry closed his eyes. "Steve's a sadist. If he started the fire, he'll hide to watch the barn burn, which means he knows Chelsea got me out. Cover my head and let him think I'm dead. He's not done yet. If he thinks I spoke to Chelsea, she's in danger."

"All right."

As Sharon and Colm wheeled Jerry out, Hunter followed. Several vehicles were parked on the other side of the picket fence and a small group of neighbours stood transfixed, watching the firemen fight the inferno. Among them was Reece Nolan. They all stared across the open yard as the ambos loaded Jerry, but no one made a move to investigate. Once the ambulance drove away their attention reverted to the burning barn.

Without solid proof, Hunter could only take Jerry's word for what happened. His gut feeling was to trust no one. They couldn't prove Steve started the fire or that he was working alone, not until they had hard evidence and all three Eckfords had been interviewed by police.

Hunter jogged over to the fire chief who stood watching his crew directing the powerful gush of water over the remaining flames. "Hi, Kel, did Riley bring you up to date?"

"Yeah. I'm glad you got the horses out. I take it that was Jerry Eckford they loaded into the ambulance?"

"Yeah, I can't say too much at this stage." Hunter made no attempt to lower his voice as others gathered round. "It looks like Jerry was locked in a stable before the fire started. Chelsea found him barely conscious. Once all the excitement dies down, Riley will find out if Jerry was able to tell Chelsea anything. She's suffered some smoke inhalation and is in shock. Dr Fahey has given her a sedative." Another lie, but necessary for Steve to incriminate himself.

Kel frowned. "What was Jerry doing in the barn?"

Reece pushed through the crowd. "Maybe he saw the cattle truck pass his place and came to investigate, like me?"

"Anything's possible." Hunter glanced at the house, making a point of raising his eyes to Chelsea's room. "We'll know more in a few hours." He gave them a nod then jogged back to the kitchen, where Reid, Riley, Jake and Abby were talking quietly.

They adjourned to Chelsea's room where they laid out a plan to trap their quarry then they all dispersed to play their part.

Chapter Forty-Three

It was almost seven and promised to be a hot day. Hunter stood by the burnt-out shell of the barn with Reid, Riley and Jake. They watched the last of the spectators and fire truck drive away.

"Let's do this." Reid shook Riley's and Jake's hands then hugged Hunter hard. "I'm taking Emma home. Steve might not show, but if he does, be careful."

Riley turned to Hunter. "Dodge and Roman are watching the Eckford place. No one has come or gone. Steve's got to be here somewhere. Jake will drive Chelsea's ute into town. He'll cut back through Angus McGregor's place then hotfoot it to the ridge. When everyone's in place, we wait for a sighting then close the net. Any questions?"

"Nope, I'm good."

"Okay, don't be a hero. Your job is to prevent anyone getting near Chelsea."

"Will do." He turned to Jake who wore one of Riley's old uniforms. "Get moving so we can catch the bastard."

Jake and Riley shared a look then Hunter followed Jake to the picket gate. Being identical twins, no person watching would question that the cop striding towards Chelsea's ute was anyone but Riley.

Jake turned back and yelled. "Chelsea will sleep for hours. I'll be back after lunch to talk to her. You should catch some sleep on the sofa."

"That's my plan."

As Jake drove away, Hunter looked at the pile of burnt timber, twisted metal and ash. If Steve hadn't been watching, he'd know via the grapevine that no human or animal remains had been found in the burnt-out shell.

Hunter glanced up at Chelsea's open window, an easy climb via the water tank and verandah roof. He hoped Steve took full advantage. After one more look around, he entered the kitchen and locked the door. He paused by the family room to study the lump under a blanket on the sofa. With the curtains open, anyone looking in would assume a six-foot male was dead to the world.

He moved on, up the stairs and along the hall to the master bedroom. Chelsea lay on the bed dozing.

Abby stood by the edge of the side window. "All good?"

He nodded. "I hope this works, because if Jerry dies, we can't prove a thing."

"We've impounded the truck. Forensics might get fingerprints."

"Jerry's."

She shrugged. "I've had dealings with Steve Eckford when he's had too much to drink. Usually when he refuses to leave a pub or the bowling club.

He likes to get right up in other patrons faces and intimidate them. Not a nice guy."

"Once a bully, always a bully." Hunter edged up to window. "He's not the most athletic of men these days. He could decide to come through a downstairs door or window."

"Not with someone asleep on the sofa," murmured Chelsea. "Riley dragged the barbecue over to the water tank to make it more accessible."

"All we have to do is be patient." Abby stiffened. "Over there by the chook shed."

Hunter edged closer, keeping the blind steady as he peered through. Steve stood plastered to the shed. "Hell, he didn't wait long."

"He won't make a move until he's sure you've had time to fall asleep. I'll send out the alert to close the noose. The army, SES and our guys are in place. When he approaches the house, I'll get into position."

Hunter spent the next thirty minutes relaying messages between Abby and Riley, checking his watch, spying on the chook shed, and watching over Chelsea. Her breathing sounded normal, but the stubborn woman refused to sleep in case she was needed.

Finally, Steve Eckford made a run for the water tank.

"I'll alert Riley and get into position." Abby left the bedroom.

Hunter hesitated, unwilling to leave Chelsea.

She waved him away. "Go, I can't be your back up if you stay here."

"I'd rather lock you the ensuite." With an exasperated sigh he left, closing the bedroom door quietly behind him.

Abby lay in Chelsea's bed with the covers tucked around her head. Being blonde, she made the perfect sacrificial pigeon. He glanced at the wardrobe where one door had been cracked open.

"Looks good." Satisfied, he took up his position in the room across the hall to wait.

Climbing off the bed, Chelsea peeped through the side window blind. "Drat." She couldn't see a thing from here. The fire truck had left and there wasn't a person or vehicle in sight. She felt decidedly wrecked and sore, yet sleep was the furthest thing from her mind.

A loud creak had her jumping back against the wall. Warily, she tiptoed across the room to her parents' front window, which looked over the house paddocks and drive. Her heart caught at the sight of Muscat, Tucker, Buck, Monty and Zeus, grazing alongside her mother's old mare under the jacaranda tree.

She turned away, kicking her toe on her father's bag of golf clubs. He'd won them in a raffle and had yet to learn how to use them. Hopping around, clutching her toe, she silently cursed them to Timbuktu.

On second thoughts…she withdrew one of the wooden clubs then padded to the door. Edging it open, she peered into the hall. The house was eerily silent, even though she knew four people were hidden within.

She took up her position outside her parents' room to wait, freezing when she heard a muffled scream.

Was she needed?

She flinched as a mighty crash resonated from within her bedroom. Then came a ferocious roar, followed by grunts and a woman yelling.

"Police! Freeze!" It was Abby's voice.

Someone smashed into the door, shaking the whole wall.

Chelsea gasped and jumped sideways, into a wall of muscle, her shriek muffled by a large hand covering her mouth.

"Shush, honey, it's me." Hunter's gruff murmur against her ear saved him from a golf club to the crotch, which could have caused a serious hiccup for her baby plans.

More grunts and shouting drew her attention back to her door. "What's happening?"

"I'd say Steve attempted to suffocate you and discovered Senior Constable Taylor." He pushed her behind him and opened the door.

Abby stood in a corner with her gun trained on the two men near the window.

Riley had hold of Steve Eckford's fisted hand, which held a long-bladed knife. They staggered back and forth, knocking the hanging wardrobe door off its remaining hinge.

Abby kept her gun on them. "Drop the knife, Steve. It's over."

Steve's eyes held a madness that scared Chelsea. He smashed an elbow into Riley's solar plexus, winding him and got his wrist free.

"No." Chelsea dashed around Hunter and swung the golf club, hitting Steve's wrist with a decisive crack.

He bellowed like a demented bull, falling against the wall, clutching his wrist.

"That will teach you to burn down my father's barn and steal animals that don't belong to you."

"You bitch." Spittle ran down Steve's chin. "I should have run you and that bastard over when I had the chance. And, I should have shot your bloody horses."

"Bastard." Hunter slammed a fist into Steve's nose. It crunched and blood spurted like a fountain. Hunter swung another punch into Steve's chin.

"Enough." Riley shoved Hunter aside then cuffed Steve's hands behind his back.

Running feet and slamming doors sounded outside and downstairs. Blood poured from Steve's warped nose, soaking into the carpet and spreading like a creeping tide. The carpet would need replacing along with her wardrobe door and the barn.

Chelsea released a shaky breath. Her parents would never leave her alone again.

Chapter Forty-Four

Taking a deep breath of fresh air, Chelsea looked out over the golden fields. Early morning really was the best time of day on Hickory Ridge. The last two days had felt like she'd been caught in a whirlwind.

Ali and Sam had insisted that it was only right their parents be notified of the fire. Thankfully, they'd decided to finish the cruise. It had taken far more effort to convince Ali, Sam and her brothers to return to Coffs Harbour to continue their holiday.

Hickory Ridge had been inundated with insurance assessors, forensic investigators, detectives and well-wishers.

Jerry Eckford basked in attention at the hospital with a cracked skull. As the banks all but owned his farm, he'd accepted an offer from Hunter and Reid to buy him out. Jerry would remain in the house and work for them.

Steve Eckford had been arrested and faced charges of attempted murder, arson, rustling, truck theft and driving without a license. Mrs Eckford faced a minor charge of hiding a crime after the fact. She'd gone to stay with her sister in Brisbane with no intention of returning, much to Jerry's delight.

Along with Jake, Riley, Hunter and Reece, Chelsea had been declared a hero for running into a burning barn to rescue either horses or humans and were to receive bravery awards later in the year. Reece was especially delighted as the older ladies of Bindarra Creek had decided to overlook his fall from grace but would be watching him.

Tucker and Buck grazed in the house paddock, none the worse for their harrowing experience, so where was Muscat?

She reached into the pocket of her jeans and pulled out the note she'd found on Hunter's pillow, where his head should have been.

My wanton ray of sunshine. As you love your morning rides, I've got a surprise for you. Wear your riding boots and meet me on the front verandah at six-thirty.

A horse whinnied from the side of the house.

"You're late, Sullivan."

She heard his deep chuckle before he appeared, leading Monty and Muscat. Both horses had been saddled. The fancy western saddle on Muscat looked brand new.

Excitement buzzed through her body. "What's this?"

"You're mine for two days, remember."

"I wasn't likely to forget, darling." She stretched up to kiss Hunter then accepted Muscat's rein and mounted.

They cantered across the grassy fields of Hickory Ridge and took the back gate onto Tulachmhor, then galloped through Tully Flats. Eagles flew high in the sky, other birds chirped and whistled. In the fields, lambs bleated and searched for their mothers.

A comfortable silence fell over them as they walked the horses up through Red Gum Gully to the dam where the family of ducks were having their morning swim. To her amazement, a massive tent had been set up by the dam.

Leaving Hunter to unsaddle the horses, she ran to investigate. It was the most glamourous set up she'd ever seen. A massive round bed stood to one side, covered in soft, multi-coloured throws and cushions. An old-fashioned tin bath, filled with soapy bubbles had been set against the back wall. Huge lounging pillows and a low table spread with a feast fit for a sheik took up the left side. Rugs were scattered about and an Indian dream catcher hung from the centre pole. Billowing pastel veils hung from the peak of the tent to the far edges, creating a decadent and romantic boudoir. All she needed was her sheik.

His arms came around her. "Does this please you, sunshine?"

"Very much. Where? How?"

"I know a couple who set up glamping tents for every occasion. Ali and Sam helped me add a few extra touches. I thought we might start with breakfast." He gave her a wicked grin. "Tonight, we can lay under the stars and search out the constellations."

She smiled. "As long as we sleep in here, so I can fall asleep in my sheik's arms."

"Whatever you wish, sunshine." They shared a

long pleasurable kiss, then he swung her into his arms and carried her to the lounging cushions. "Will you marry me, sunshine?"

"Yes." She hugged him. "I love you to the moon and back, Hunter."

"Then will you wear this for me." He reached under one of the cushions and pull out a small, red velvet box. "You mean the world to me, Chelsea."

With her heart in her mouth, she opened the lid then stared transfixed at the twinkling solitaire diamond set on a rose gold ring.

He took the ring then slid it onto her finger. "I handled a property settlement for a jewellery designer a few weeks ago. He showed me his latest creations and offered me a discount. This ring reminded me of you. A sparkling beauty I thought to be beyond my reach. I went back yesterday and bought it."

"I love it and I love you." She hugged him tight. "Thank you."

Later that evening she lay in Hunter's arms staring at the blanket of stars twinkling in the darkness. "You do realise our wedding will be the event of the year. Three Morgans married to three Sullivans. Will wonders never cease."

He chuckled. "That's one wedding I'm looking forward to, and by New Year's Eve, we will have something else to celebrate with our families and friends."

"You're very sure of yourself, Sullivan."

He chuckled. "I assured Reid I'd have you married to a decent guy and pregnant by New Year's Eve. It's a promise I intend to keep."

"In that case, we will definitely have an April wedding. I want Ali, Sam, Emma and Lindsay as my bridesmaids, and Kaylee Myers can be our flower girl. Let's get married in the garden at Tulachmhor. Can we have a honeymoon somewhere romantic?"

He gave her his indulgent amused smile. "Whatever you want, sunshine." His words made her heart sing, but she had more important things on her mind.

"Kiss me, Hunter."

The End

Thank you so much for taking the time to read *A Twist of Fate* which is part of the group writing venture – **Bindarra Creek A Town Reborn series**.

All reviews are appreciated.

If you enjoyed reading A Twist of Fate, please recommend it to your friends. Word of mouth is a wonderful way of discovering new books and authors.

If you are able to leave a written review on your favourite e-platform, I would appreciate it.

Bindarra Creek
A Town Reborn

Welcome to Bindarra Creek, a struggling country town where people work hard and love deeply. Set in the picturesque tablelands of New England, Australia, Bindarra Creek is a fictional, drought stricken community full of intrigue, adventure, drama and romance.

Life and love in a small country town has never been more challenging.

Bindarra Creek A Town Reborn series consists of eight romances written by eight Australian authors and published individually beginning in July 2019.

In order of release:

Take Me Home – Suzanne Gilchrist
(aka S E Gilchrist)
In the Heat of the Night – Susanne Bellamy
No Looking Back – Linda Charles
Worth the Wait – Annie Seaton
With Every Breath – Lauren K. McKellar
Stealing Her Heart – Simone Angela
A Twist of Fate – Erin Moira O'Hara
Promise Me Forever – Juanita Kees

To date there are three group writing venture 'series' set in our fictional small town of Bindarra Creek all written by best-selling Australian romance authors. Our latest series is A **Town Reborn.** A Collection of short romances, **Bindarra Creek Short & Sweet,** was released in January 2019 and our first series, **A Bindarra Creek Romance,** was released during 2015/2016.

All books are available as ebooks, some also have paperback versions.

Each series has one theme running throughout, while every romance depicts the changing lives of the townsfolk as our small town begins to grow and thrive despite the dramas of everyday life.

Bindarra Creek Short & Sweet Collection
comprised of:

What's in a Kiss – Linda Charles
My Forever Valentine – Sandie James
Pearls and Green Beer – Susanne Bellamy
Full Circle – Annie Seaton
Date with Destiny – Erin Moira O'Hara
A Letter from the Queen – Lee Christine
Love's Sweet Challenge – Suzanne Gilchrist
(aka S E Gilchrist)
The Widow Maker – Lauren K. McKellar
Out of the Blue – Noelle Clark

Books in the first
Bindarra Creek Romance series:

Bindarra Creek Makeover – S. E. Gilchrist
Shadows of the Heart – Lee Christine
Second Chance Love – Susanne Bellamy
The CEO Mechanic – Sandie James
Reach for the Stars – Kerrie Paterson
Home to Bindarra Creek – Juanita Kees
Stolen Sanctuary – Stacey Nash
Tempting Fate – Erin Moira O'Hara
One More Day – Linda Charles
The Vine – Lauren K. McKellar
The Ghost of His Past – Simone Angela
Joanie's Dilemma – Marianne Theresa
Buckley's Chance – Noelle Clark

For more info on Bindarra Creek Romances, please
visit www.bindarracreekromance.com

Acknowledgments

Thank you to my friend and brilliant editor Juanita Kees, Amy Atwell for her formatting skills, and Paradox Book Cover Designs for my beautiful cover. A special thanks to Suzanne Gilchrist and the wonderful group of authors involved in this delightful rural romance series. It's been a fun journey.

About the Author

Erin Moira O'Hara grew up in the Blue Mountains of Australia, with a garden backing onto native bushland, hidden caves and fabulous lookouts. Weekends were spent exploring, climbing trees and creating secret bases. Her love of reading began with visits to the local library, where she became absorbed in a world of intrigue, fantasy and action-packed adventures. The moment Erin read her first romance; she recognised the importance of finding the right man to share her life. She now lives with him close to the largest saltwater lake in Australia. Their home overlooks bushland and is surrounded by an abundance of bird life and an ever-growing garden.

Erin's writing encompasses everything she loves—intrigue, suspense, passion and romance.

If you would like to know more, please visit:
http://www.erinmoiraohara.com

Also by Erin Moira O'Hara

The Knight of Castle Kildare

Conspiracy in Emilia Romagna

Beat of the Jungle

Steele Ops Series

The Kalista Diamond

Precious Gems

Jewel of the Kimberley

The Amethyst Code

Bindarra Creek

Tempting Fate

Date with Destiny

A Twist of Fate

www.ingramcontent.com/pod-product-compliance
Lightning Source LLC
Chambersburg PA
CBHW031942110726
47902CB00001B/263